What They'r
A Long and Stony Road

We know the history of the tumultuous and violent times of the South during the Civil Rights Movement of the 1950s and 1960s. Author Jack Saarela brings it up close and personal... as he makes us feel the emotional toll on actual participants. Through his two fictional main characters' inner thoughts, motives, and dialogue we witness the atrocities and gain a higher level of understanding as the practice of Non-Violence grows and begins to make headlines. A movement that caused changes in our nation that still have effects today.

Wendy Wyatt – Author

In *A Long and Stony Road*, author Jack Saarela invites us on a journey beginning in the mid-1950s during the Jim Crow era of the American South, taking us to some of the pivotal early events... Perhaps not surprisingly, given that the story is told from the perspective a pastor, and much of the leadership and participation came from clergy and church folk, the faith perspective of the Movement was an overarching presence, I found that to encouraging. These events and personalities of the Movement, recounted in a personally relatable way, serve to remind me how the issues, events and courageous people of that era resonate still in our troubled time.

Tom Lurvey, Winnipeg, Man

This historical novel is read through the eyes of two men embarking on a tour of the deep south to explore the gains of the civil rights movement. Everyday events are interwoven with history unfolding as they encounter giants of the movement as well as the everyday unnamed heroes who also played pivotal roles in its evolution. Saarela does a beautiful job at creating a humanized perspective which evokes resonance and pride, but it is also painful in spots as we experience, at a deep and personal level, their fear and pain as they live through key historical milestones throughout their journey.

Jean Mackie Sutton, Cheltenham, PA

This historical novel by Jack Saarela covers a lot of ground: a tragedy, a love story, episodes of violence and confrontation, and others of courage and grace. It tells of a second American Revolution, the one that happened in the 1950s and the 1960s. Perhaps the biggest takeaway for this reader is a changed perspective. It has changed how I look at today's headlines: Every episode in history is linked inextricably to another. Rev. Raphael Warnock, newly-elected black Senator from Georgia, modeled his life on that of Rev. Dr. Martin Luther King, Jr. A full circle.

Lynn Aber, Durham, N.H.

The
Long
and
Stony
Road

Jack Saarela

The Long and Stony Road
Copyright © 2023 by Jack Saarela

ISBN: 978-1-7365979-7-2

Published by
Can't Put it Down Books
Willow Spring, NC 27592

Cover design by Eric Labacz
www.labaczdesign.com

A Long and Stony Road is dedicated to the brave men, women, and children of the Civil Rights Movement of the 1950s, 1960s, and beyond who risked life and limb in the struggle to make America faithful to its founding ideals enshrined in the United States Constitution and the amendments attached to it.

To the men, women, and children who no longer accepted passively their status as second-class citizens of the United States to which they were assigned by white society for centuries since the centuries of chattel slavery, until they were animated by a new spirit of freedom that inspired a hope and vision of a beloved community of black and white together.

To the generations of men, women, and children who endured a daily diet of humiliation and were force-fed the lie that because of the color of their skin, black men, women, and children were less than human.

To the men, women, and children who demonstrated to the world that a repressed group of people could conquer the violence to which they were vulnerable by acts of nonviolence, revealing the inhumanity of many against them by an attitude of humanity toward those who dehumanize them.

To the men, women, and children who sought to overcome the natural human urge to meet violence and barbarism with steadfast self-discipline, love, and forbearance.

To the leaders and visionaries of the Movement including the Rev. Dr. Martin Luther King, Jr., the Rev. Ralph Abernathy, Diane Nash, and Daisy Bates who led the people with a vision of nonviolence and the absence of retribution, tireless organizing and strategizing a clear and articulate rationale for courageous action.

Chapter One

Stony the road we trod
Bitter the chastening rod
Felt in the days when hope unborn had died
Yet with a steady beat
Have not our weary feet
Come to the place for which our fathers sighed?

"Lift Every Voice and Sing"
James Weldon Johnson

THE REVEREND HENRI ESPER found a seat in one of the coaches marked for "colored passengers" as he boarded the overnight train for Little Rock, Arkansas, at Union Station in Washington, DC. It was nearly a nine-hundred-mile trip, and because of stops in towns and cities on the way, it was more than a sixteen-hour journey on the train.

It was nearly midnight as the train pulled away. He stood up by his seat and placed the sack of sandwiches in the overhead shelf beside his suitcase. The kitchen staff at the Cadillac Hotel had kindly prepared them as fuel for the journey. It would be a long night in the dark countryside before there would be enough light to read. The colored cars didn't have any personal reading lights.

Henri got as comfortable as he could, taking off his raincoat and resting his head against it in the seat that he judged had been transplanted from a coach no longer in service. Within a short time, his eyes grew heavy. He was lulled into a trance halfway between wakefulness and sleep by the hypnotic "clickity-clack" of the train's wheels beneath him. His eyes gave up the struggle to stay open, and his head began to bob up and down. His ears, however, still registered the rhythm of steel wheels against steel rails, his drowsy mind translating the sound into the words, "Rosewood Town. Rosewood Town. Rosewood Town." He didn't know why the wheels would repeat the name of that small Florida burg that he hadn't thought about for at least a couple of decades.

But he did remember the first time he had heard the name Rosewood and the story of its short life and tragic demise. It was back in one particularly memorable class in fifth grade at the public school in his tiny village of St. Vincent, one of the northern gateways to the Adirondacks.

It had been Mr. Cletis Tanner, the only Negro member of the faculty, who first mentioned the name Rosewood. Henri had never forgotten it.

It was a lesson that he remembered well.

Mr. Tanner gave no introduction to the story of Rosewood. He jumped right in.

"...the whole bloody incident of Rosewood began with the frantic cries in the in the middle of the public street by Mrs. Fanny Taylor."

Some of the boys, including Henri, tittered self-consciously when he spoke the word "bloody."

"Help! Someone please help me! I've been beaten."

She was the wife of a white mill worker in a small town named Sumner, Florida. A tiny crowd of female neighbors gathered around the shrieking woman to comfort her. She burst into terrified tears once she cried out for help, so the neighbors could barely make out what she said had happened.

"The man was big. He didn't rape me. He beat me with his huge fist and kicked me with his boots when I fell on the floor." Her voice was getting louder. She clenched her teeth. "He was...a nigger!"

The women in the crowd repeated Fanny Taylor's words. "A nigger! A nigger raped her!"

By then, some men from the town, some of them husbands of the women, joined the small crowd of women surrounding Mrs. Taylor.

"What happened here? What's the matter?" the men asked.

"Fanny has been beaten by a nigger," several women answered in unison.

"Fanny's been raped by a nigger," one man repeated to another man who said he couldn't hear what the women had said.

"Rosewood!" several of the men hollered. "It *has* to be someone from Rosewood!"

"Yeah!" several men agreed. "There ain't any niggers in Sumner except the few who come from Rosewood to work at the sawmill."

"The sheriff warned us about an escaped prisoner named Jesse Hunter probably hiding among those other niggers in Rosewood," said Buck Ewing. "Sounds like a likely suspect to me."

The news caused the men to look at each other and reduced their disorderly howling to a more subdued murmuring. "I'll go to Bronson to notify the sheriff. Duke, gather the men by the sawmill..."

As Duke Purdy hurried off to follow his order, Ewing added, "And tell them to bring their guns and rifles."

The Sumner townsmen hollered and cheered as one by one they regathered in front of the sawmill. James Taylor, the bashful husband of the young Fanny, was in the impromptu search party, too. He was at the front reluctantly but figured that because Ewing had ordered Duke to muster this provisional militia in pursuit of the nigger deemed most likely to be guilty of beating his wife, he needed to display gratitude to them.

"We'll get the lousy son of a bitch, James. Count on it," Purdy reassured Taylor.

One of the women had assisted Fanny Taylor to a chair on a house porch across the street from the sawmill and overlooking the gathering posse. She overheard Purdy's self-satisfied bravado. Her face revealed a strange discomfort with Duke Purdy's zeal for retribution. Her glance met that of the handsome blacksmith in the gathering of men, Robert Patrick, whose skin was as white as that of any of the others. He immediately lowered his gaze from her to the ground. But Fanny's eyes betrayed a furtive intimation of shame that only Robert understood.

Sheriff Walker, followed by Buck Ewing and several armed deputies, arrived on horses from Bronson, the county seat.

Ewing and Purdy stepped back a few steps in front of the posse and ceded leadership to the sheriff. The burly, bearded man was trying hard to emulate the threatening posture of a sheriff, but he knew that both the county commission and the more persuaded of these men in Sumner were dissatisfied by his ineptness in handling "the Negro problem" in Levy County.

"We all present now? Anybody we still need to be waitin' on? If so, they'll just need to come to Rosewood on their own and join us there. The rest of you, hitch a ride on someone's wagon. We're moving on to Rosewood to snare this nigger who's escaped from the custody of the state. Make sure your firearm is loaded but don't shoot until the order to let loose comes down from me through either Purdy or Ewing. That clear?"

The men hurried and found space on one of the four or five wagons driven by their fellow townsmen. The posse of twenty or thirty was compliant with the sheriff's commands and, for the time being at least, respectful of his civic authority.

Ewing spoke privately with Sheriff Walker. "If the bastard is hiding out in Rosewood, he's likely with the schoolteacher Sylvester Carrier. If not there, then with Sam Carter, the other blacksmith in town. Both of them hate us white folks."

Walker replied, "I'm familiar with Carrier. He's been brought before me twice or three times for various offenses. Purdy, take one group of men with you to Sylvester Carrier's. Ewing, do the same at Carter's. But remember, both of you, I want Carrier and Carter taken alive, not dead."

CARRIER'S TWO YOUNG SONS were in the pinewoods in front of their home playing cowboys and Indians when they heard the rustling of feet on the forest floor not far from them. They looked at each other with trepidation They couldn't see who was making the rustling noises, but they knew almost instinctively that the approaching gang of rustlers meant trouble. They slinked off toward their home.

"Dad," one cried out inside the log house, "there's someone creeping our way. We didn't stop to see who they were but it sounded like there was a whole bunch of them like when the Klan came to threaten us about the lessons you were teaching at the school."

Just then Frank Irwin barged in through the front door. He was trying to catch his breath so he could speak. "Sylvester...there's a posse of men from Sumner comin' this way...with Sheriff Walker. They don't...look like they's intendin' to pay you a social visit...They've got guns...and rifles, Sylvester."

The initial look of confusion on Carrier's face sharpened, his eyes acutely vigilant, his lithe body ready to spring into action.

"Everybody, kneel down on the floor and keep your head down," he shouted as he himself bent low and crept along the floor toward the large window in the wall.

He saw Sheriff Walker at the head of a column of twenty or more white men who looked aroused and inflamed with single-minded hungry determination. Carrier's heart raced as someone threw a rock through the window. The crack of the window breaking was echoed by the women's shrieking.

"Keep low, dammit," Sylvester shouted.

He stood erect, though, from his crouched position and aimed two shots through the gaping hole in the glass. The shots rang out, and they could hear one of the posse cry out, "Shit! I've been hit in the leg!"

Sylvester's Aunt Thelma came over to him and tried to comfort him with her embrace.

"This shootin' at one another won't solve nothin'. I want to talk to Sheriff Walker, Sylvester. He knows me. He'll listen to me. We've helped each other several times—"

Sylvester cut her off and pushed himself from her arms. "You ain't goin' out there in front of angry men with guns, Thelma!"

"That's all crazy talk, Aunt Thelma," said Sylvester's wife, Emma. "You listen to Sylvester now."

Instead of heeding their words, Thelma ran to the door out to the front veranda and slipped out. Sylvester tried to grab his aunt by the arm, but she was too fast and determined. She stepped out carefully onto the veranda.

When the sheriff saw who it was, he ordered, "Put your guns down, men! Nobody shoot! Thelma, what are you doin' comin' out here like a crazy fool?"

Thelma's hands were outstretched. "Look, Sheriff Walker. My hands are empty. I ain't got no gun. I want to know what this fuss is all about."

"We're looking for an escaped prisoner. He's one of your people. We have reason to believe he's hiding out here in Rosewood. Is Jesse Hunter in there with you? Somebody said that he knows Sylvester."

"No, Sheriff, we don't know no Jesse Hunter, and he ain't in there. We don't know nothin' about an escaped prisoner."

"Who you got in there with you?"

"It's just us. Sylvester, his wife Emma, the three children, and myself."

Walker looked at the men in the posse, especially Duke Purdy.

"You sure that's all who's in there?"

"Sheriff, I midwifed more than half of you men into the world. You know I haven't lied to you before, and I ain't lyin' now." Thelma began to say something else but paused. "Sheriff, I saw the man who beat Fanny and almost killed her...he was...white."

Without warning, the sound of a firearm at close range resounded in the yard. The front of Thelma's apron was blotched with her blood. Her voice was stilled. Her eyes grew as large as plates as though she couldn't believe what had happened.

"Aunt Thelma!" Sylvester cried out from within the front room. Another two shots rang out from the house through the door, striking one of the posse in the leg.

Sylvester jumped out of the house onto the veranda, took hold of Thelma's ample frame, and dragged her through the door onto the floor of the front room. Emma and the children crouched behind various pieces of furniture. Emma crawled over to Thelma and cradled her head in her arms.

"She's dead, Sylvester," Emma sighed. "My God. They shot her dead."

Sylvester stood up from his crouch, aimed his rifle at the hole made by the thrown rock, and angrily emptied his rifle at the crowd outside.

Two or three more of the posse were hit; they crawled on their bellies in the direction of the pinewoods, trailing streams of blood.

Sheriff Walker held up his right hand to get the attention of the posse. "Retreat, men. Get your asses the hell out of here. Retreat, I say! Back to the horses and wagons and then back to Sumner. Come on, men. On the double!"

As the posse was retreating to the wagons, the sheriff's deputies tossed live torches of flame onto the wooden front porch and left the scene.

WHEN MR. TANNER CONCLUDED his story, he looked exhausted. The class was absolutely silent. Never had they heard such a story in school. They didn't know how to respond. With respectful silence in Aunt Thelma's honor? With silent shock at such unexpected violence? Astonishment at the crude language Mr. Tanner dared to use?

Henri didn't know how to respond either, but he maintained a stoic silence and stood up with appreciation for Mr. Tanner for taking such a risk in relating a story deeper and more vivid than the usual dry reports from their history books. Surely, Mr. Tanner was taking a big risk in telling the story. If Mr. Christopher, the principal, ever found out, he bet Mr. Tanner would be in trouble.

"That's part of the true story of a place called Rosewood. It's a story from real life. Rosewood was an actual place where people lived and worked and worshipped God and had families. Folks like some of us, boys and girls. Negroes. But if you look it up in an atlas of Florida, you'll find nothing at the place where Rosewood is supposed to be."

The children looked at each other quizzically.

"That's because it's not there anymore. There is no more Rosewood."

The children were silent, staring into the space in front of them, oblivious to the presence of the others. "There is no more Rosewood." It sounded so final and irrevocable.

"Why is there no more Rosewood, Mr. Tanner?" a tiny pig-tailed girl asked.

"The events of the beginning of the story that I related to you were followed by more terror, more death by gunfire, more homes burned to the ground. There has been no Rosewood since 1923— before you were born. But say the name Rosewood to your parents and grandparents and aunts and uncles, and they will know about it. They will remember that every building except one was burned by mobs. Every single man, woman, and child whom the posse could lay their hands on when they came back the next day from Sumner was shot and killed in cold blood. The few that survived the massacre escaped and spread out over north Florida."

"Just one house was left standing?" one of the boys inquired. "Which house, Mr. Tanner?"

"The home of Mr. John Wright and his family, the owner and operator of the town grocery store. He was a white man.... As I say, your parents or grandparents will know the story. Ask them to tell it to you."

It figures that it was the *white* family's house that was spared," said Henri, the one Negro in the class and one of only three at the Upstate New York school. He and his family had moved to Cape Vincent a few years ago from across Lake Ontario in Upper Canada. His family were descendants of United Empire Loyalist refugees from the colonies during the Revolutionary War.

Mr. Tanner looked proudly at his star pupil but tried not to betray any favoritism. He paused before commenting cautiously on Henri's observation.

"That's right, Henri. That's one reason why I told the story of Rosewood. I wanted the class, our future citizens and leaders, to become aware of some of the inequities between white and black people and communities in our country. Most Negroes are descendants of slaves who were brought to these shores in ships by white traders. Sure, you've heard that many slaves were set free after the Civil War in 1865. But let me ask you, Henri, can I put you on the spot?"

Henri shrugged his shoulders. He was sure that Mr. Tanner would ask the question anyway.

"It's been ninety years since 1865. Honestly, do you feel perfectly free?"

The question stunned Henri. All eyes in the classroom were riveted on him.

Henri pondered Mr. Tanner's question before venturing to respond. Mr. Tanner and Henri's classmates waited silently while he formulated an answer.

"Well, I don't think about whether or not I'm perfectly free most days. I am free enough to come to school and go out to the playground and play with my friends, white or Negro. But I also know from the newspaper and watching the news on TV with my dad that not every Negro pupil in our country is free to play in the same playground as the white kids, or to go to the town school like this one or the school right in their own neighborhood of the city because many schools do not allow Negro pupils to go there. They have to ride a bus to a school for

Negroes. Their state says that keeping Negro kids out of white schools is against the law, but they ignore it. So, if I was one of them, I wouldn't feel I was perfectly free."

"How do you think your parents would answer my question about being perfectly free?"

"When we decided to come to Cape Vincent," Henri said, "my father applied even before we left from Ontario for the job as supervisor, what's called the 'ferry master,' on one of the ferry boats that goes across the river to Wolfe Island. But when he got here, the bossman told him that the job had been given to another man. My dad saw that the new ferry master was a white man while he was just part of the crew. So, I don't think my father feels that he is perfectly free."

"Thank you, Henri," commented Mr. Tanner.

Henri felt proud that Mr. Tanner appreciated his remarks. At the same time, however, he wondered how his comments about "white schools" were being received by his classmates who were all white.

Billy Franklin, a tall, athletic white boy, asked, "So, what are you going to do about it, Henri? Isn't that just the way things are and have been for a long time?"

Henri glanced at Mr. Tanner who nodded at him, presumably to encourage Henri to answer Billy's rather sardonic if not contentious question. Henri would rather that he hadn't urged him to continue.

"I'm not sure I can do a whole lot about such unfairness all by myself. But I know that there are groups of people all over the United States determined to make change happen. I guess I'll just have to read and listen to the news to keep up with what's happening."

Mr. Tanner reserved the privilege of having the last word.

"Who knows, Henri? Maybe someday you will go down to Rosewood and see with your own eyes what's left of it, or to other places where these individuals and groups you mention are not satisfied with the way things are and have been and are working to change things."

Chapter Two

I think the picture in Jet magazine showing Emmett Till's mutilation was probably the greatest media product in the last forty or fifty years because that picture stimulated a lot of interest and anger on the part of blacks all over the country.

Congressman Charles Diggs, Michigan

A letter to Emile Esper
February 17, 1958

Dear Brother,

I'm writing to let you know that I arrived here in Washington, DC, on time as planned. Would you please let Mama know that I'm safe in the nation's capital? I know she's worried. The reality of the situation here is not as bad or dangerous as she imagines. I haven't been mugged, and no one has tried up to now.

Let me tell you about one of the last things I did before I departed from New York. A part of me wishes I hadn't.

You read in the papers a couple of years ago, I am sure, of the terrible and tragic death of fourteen-year-old Emmett Till. He had been sent by his mother in Chicago for the summer to visit her father and others of his extended family in Money, MS, in the Mississippi Delta.

Till was forcefully abducted from his great-uncle's home—just a ramshackle shanty back in the piney woods—by at least two white men, beaten mercilessly and shot in the woods. His mutilated body was heaved unceremoniously into the Tallahatchie River.

His slender body was recovered three days later. Newspaper reports have it that when they fished him out of the river, Till's face was barely recognizable as human, so disfigured it was, one of his eyes totally missing and the other forced shut by the swelling of his cheekbones.

I had difficulty reading the reports in the newspaper. I admit that a small rivulet of tears started to flow down my cheeks, and it grew into a veritable flood with each new story I read about Emmett that was more barbarous and violent than the one preceding it.

My God! The poor boy was in over his head the moment he

stepped off the train in Jackson. He had no idea of what Mississippi was like, how some white men there treat black lives like disposable paper cups and plates. I wonder if, before he left Chicago ,Emmett's mama told him anything at all about what white people are like where she had come from? But it's not fair, I admit, to place responsibility on her for her son's horrible slaughter. For all we know, she might have been trying to speak sense to the boy who was barely a teenager. He was probably so full of excitement about the trip south and of being independent that he didn't hear a word of what his mother might have been trying to tell him. Or he was so cocksure that he thought he didn't need any unsolicited advice from his mother, that he was smart enough to make his own way in the swamp that is Mississippi. I've detected the same attitude in our nieces and nephews who are about Emmett's age. (Of course, neither you nor I ever dismissed our elders' advice like that when we were growing up!)

One of the two men eventually apprehended by the police and charged with the murder was the proprietor of Bryant's Grocery Store, which the alleged precipitating event involving Till is said to have taken place. It's a small world! What really happened is still under dispute two years later. According to the grocer's testimony to the police, when his twenty-one-year-old wife, Carolyn Bryant, came to the store, Till whistled at her suggestively, flirted with her, and made other physical and verbal advances in plain sight and hearing of other customers.

A jury of her peers did not find the woman's testimony credible, as you probably know. The judge, in fact, didn't admit her testimony in its entirety into the court.

Nonetheless, the all-white jury found the two suspects not guilty, and the judge ordered them released from custody. What the hell did they expect? An all-white jury!

Apparently, the purported encounter between Till and the young woman violated the strict Jim Crow regulations of the interaction of a Negro male with a white female, if not an officially recorded legal code as a long-accepted ethical custom in that environment, but just as binding.

In addition to my profound sadness, reading about Till and this tragic event hit me with a sudden jolt of anxiety and even dread. On the very eve of my departure for the South as a Yankee Negro, the thought of an unsuspecting violation of a long-held cultural taboo in an unfamiliar part of the country made me realize suddenly that there was much about the deep South, frankly, that is still an unfathomable mystery to me in spite of all the reading I have done to prepare for my journey. I think I can say categorically that even if my eyes find a young lady like Carolyn Bryant attractive or sexually alluring, I will not dare to whistle at her or make any other kind of suggestive remark to her. "Just look at the candy with your eyes, but don't try to taste it," right? Wouldn't the cops just drool over the prospect of nabbing a Negro pastor flirting with a white woman?

But beyond that, how can I be sure that in my dealings with people I will not violate some other unspoken taboo? What if I look at someone in a way that people in a Jim Crow environment interpret as inappropriate? Or speak in a tone of voice that in the South is heard as terribly offensive or say something that to you and me might sound innocent enough but in Atlanta or Birmingham or rural Alabama or Mississippi is considered as outright reprehensible?

I recalled that Lucius Smallwood was the only Negro classmate I had back at Union Seminary who was from the deep South. I might have mentioned him to you in one of my letters from Union. The other Negroes were all from the big northern cities. I managed to track down Lucius's telephone number. He's now a Baptist preacher down in Crawfordville, Georgia. We had a long talk over the telephone. We got caught up with each other's lives since Union. He congratulated me on winning the Howard Thurman sermon writing contest, which I appreciated.

Then I told him how I was using the cash winnings awarded by the Thurman Foundation to do a self-guided tour of the deep South to explore the tremendous gains there in recent years made by the up-and-coming civil rights movement.

"I came to study theology in the north, in New York City," he responded, "to get the hell away from Jim Crow. Why in heaven's name would you choose to spend good money touring these states that are in Jim Crow's tightest grip?"

"Well, my mama is puzzled about the same thing. Just curiosity, I guess. There's a furious battle going on there over segregation. The civil rights movement that is trying to rid the country of the sin of segregation is motivated by Christianity and supported largely by black Christians. But at the same time, from what I read, a great deal of the adamant and sometimes violent resistance to desegregation arises from Christian churches and is couched in the language of traditional Christian biblical theology. What sense do you make of that? How can two groups of well-meaning Americans arrive at such diametrically opposed conclusions from reading the same Scripture? Maybe you've figured that out, Lucius, but I'm baffled. I know that in our history as Christians, this antithesis is not new. We've been pondering theology and the Bible for centuries and landing at radically different understandings ever since the church was born. But here it is happening right in my own country. I'm eager to explore the phenomenon here for myself. At the very least, it'll give me plenty of fresh fodder for informative sermons back in Harlem."

"I imagine then," Lucius responded, "that the folks who award the Thurman Prize would be proud that you are pursuing such a first-hand personal introduction to a social problem down here that many of us fear may be intractable and ultimately beyond human resolution."

"I hope you're wrong about that, Lucius. But except for those brief years at Union, you've lived in Dixie all your life, so I owe it to you to give your ideas serious thought. After Dr. King's surprise victory over the Montgomery city bus system last year, he and his followers are encouraged that this civil rights movement, particularly the practice of nonviolent resistance, can pull off a miracle and resolve an apparently intransigent issue."

I asked Lucius for a favor. In light of Emmett Till's sad fate, would he orient me on the more subtle, perhaps hidden quagmires in daily interactions in the Jim Crow South, particularly with whites, where I could inadvertently get trapped and be guilty of breaching some long-held custom of southern decorum and end up in pieces like Emmett Till?

Among other things he warned me about, Emile was to "never forget that in the South, the white man is in charge for the reason that he believes that God has decreed that it be so. Sure, slavery was banished over nine decades ago, but many if not most whites down here still feel they have a divine right to keep people who look like you and me subservient in every way.

"For instance, never presume to say good morning to a white person unless they greet you first. And even then, never look the white person straight in the eye. Don't make him suspect that you consider yourself his social equal. That was Emmett Till's unforgivable sin. He forgot the place in the social order assigned for him. The white man doesn't appreciate, to put it mildly, when a

Negro thinks and behaves as if he's not subject to his preeminence. There are few if any laws in the South to protect that Negro from the unfortunate and sadly often violent consequences if he does. Hence, Emmett Till. You get my point?"

Lucius paused to allow me to ponder this. "Still want to come south, Henri?"

I smiled a silly, anxious grin. I'd seen the graphic photographs in *Life* magazine of the young Emmett Till's disfigured body. Ever since my eyes came upon them, I couldn't erase them from my mind. I didn't want Mama or other siblings to ever see me like that. Truly, my innards weren't certain anymore that I was up to this purely voluntary tour I had planned.

But Rosa Parks risked a lot to keep her seat on the Montgomery city bus last December and not give it up to a much stronger white male. Can I do any less than emulate the courage of this tiny seamstress?

"I'm planning on being on the train to Washington and beyond tomorrow, Lucius," I promised.

Gotta go, brother. Still got some packing to do. And some contemplating and praying before my day is through. Stay well and take care of Mama.

With much fraternal love, your older brother,
Henri

Chapter Three

The only justification for continuing to have separate white and black schools was to keep people who were slaves "as near that stage as possible."

Thurgood Marshall

THAT AFTERNOON, HENRI DROPPED the letter to his brother in the mailbox outside the entrance to his rooming house and headed to meet the first person on his list. He had been encouraged by Negro leaders in New York to pay a visit to the N.A.A.C.P. office in Washington. There were a couple of secretaries at the office when he stopped by.

"May I help you?" an attractive twenty-something staffer asked.

When Henri said he was hoping to have a word or two with Thurgood Marshall, she reported that unfortunately Mr. Marshall was out of the office at present. "He should be back later this afternoon, Mr....?"

"Esper. I'm Henri Esper. Actually, the Reverend Henri Esper from New York."

She smiled. "I'm confident, Rev. Esper, that Mr. Marshall will be back in the office by say, 4 p.m., or shortly after that. I guarantee you that he will come in carrying a fat briefcase stuffed with briefs regarding the N.A.A.C.P. or angry letters from whites, protesting his role as the Brown family's attorney and winning the case outlawing the separation of school children on the basis of race. I'll tell him that you stopped by...Wait! I believe Mr. Rustin is in the office. I'm sure he would be happy to help you if you have concerns."

"You mean Bayard Rustin? Why, yes, if Mr. Rustin can spare a few minutes, I would like to meet him."

"Surely, Reverend Esper." The young lady escorted Henri down a short corridor and introduced him to Rustin.

Rustin's cramped office was orderly almost to the point of being obsessively neat. Henri noticed the desk held orderly piles of papers and a stylish pot on the desk in which a houseplant was thriving. So was the taller and very healthy-looking plant that towered over the scene in a ceramic planter nestled smartly in a corner.

"Mr. Rustin, it's good to meet you. Thank you for agreeing to meet with me on such short notice. You are most kind. I'm making a freelance tour of the southern states to explore some of the places in which our people have been struggling for their civil rights. That's one reason I stopped by this office today: to meet and, if possible, converse with Thurgood Marshall."

"Yes, Mr. Marshall is a veritable star in civil rights. He's among the civil rights aristocracy. But have you considered making contact with some of the contributors to the movement who are more accessible to the common man? They are key players in the movement who will never get their names in the history books. I call them the 'hidden heroes' of our movement."

"Well, sure, Mr. Rustin. I'd love to interview some of those."

"Let me ask you if you need a haircut, Rev. Esper?'

Henri was puzzled by Rustin's question.

"Whether you do or not, you would enjoy meeting Mr. Gardner Bishop. He's a committed leader of young schoolboys and some of their mothers. He'd say he's just an 'ordinary barber,' but I'm sure you'll agree with me that he's not 'just ordinary' at all. He's one of the 'meat and potatoes' people in the movement here in Washington. We couldn't survive without the likes of him. His shop is right on 7th Street in Shaw in the Northwest."

The next morning, Henri took the bus from his hotel in the Logan Square neighborhood north on Rhode Island Avene and got off at 7th Street. Rustin told him that the barber shop was just a few blocks up 7th near Florida Avenue, so he could walk and get a taste of the neighborhood.

The loquacious male server at breakfast in the Cadillac Hotel dining room had mentioned that Shaw used to be the "Negro Broadway." "There were more than a few fancy theaters on 7th before the Depression just as fine as any you'd find in Manhattan." He didn't add that he and his girl would have to bypass the luxurious ticket lobby and go around to the back of the building, purchase a couple of tickets at a small window in the brick wall, and go up to their seats in the second balcony using the back stairs.

Sure enough, there were the shells of a couple of formerly grand theatres amid the pawn shops, liquor outlets, and tiny quick food counters on 7th. There were telltale indications that the neighborhood had seen better days. The shuttered shops along the avenue conceded that the Great Depression had left its mark here, and that it hadn't enjoyed the economic benefits of the post-World War II theater renaissance as much as the rest of the country.

Merchants had house radios on portable tables in front of their establishments, some of them broadcasting jazz tunes and others the big band sounds of Glenn Miller or Woody Herman and his orchestra.

Amid the cacophony, Henri heard the singing of songs of another genre. As Henri continued on 7th, the singing became louder and more distinct the further north he progressed:

Oh, freedom; Oh, freedom; Oh, freedom over me
And before I'll be a slave I'll be buried in my grave
And go home to my Lord and be free"

sang a mixed chorus of older women and robust younger teenage and juvenile voices from a space down the stairs from the sidewalk.

A church service on a sunshine-washed weekday noontime with old and young Negroes revisiting the Source of their hope and tenacity, Henri thought.

Down a similar staircase from the level of the sidewalk at 7th and N streets to a basement was the barber shop he was looking for named "Bishop's Place." The door to the outside air was open as a suggestion of welcome. Henri went down the five or six concrete steps, entered, and was surprised that at midday the shop was silent and devoid of customers. There had been an increasing number of men mingling and joking around out on the sidewalk in the northern reaches of 7th, some of them standing in groups or a small circle with a shared liquor bottle in a brown paper bag passed among them. Evidently, they weren't interested in a haircut and were content to remain outside. Bayard had told him that Mr. Bishop was in his early or mid-sixties and perhaps happy just to maintain his long-time customers but not ambitious at this stage of life in expanding his clientele.

In a tiny vestibule-like space just beyond the salon but still in view was an old barber's chair, which Henri surmised hadn't been used for hair cutting for a long time and was probably no longer in use, with a man in it enjoying an early afternoon snooze. When he got closer to him, he could see the name "Gardner" sewn in stylish cursive letters on the front of his white barber's smock. It was none other than the proprietor of the establishment. The telephone in the salon rang, waking Gardner from his catnap. He was disoriented and then startled when he saw Henri, an unannounced stranger, standing just a few feet away.

"Your telephone is ringing, Mr. Gardner," Henri informed him gently.

"Oh, it's probably just a customer checking to see if we're open for business today. Or if there's a long line of people wanting a haircut and wondering if he should wait until we're less busy later. But it's not Saturday, and the crowd don't come on Tuesdays. Anyway, how can I help you? You need a haircut?"

Gardner Bishop looked rather distinguished in his graying hair. Henri had always been grateful that the contrast between Negroes' black skin and grey hair was so much more attractive than the anemic contrast on whites.

Henri smiled and took off his fedora so that Bishop could see that he didn't really need a trim yet.

"Not today, Mr. Bishop, I'm sorry. But I have come here to see if I can talk with you. I'm the Reverend Henri Esper from New York. I'm doing a self-guided tour of some of the places, particularly in the South, where the civil rights movement has been active lately. You were recommended to me by Mr. Bayard Rustin."

"You mean that certified homosexual from Harlem? I don't know how he knows me. I'm not one of them."

"Well, Mr. Bishop, yes, there have been rumors to that effect, but they are only rumors. Mr. Rustin has a long history organizing Negroes to secure and protect the rights that are theirs even though they are often denied to them by the political powers that be. He advised me to stop by and interview you about the struggle for equity in access to quality education in Washington despite the Supreme Court ruling. He said you have quietly been providing leadership to some Negro students in the neighborhood and their parents who are determined to gain access for their children to schools traditionally reserved for white students only."

"You say you are touring the South to visit places 'where the civil rights movement has been active lately.' I'm afraid I may disappoint you, Reverend, because the civil rights movement hasn't been involved in our little project. It's strictly a private effort by a simple barber and some local students and parents."

"I think that qualifies as forward movement in civil rights regardless of whether or not the individuals and parties leading the push are well-known by the greater Negro community and doing so with the support of one of the formal civil rights organizations. First of all, on behalf of myself and everyone who has rolled up his sleeves or put on her marching shoes for the sake of the cause, I came by to congratulate you for your daring initiative and thank you for your courageous leadership. I want to hear more about your struggle. I may learn something. I will be inspired and encouraged. Who doesn't need that? That's what makes this a movement. We join hands, even if only figuratively, and sing with our combined voices to bolster and give one another motivation and support to continue the struggle and keep our eyes on the prize, as people sing at our rallies."

"Reverend Esper, all I have been doing is listening to the gripes of the kids who come to the shop about their experiences in schools that barely take notice of the Negro students. I think to include me among 'civil rights leaders' would be an embarrassing exaggeration. I'm no W.E.B. Dubois or A. Philip Randolph. I ain't gone to Harvard or started no labor union. As I say, I'm just a college dropout who's now cuttin' hair and trimmin' beards and who listens to the gripes of a few neighborhood boys every now and then."

"Don't underestimate the value of listening, Mr. Bishop, and letting our youth know that they are being heard and their grievances taken seriously. Isn't what you are doing a movement for the civil rights of those kids? By the way, Mr. Bishop, how long have you been listening to the kids and their parents?"

"I ran out of money to pay for my college education at Shaw University in Raleigh. I had to drop out and come back home here in D.C. That was back in 1940. My late father was a barber, and I picked up a few tricks of the trade from him in his shop, which was just a few blocks from where we're sitting. Cuttin' hair and trimmin' beards are the only things I knew how to do, even if only marginally. So, I borrowed the money from one of the few banks that would do so and bought this shop. I started to know some of the boys when they came into the shop on Saturdays for their weekly trim. They are good kids, Reverend. They just need somebody older and supposedly wiser for advice and direction."

He paused to take a sip of his coffee from a paper cup. He seemed so eager to tell his story that it's doubtful he paid attention if the coffee was fresh or not.

"Some of the guys confessed that they weren't doing very well in school and that they didn't like school one bit. I remember that in my own school days there were times when I felt the same way. When I asked them why they didn't like school, more than one said that they weren't learning a lot in their arithmetic lessons. It didn't seem to them that the teacher had learned much either about arithmetic in her preparation to be a teacher. That became more glaringly apparent when the lesson plan switched from arithmetic to science."

"You had some words of wisdom for them?"

"Not many, really. Just to be patient with their elderly teacher and try their best to learn what they could because arithmetic is pretty important. Ask the teacher if there is a tutor available to help fill in the gaps in their knowledge. But mainly, I just listened patiently and finished cutting their hair. Then we'd change the subject and laugh together about the futility of the Senators ball club at the bottom of the American League again. "

Henri chuckled at that. It was like being a Dodgers fan in Brooklyn. "Isn't that one of the biggest and most important gifts we can give to one another, that we stop to listen? In fact, genuine service to others begins in listening to try to understand their real problem."

"Well, I suppose a barbershop is one of the few places where people can go to share parts of their lives and have someone listen. I know that some of them come only incidentally for a haircut."

"Like right now, for instance, Mr. Bishop. You're being invited to share your story with me in your own barbershop."

"My story isn't terribly thrilling. I hope you haven't come all the way to Washington just to hear it."

"No, it's actually the first stop on my journey. But what you say really is interesting to me. I'll be leaving for my next stop sometime tomorrow."

"Where do you go next?"

"Little Rock, Arkansas."

"Oh, boy! I hear things are rather tense down there these days. The white folks have surely been whipped into a frenzy of anger by those Negro kids' daring to come to what they consider to be their school."

"Bayard told me that you, the students, and the parents have experienced some resistance from white parents and the school board, too."

"True, but we haven't had nearly the same rancor or the loud shouting for our kids to go back to Africa. Not yet, at least."

"Oh, do you think that things might devolve someday here in Washington, D.C., into similar anger?"

"The folks in Little Rock are way ahead of us at this point. These kids are not at the stage yet where they're ready to force their way against the tide into the white schools, although there are a couple of firebrands among them who might try it if they continue to be told that they're not welcome at those schools no matter what the court says. Actually, I have a hunch that most Negro students don't have the least bit of interest in going to one of those schools. They're satisfied with the way things are and, as far as they know, have always been since Adam and Eve."

He shook his head in discouragement. After a while, near closing time, a small delegation of the boys' mothers came by the shop. Henri knew they hadn't come for haircuts. At first, Bishop told him, when the mothers came to his shop, he feared that they suspected that he was showing too much interest in their sons and came to warn him to back off. "There have been some unfortunate incidents in the city where grown men have behaved perversely with naïve, unsuspecting boys. You catch my drift?"

Mr. Bishop was awkward and embarrassed as he spoke about it with a man of the cloth and apologized for talking about such things.

"Mr. Bishop, I assure you that I'm not offended. In the course of our work, we clergy encounter all kinds of sinful behavior. It doesn't shock me."

"I suppose so, Reverend. I don't understand how you preachers can stand some people. But to get back to the boys' mothers, I repeated the same process with them that I had with their sons. I sat and listened, usually silently, so that I wouldn't get in the way."

"Hopefully, they didn't come by to chastise you."

"Actually, they came to thank me for taking an interest in their sons' education. 'Lord knows,' one said, 'it seems that no one at their school does. The principal is too preoccupied, and the teachers are all tired…'

"'Their school is not very well run or organized…,'" another added.

"And another said, 'The school building is very dilapidated. On some days, the toilets aren't flushing and overflowing with sewage. You can imagine the aroma…'

"The mothers were forming a speech choir, one chiming in after another without so much as a breath.

"'There's no clean water the kids to wash their hands…'"

"'Last week Reggie brought home his social studies book. My

God! There were obscene words scrawled all over the pages that he denies writing, especially the racist phrases. One of the book's covers was just about to fall off, so many years has the book been handed down from the kids in the white school and then from one Negro kid to another...'

"The mother who initiated the recitation concluded, 'The principal resents when we go down to report these kinds of things to him. He throws up his hands and asks, 'just what do you suggest I do about it? It's just the way it is and always will be.'"

"The schools in Cape Vincent New York where I was raised weren't pristine by any stretch of the imagination, but these schools sound a lot worse," said Henri.

"The mothers brought me up to date about the school board budget in which year after year the Negro schools were receiving far less than their fair share of tax dollars based on the numbers of Negro children enrolled.

"Our sons' school was operating at double its capacity. Double! There have been so many new Negro children who arrived with their parents or grandparents in the 'Great Migration' from Alabama and Mississippi and beyond that the schools can't handle them all. The learning conditions here are hardly an improvement over what they were used to down there. For God's sake, this is supposed to be the nation's capital!"

"When the school board—overwhelmingly white, naturally—was made aware of the overcrowding," Mr. Bishop chimed in, "they unilaterally adopted a schedule of shifts that resulted in students' receiving only four and a half hours of school per day. Trouble is, the state requires students to attend school for a minimum of six hours a day. Geez, this imprudent proposal, totally ignoring the matter of overcrowding, was particularly galling to these mothers. To me, too, for that matter. The board attempted to remedy the situation by implementing the use of two adjacent white schools that had been abandoned and left to the rats. Hand-me-downs again! Meanwhile, several white schools nearby were operating under capacity and had room to accommodate more students—if they were white."

Chapter Four

The controversy in Little Rock was the first fundamental test of the United States' resolve to enforce civil rights in the face of massive southern defiance during the period following the Brown v. Board of Education of Topeka decisions.

William Clinton
Arkansas Governor, 1979-1981, 1983-1992

AS HENRI WALKED TO THE HOTEL in the mild evening, he thought of the courageous and tender young people in Little Rock whom he hoped to meet face-to-face later on this trip. Till now, he had only known them in correspondence he conducted before his departure from New York. Their letters described an awakened hope and excitement engendered in their hearts by Thurgood Marshall's landmark victory before the Supreme Court of the United States in 1954.

In Henri's mind, these gallant youth—Charissa, Daphne, and Emmalene—were precisely the ones *Brown v. Board of Education* was intended to champion and foster. Henri prayed silently as he walked that their hopes indeed be realized, that indeed, Charissa would become a doctor and Emmalene a dedicated teacher of the next Negro generation.

Henri found himself thinking intensely about these promising youth every day. *Why?* he wondered. *What's going on? Why are my thoughts so firmly fixated on them and their education? So frequently, almost—dare I think it and name it?— to the point of being obsessive?*

These young ladies were still just that—at least twenty years his junior. He felt no sexual fantasies, no romantic delusions about them. What, then? Why am I so fiercely curious about them when I am a total stranger who wrote a letter to each of them out of the blue to ask about their educational aspirations in the wake of Brown v. the Board of Education and to congratulate them on every step they took successfully toward their ambition?

Does the word "protective" describe my feelings for them? Have I stepped into a drama in which the youth play the role of "damsels in distress" while I portray the protector who would show up in the nick of time to rescue them from the evil designs of the debased segregationists who intend to block their way to their aims by denying them admission to superior and better equipped segregated white schools?

The thought of "damsel in distress" reminded Henri achingly of Riina, a young parishioner recently married who had come by the office panicked when she had been informed that her husband had been caught stealing items at the store where he worked. He hadn't been home for the night as promised because he had been arrested for shoplifting. As Riina was leaving his office, she told Henri she was due that evening for dinner at her parents', and she'd have to tell them that the man she had chosen to wed against their express wishes was, as they warned her, nothing more than a common thief. Henri couldn't eat a bite that evening, feeling her anxiety and fear and bitter disappointment of having been let down by the man she loved.

He was drawn into the pain and fear of this "damsel in distress" and caught playing the part of her rescuer in the white hat, even though he couldn't rescue her at all but merely commiserate with her in her disappointment. Was this happening again in his deep concern for the young female students?

What am I doing anticipating their potential distress should the segregationist culture, which has victimized them based only on the color of their skin, erect insurmountable barriers to the progress of their education? Why am I foreseeing the potential distress when it is they who will have to cope with it and try to surmount the obstacles, and in one or two cases will have the resources within themselves to succeed? Am I presuming to do for them what they desire the dignity of doing for themselves?

Henri grew increasingly ashamed the more he considered the situation, remorseful that even after the incident with Riina and other damsels in distress in later pastoral encounters. *Have I learned nothing?* Not much, apparently. About the young high school students he was thinking about day and night, his circuit counselor or bishop would agree that he needed to remember where his life ended and theirs began, what were their concerns and feelings, and what was his own, then ask himself if he had the right to transgress the emotional boundaries between him and them.

THE VERY NEXT MORNING, Henri skimmed a copy of the *Washington Daily News* in the hotel dining room. His attention was captured by one particular article that cast a shadow over his happy thoughts about the three high school women in Little Rock, and certainly poured cold water over the optimism and elation he felt after talking with Gardner Bishop the prior afternoon. The article informed the *Daily News'* mostly Negro readership that on the day before, ninety percent of the total congressional delegation from the southern states had voted on a motion introduced by Senator Harry Byrd of Virginia jointly with Representative Harry Smith from the same state. Ninety percent? My Lord, has that body ever achieved such unanimity on any matter before? The motion proposed the so-called "Southern Manifesto," which soundly denounced Marshall's pride and joy, the *Brown v. Board of Education* ruling, as a "clear abuse of judicial power" and vowed to "reverse the ruling by using all legal means."

Suddenly, amid the usual noises of the breakfast room, patrons heard an emphatic "Whack!" It caught everybody's attention. The room became absolutely still. All eyes looked in the direction of Henri's table. He had folded the newspaper and slapped it down indignantly on his breakfast table. He was trembling and staring irately at the partially opened newspaper and trying not to look up at the other curious diners who were startled by this sudden eruption of ill temper. How would Charissa, Daphne, Emmalene, and other young Negro students like them react when they heard the news? What emotions were they feeling? Would their high hopes and expectations of their nation still be intact?

He continued reading the article. Arkansas Senator J. William Fulbright was one who had voted for the motion and spoke in Congress affirmatively about the bill. Fulbright had been one of Arkansas' senators since 1945.

Henri's mind raced so chaotically he could barely eat a thin piece of toast with his coffee. He was filled with acidic venom at the southern Congressional opposition to the Supreme Court ruling. *I cannot even begin to fathom how these public servants could possibly object to the Court ruling. The injustice and inequality of the Jim Crow is so clear and obvious to me. What do I see that the Congressmen cannot? Or would not? Is the problem that they don't want to see it, and so they don't?*

His white-hot righteous anger stirred in him a burning urgency to express his bitter disappointment at the Arkansas' Congressional delegation's action, to shout obscenities at them, not just on his own behalf but, more importantly, for the sake of Charissa, Daphne, and

Emmalene. And for the sake of the boys and their mothers from Gardner Bishop's barbershop—and the untold thousands of other cheated Negro youth who wanted to improve their chances for their future with a better education.

Although Henri had planned to enjoy a leisurely breakfast and then relax in the Cadillac Hotel's comfortable community room with another cup of coffee, he decided to alter his plans. He was too flooded with adrenaline to stay still. He had until late morning, until almost noon, in fact, before he had to be at Union Station to purchase a ticket and get on the train for Little Rock. Enough time to bolt over to the library at Howard University. He needed to consult an atlas of Arkansas and see if Fayetteville, home of Fulbright's local Arkansas office, was on the same train line as Little Rock and whether there was a station stop scheduled there. Perhaps he could catch the Little Rock train but get off at Fayetteville en route and pay a visit to the Senator's office.

It occurred to him that for Senator Fulbright to take him and his grievance more seriously, he needed to fabricate a story that he was a representative of some bona fide, authoritative organization. He couldn't just say that he was making a freelance personal tour of the South. He couldn't just show up unannounced at the office of a United States Senator.

At the reference library at Howard he looked up the name and telephone number of the bishop of the New York Conference of the African Methodist Episcopal Church. Because the bishop had only recently been assigned to the New York Conference, Henri hadn't had an opportunity yet to meet him. But no matter. Henri could still introduce himself at Fulbright's office as representing the bishop. Surely, that would be adequate for the purpose. What is Fulbright going to do? Order his staff to check and see if my story is true?

Henri dashed out in a rush into the foyer with the intention of asking the kind-looking maître de if he could leave his suitcase at the hotel for a couple of hours until he returned for it.

"Oh, Reverend, here," the fastidious attendant said, holding up an envelope just as Henri was almost out the door, "This arrived just a half-hour ago."

Henri was visibly befuddled. He stopped and took the envelope even though he wasn't expecting mail. *Who could possibly know where I was spending the night? How would they know?* He hadn't left a detailed itinerary with anyone, though it struck him now that it might have been a prudent idea. Emile? He hadn't mentioned to him anything about being at the Cadillac, though he might have and just didn't remember.

Who was left? Only Lucius. *Did I say anything to Lucius during our long telephone call the night before I departed New York? We talked about a lot of things. But I couldn't have named the Cadillac because I didn't know about it until I found it in The Green Book and didn't make a reservation here until the next day.*

Henri hurriedly borrowed the letter opener on the registration counter without asking for permission and inserted it in the envelope. He put the envelope aside and opened the pieces of paper inside. Sure enough, they were from Lucius Smallwood.

"Hey, buddy. How are you faring in your travels? You're surprised to hear from me, I wager. I was overjoyed to talk with you. Your questions to me on the telephone were a little unsettling for me, however. Now, don't take this the wrong way. Your questions were altogether appropriate and fitting ones to ask when you were about to venture all alone into what to you is totally uncharted territory. I'm flattered, frankly, that you remembered me from Union and felt free to ask such questions.

"It's just that I woke up the next morning feeling mighty concerned for you. More specifically, for your safety. There are a lot of myths about the South, especially among you Northerners, and they lead to some misconceptions about it. It's the way many Southerners have the paranoid belief that no one is safe walking the streets of Manhattan. My family was certain that I'd never survive three years at Union in the middle of that den of violence and Yankee iniquity.

"The Emmett Till episode that put such fear into you is not typical nor an everyday occurrence, even in God-forsaken Mississippi. I think the torrid heat and humidity there can drive some of the white people plain loco.

"In any case, if I were you, I wouldn't let poor Emmett's horrific experience and cruel fate give you the wrong impression. Just behave properly, as I know you always do, and don't do anything stupid, and you'll be all right.

"Yet, you couldn't disguise the real apprehension in your voice on the telephone about the wisdom of stepping out on your trip in the South alone. That made me nervous, as I say. It got me thinking that I should offer to come along and be a guide. I wouldn't want to be a

chaperone or escort, just a travel companion who might impart a little practical southern wisdom. Kind of like the ushers at the church who show the worshippers their way to a pew.

"Listen, Henri. For reasons I won't take time to go into right now (all good), I'm suddenly a free man. For a month or two, I am relieved of my ministerial duties at St. James. (Again, not for any misconduct or dereliction of duty or any such thing.) If my idea works out, I can lay out the details when we're on the road.

"Henri. What I am saying is that for now, I'm footloose and fancy free. I'll go home to Louisville for a few days to see my family, but I don't want to stay there too long. In February and March, the weather isn't very hospitable. Freezing rain or sleet most days if it's not snowing...

"So I thought of you, equally free as a bird but all by your lonesome somewhere in the Jim Crow South, probably in climes more suitable for Southern folks like me.

"Want some company?"

HENRI HAD MISPLACED THE NUMBER to call Lucius, so he wrote back right away that same afternoon. Scribbling, he told him of his excitement about having a travel companion.

"Hopalong Cassidy had his grizzled sidekick Gabby Hayes, the Lone *Ranger had the faithful Tonto, and Don Quixote had Sancho Panza to provide Spanish proverbs and wisdom for their journey. You're not nearly as good-looking as Gabby and Tonto, but you'll do."*

Lucius called Henri by telephone at the hotel the next day after receiving his letter. Henri had decided to delay his trip to Little Rock to wait for Lucius to join him. It wouldn't be very far from Louisville for Lucius to travel south to Little Rock. They agreed to catch up with each other at Little Rock's Union Station.

Chapter Five

The nature of inequalities and divisions between the races was a matter not merely of formal civil status and law, but also of deeply etched economic arrangements, social and political conditions, and cultural outlooks and practices.

John Hope Franklin
The Color Line

"OH, MR. HENRI," MRS. WILLIAMS, the proprietor of the Cadillac Hotel greeted Henri at breakfast. "Here's a telephone call for you. I am sorry that I cannot pronounce your last name."

"Don't worry, you're not the only one. It's actually pronounced 'Les-per-awnce', but I usually shorten it to 'Esper.'"

"I appreciate that, Mr. Esper. I'm sure the others do, too. Oh, I'm keeping you from your phone call."

"Thank you, Mrs. Williams."

Taking the receiver, Henri said, "Hello. This is Henri Esper."

"Henri, I'm so glad I caught you before you're out on the town for the day." It was Lucius calling from Kentucky. "My meeting you in Little Rock will have to be delayed once again. My father's gotten sick...very sick...a stroke, we think. I need to hang around here and help Mama care for him until my sister arrives from Jackson, Mississippi."

"I'm sorry that your father is ill, Lucius. How is his prognosis? You say, 'he is very sick.' How sick? Do you think you'll still be able to join me as a travel companion?"

"I wouldn't miss it for the world, Henri. As soon as my sister gets here, I'll get on the road and meet you, where? Somewhere in Little Rock in a few days, you said, didn't you?"

"I'm relieved you're still looking forward to our adventure, Lucius. I have an appointment scheduled with Senator Fulbright's head of staff in Fayetteville on my way to Little Rock. I'll get settled there somewhere and let you know where to meet me."

IT WAS A FEW MINUTES AFTER 7:30 p.m. when Henri's train from Washington pulled into Fayetteville. He had been on the train since around midnight of the day before—more than thirty-six hours. An unexpected stop in North Carolina to correct a mechanical problem had added several hours to the travel time. Henri had tried to remain awake so as not to sleep through his stop. He gathered his bag and books and stepped off the train at the main station of the Arkansas-Missouri Railroad, not in Fayetteville proper, mind you but in a small neighboring town named Springdale.

Only one other passenger got off the train, obviously, a student at the University of Arkansas, judging from his telltale, bright red Razorbacks' jacket. They stepped into the terminal, Henri through the entrance allocated for Negroes, the Arkansas student through the whites' entrance. The terminal was almost totally abandoned at that hour of the evening except for a Negro custodian silently mopping the floor.

Henri looked in vain for any indication of some kind of diner or restaurant. He was famished after his journey. The kitchen staff at the Cadillac Hotel had put together a sackful of ham and cheese sandwiches, as well as a few legs of fried chicken.

"Mr. Henri, these are for you to refuel on your trip," Mrs. Williams had said as she came out of the kitchen carrying the brown-paper sack. "It will save you from having to search for a diner at stops along the way. You may find a diner, but one that serves folks like you and me, I suspect may be another story."

It looked as though there were enough sandwiches in the sack to last the day-and-a-half trip into the heart of Arkansas and still have enough to feed a small company of strangers on the streets of Fayetteville. By the time Henri got off the train, all he had left was an empty sack. *With all due respect to Mrs. Williams, I hope I never see another ham sandwich again.*

Henri did find a small restaurant in the station but it was closed. A handwritten sign adhering to the glass on the entrance door said that the establishment would be open again at 7 a.m. the next morning. He noticed the other sign posted just beside the one listing the hours of business: WHITE PATRONS ONLY. NEGROES NOT SERVED.

Now, in addition to his hunger, he had the logistical problem of not having a place nearby to get something to eat after a long, restless night on a train. But there really wasn't much space in his brain for such mundane matters as he struggled to put a lid on his anger. He had succeeded in doing so during the train ride but now his emotions again threatened to explode at the sign in the restaurant's door, at Fulbright, and at the other signers of the "Southern Manifesto." His anger at Fulbright, initially provoked yesterday by the article in the *Daily News,* had been under control while on the train, but now he knew he had to discipline and restrain it before going to Fulbright's office. He couldn't go in there foaming at the mouth and spewing invective and hope to be listened to and taken seriously.

Out of the corner of his eye he saw that the college kid was now observing him closely. Self-consciously, Henri pretended to be examining the signs on the restaurant's door. Was this young white student's scrutiny of him from a distance a friendly sign, or one of which he should be apprehensive? Was the fellow trying to read Henri's mind, suspicious of his intentions, wondering what this solo Negro was up to?

Henri stood still. Was he revealing his heightened nervousness about this young man surveilling him? The student started walking toward Henri cautiously, as if he had come across a snake in the grass. *Am I in danger?* Why would he move closer to a Negro stranger in a near deserted railway station?

Henri felt quite uncomfortable. He dearly wanted to communicate to the young man that he was not a threat to his safety—that he was friendly and approachable. *How do I do that? I don't know the etiquette. Should I smile and nod my head at him in greeting?* Maybe just subtly. "Certainly not, Henri," Lucius would warn him. "Don't speak to a white person until he or she has first spoken to you. Always remember that the white man, even if just a teenage college student, assumes that he's in charge of the encounter."

He wished that Lucius was there in person to provide guidance. There was so much he didn't know. He disappointed himself at how incompetent and helpless he felt and how unsure he was about what to do in what was probably, he hoped, just a relatively innocuous circumstance.

His quandary was resolved when the young man did come over and introduce himself most cordially. "Mornin'. I'm Wallace Vandorf. I'm a student at the university. I hope you don't mind my sayin', sir, you look a tad lost, like you're looking for something or someone—your ride home, perhaps— you expected to find here but couldn't. Can I help?"

This young student must have been raised in a good family. Nothing "good ole boy" or "redneck" about him. His parents had taught him the essentials of being polite to strangers, even to a Negro one. Henri felt reassured.

"I'm glad to meet you, Wallace. I'm Henri."

"You're not from here, are you, Henri?"

"Is it that obvious? No, it's my first time south of the Mason-Dixon line, actually. I'm from way up north in the far reaches of New York State, but I live in the city now, New York City."

"New York City! Man, what brings you way down here to Arkansas? I was born right here at Fayetteville General. I've never lived anywhere else. I haven't even left town to go away to college. There's a good university right here in town so I chose to stay close to home. How very unAmerican of me, right?"

"Not really, Wallace. I went to St. Lawrence University in Canton, New York, just fifteen or so miles from my home in Cape Vincent. I had gone to high school in Canton, so I figured why not just stay in a place you know well?"

"My father is head of the history department at Arkansas. If I had chosen some other school like most of my friends and classmates, I was afraid he'd think I was turning my nose up at the institution where he teaches."

The conversation so far was pleasant and comfortable enough, but Henri feared that they would soon run out of common topics to talk about. Then what? How so very unlike a preacher to be close to running out of words and things to converse about.

Wallace might have been feeling the same way, Henri speculated. Henri didn't know how often Wallace might have approached a Negro before and struck up an easy, informal conversation. But to his relief, he didn't seem at all awkward or the least bit skittish about chatting with Henri.

"Man, that was a long train ride," Wallace sighed. "I got on in Richmond. I'm so hungry now that I could eat the hog they make bacon out of."

"I got on in Washington. I'm with you, friend. I'm also hungry."

"Listen. I have a car out in the south lot. There're not many places for a bite to eat out here in the sticks. But I know there's a new IHOP diner not terribly far from my dorm, It's open until midnight most nights. Do you want a ride there?"

Henri was a little stunned by Wallace's overture. How was he supposed to answer? A white man's offering a ride in his car to a Negro he didn't know was unusual, even in the North. He'd also heard many tales of suspicious predators cruising train stations for unsuspecting easy marks.

Wallace perceived Henri's hesitation. "The IHOP is a very casual, laid-back kind of place near the university campus. You don't need to be concerned about having to change your shirt and slacks. No one is that formal there."

"Wallace, in that case, that's right kind of you to offer. I really don't have any other way to get anywhere except a cab. I pictured this as a train station in the heart of the city with all kinds of shops and places to eat as in New York and Washington. It's probably too far to walk from here to the IHOP, isn't it?"

"Yes, I'd say a bit too far to walk. Besides, why walk when you can ride in a car?"

"Then I think I'll take you up on that ride."

WALLACE DROVE THE BLUE VOLKSWAGEN Beetle expertly through the rolling farmland between Springdale and the university town. He slowed his speed as they crossed the city limits of Fayetteville but drove in a way that showed his familiarity with the city. The street Wallace had chosen to enter the city, Garland Road, changed its name to Razorback Drive, a certain indication to Henri that they weren't far from Wallace's dormitory.

"As soon as you see an open parking spot, Henri, let me know. We can walk to the IHOP from here."

There weren't many free spots, but they finally found one. They got out of the VW and started walking in the direction that Wallace indicated.

They stepped in the door to the IHOP. The place was very busy, mainly with what Henri thought were a few white working men in their industrial uniforms and some middle-aged Negro couples. Country and Western music played on the jukebox. One large table was occupied by a large party of white male college students with an occasional female date squeezed in.

As they progressed behind the IHOP hostess through the aisle between the tables and booths, people seemed to interrupt their happy chatter and regard the new white and Negro guests carefully. Even after Wallace and Henri were seated in their booth, the curious eyes of the other patrons continued to examine them.

Henri was reflecting pensively on the curious reactions of the other guests. Wallace didn't talk right away, but then looked Henri directly in his face and asked, "Henri, did you notice the sudden muffling of the chatter when we entered the restaurant?"

"As a matter of fact, I did. I was just contemplating what it all meant. I guess they're not accustomed to a Negro's entering their dining space."

"I don't think that it's just your presence alone here that confounded them. They've seen Negroes here before, and some are here now. There are exceptions, I'm sure. But most white students are getting more accustomed to places that are no longer segregated."

"But why, then, were they confounded, as you say?"

"If we had already been seated and digging into our dinner, some might have taken a second look. Then they'd go on with their business. It's seeing a Negro and a white guy coming in together for dinner. They may be finding that arrangement...well, not inappropriate necessarily, but a little novel. They are probably considering me as their enemy more than you, believe me. Folks down here are still trying to adjust to everything that is suddenly novel. Some are suffering from what I would call 'novelty fatigue.'"

"'Novelty fatigue.' I must say that that's a refreshingly positive way of understanding the situation, Wallace."

"Where are you headed from here, Henri? Fayetteville isn't normally on the itinerary of New Yorkers unless they're avid college football fans."

"Well, tomorrow I've got an appointment at Senator Fulbright's local office."

"Ah, the revered former president of this fine university, the gallant man who stuffed a giant wad of cotton or something in Senator Joseph McCarthy's mouth so he'd finally shut up! Congratulations on your choice of bigwigs to visit."

"Oh, I won't get to meet the man himself. I'm told he's at a conference at Oxford in England. I get to have my conversation with his chief of staff instead."

"And what will you talk about? The market price of cotton? The names of diners that serve the best grits?"

"About which I know less than nothing, especially the price of cotton."

Henri hesitated, not sure he should divulge his real mission at Fulbright's office. He sensed that political conversations were taboo in the South, or at least a Yankee's promoting his own personal political views was probably not wise here. But what the heck,

Wallace drove a Volkswagen, not a Lincoln. He was a little different from the mainstream.

"I want to register my disappointment, and that of the presiding Bishop of the New York Conference of the AME Church, about the senator's motion to join with those who are formulating the 'Southern Manifesto,' vowing to oppose in every way the *Brown v. Board of Education* ruling of 1954."

"You're in favor of desegregating public schools then, I presume?"

Again, Henri hesitated. *I really don't want to spoil our dinner and alienate Wallace with a political argument.*

"Well, yes, I'm one of those Yankees who has a hard time figuring out what problem William Fulbright and George Wallace and Strom Thurmond and the rest of their gang of segregationists have with desegregated schools."

Wallace was quiet now. Henri was certain he was regretting that he ever offered to help this foolish misguided Yankee Negro with the little kindness of a ride from the train station to a diner and walk into that diner together with him.

Henri tried to interpret the look on Wallace's face.

Gradually, a smile broke out on his face. "Henri, I sure do wish that more white people down here would think like you do. The whole notion of their losing their exclusive right to attend white-only schools is one of those 'novel ideas' that is just too far beyond the ability of many to adjust to. Perhaps someday, after some time. If only they would venture to meet some Negro leaders, genuinely listen to the stories of their Negro neighbors, and really honestly share their own."

Chapter Six

The southern states fought to preserve segregation after the Brown v. Board of Education Supreme Court decision.

WALLACE OFFERED HENRI A RIDE to the hotel whose listing Henri had found in *The Green Book*.

"This one is right by the university campus," Wallace said helpfully. "It's not far from here at all and ought to be convenient to the Senator's office."

Once in the car, he questioned Henri again. "What is that book where you find all these listings for hotels and restaurants? I've never even heard of some of the hotels that are listed in there for Fayetteville."

"That doesn't surprise me. If you have guests from out of town who may require hotel accommodations, they can choose just about any hotel in town and enjoy a good night's sleep. But many of those hotels that have rooms for your guests will suddenly discover that they have no vacancy when a colored man shows himself at the registration desk. It's happened to me more than once. That's why I carry *The Green Book* around with me whenever I travel; it's just about as valuable to me as the Bible."

Wallace took a quick glance at Henri in the passenger seat with raised eyebrows.

"Its marketing slogan is, 'Never leave home without it.'" Henri felt like a teacher, and like all teachers, he had to learn when to stop teaching.

"You find the names and addresses of hotels that cater to Negroes?" Wallace asked.

"Precisely. It saves us from the humiliation of being refused and turned away by a hotel that has chosen not to rent rooms to us, which is the majority of them."

"You would pay for the room with the same United States currency as I or any other white person would, wouldn't you? What's their problem? Your money not good enough?"

Henri was simultaneously growing weary of having to explain the basics of travel for Negroes in the United States yet welcoming the opportunity to cultivate a potential white ally.

"Apparently not, Wallace. I guess some of these hoteliers

perceive some kind of moral transformation happening in the dollar bill whenever it passes from a Negro's wallet into the white man's hand." His voice grew heated as he continued. "Like we have contaminated the dollar bills with some kind of 'cooties' or something. I really don't understand it. You're white. Maybe you can figure it out."

Henri calmed down and apologized. "I'm sorry, friend. You've been terribly kind to me. You deserve better than to be the brunt of my frustration."

"Man, I can appreciate your frustration," Wallace said. "I doubt that many white people would be happy having to consult an alternate travel guide while traveling in their own country."

He pointed out the new federal building where Senator Fulbright had his local office as they passed it, then pulled up in front of a squarish four-story brick building. "This the place we're looking for?" Wallace asked.

"It has the address listed in *The Green Book*. It must be it." Henri sounded a little unsure. There was no sign or any other indication visible on the building to identify it as a hotel. Henri grabbed his suitcase from the back seat, opened the passenger door, and exited the car. "I'll go inside and check it out," he said to Wallace through the open window. "Thanks for the lift and the company for dinner."

Wallace displayed a mischievous smile. "You go in and get a room. If the place is a gambling den or a house of ill repute, I'll wait here for a few minutes."

"Understood," Henri said, then walked to what may, or may not, have been the entrance door. Five minutes later, Henri came back out carrying his suitcase and looking a little sheepish.

"What's the matter?" Wallace asked him. "You didn't pass the dress code?"

Henri sounded irritated. "No, the indifferent louse behind the registration desk said that the hotel's listing in *The Green Book* has expired and is out of date. This place is not on the list any longer. And I couldn't believe that they don't even have showers."

"So where now, boss?" Henri was taken aback by being addressed as "boss" even though he knew that Wallace meant it as a good-natured joke.

"The clerk warmed up to me and told me about the nearest hotel in *The Green Book*. It's just down on West Clinton Avenue. Not far, he said. They even have showers for the guests, he assured me."

"To West Clinton, then, we go."

THE HOTEL ON WEST CLINTON WAS farther away from Fulbright's office than the first one. But Henri calculated that if he hit the sidewalk before the March sun started to heat the morning air, he could walk it.

An attractive receptionist greeted him when he entered Fulbright's office suite. Henri judged from her elegant appearance and wardrobe that she might moonlight as a model for a cosmetics company or something. The name on the plate on the table identified her as Valerie Slocum.

"Good morning, sir. Can I tell Mr. Francis who is here to see him?"

"My name is Henri Esper from New York. I called yesterday about an appointment."

"Oh, yes, Mr. Esper, I recall. But it's the Rev. Mr. Esper, isn't it?" This woman was efficient and used to being in control.

"Yes, you remember correctly."

"Well, Rev. Esper, I will inform Mr. Francis that you have arrived. Please make yourself comfortable and kindly wait here. Help yourself to a bottle of Coca Cola from the small refrigerator or a cup of coffee from the carafe."

Henri was thirsty from the walk to the office but resisted the temptation of Coca Cola or coffee. *Caffeine is not the best idea when I'm already a little jumpy about this meeting. I've never met with a Senator before, not even with a Senator's chief of staff.*

Henri chose a magazine from on top of the coffee table. *Arkansas Today*. Skimming the table of contents, he noticed the name of an article, "The Woes of Little Rock," about the crisis induced by the attempt the past fall by nine Negro students to enroll at the Central High School in Little Rock.

Henri skimmed the first paragraph. Central High was the school where young Aliza Beckwith, Charissa Sands, and seven other Negro youth were attending in spite of the odds stacked against them. Henri had been thoroughly impressed by their courage and single-minded determination to succeed when he first read about them in the press. His esteem for them only grew when they responded to his invitation to share some of their moving story with him in correspondence.

"I don't understand the interpretation of the Little Rock school crisis on the part of the editors of *Arkansas Today,*" Henri thought. "They seem to be implying that it was induced by the Negro students' attempts to desegregate Little Rock Central. It's as clear as the nose on a man's face that had the white governor not resisted desegregation as he did and enlisted the active support of the Arkansas National Guard to bar the Negro students' entry into the school, there would be no crisis."

Henri thought he'd better curb his growing annoyance at anyone with a segregationist bias, but not overregulate it to the point that it failed to energize him as it was doing.

A fortyish gentleman dressed in an impeccably tailored grey suit entered the waiting room and stood confidently in front of Henri. He introduced himself as Mr. Stephen Francis and offered him his hand. "Rev. Esper, I'm sure?"

"Yes, Sir. I'm the Rev. Henri Esper of New York. I come to represent my bishop, the Presiding Bishop of the New York Conference of the African Methodist Church, Rev. Earl Caldwell."

"It's good to meet you. Shall we step back into my office and discover what's on your mind?"

Henri reached back to the table of magazines, picked up the copy of *Arkansas Today,* and carried it with him as they proceeded to the man's office. *I may need this as additional ammunition,* he thought.

Mr. Francis's office was made to look more spacious by the conference table and chairs in the space in front of his large desk. He pulled out a chair for Henri. "Please, make yourself at home, Rev. Esper. Can I get a Coca Cola or a cup of coffee for you?"

I wonder if Fulbright owns stock in Coca Cola or represents its interests in lobbying efforts? That's twice now within a few minutes that I've been offered a Coke.

"No thank you, Mr. Francis, I'm good."

Mr. Francis is undoubtedly trained in the gracious art of small talk with a constituent. But I have no less doubt that he's already concluded that the issues that he thinks I have come here to explore are minor and largely irrelevant to the Senator's best interests. He wants to move this meeting along, escort me affably out of here, and then be free to go on to what he considers more pressing matters.

"Rev. Esper, I believe when you made this appointment you mentioned to Miss Slocum that you wanted to discuss Senator Fulbright's position on what is referred to as the 'Southern

Manifesto.' I apologize that the Senator is away in Oxford, England, meeting with other parties who are working on furthering international peace and understanding. I certainly want to hear your questions and concerns and respond on behalf of the Senator to the best of my abilities, then report your concerns to him when he returns."

"Thank you, Mr. Francis. Yes, I'd like to begin with that. I'm glad I was able to get an appointment the very next day."

"Thank you, Reverend, for caring enough about an issue that you would come see us. Now, how can I help you?"

"You may know that the African Methodist Episcopal Church is one of the largest Christian denominations ministering primarily to Negro parishioners. We consider ourselves the spokespersons for Negroes who may or may not reside within the borders of our district."

As soon as Henri had said the words, "You may know," Mr. Francis's face took on a look that Henri was sure indicated that no, Mr. Francis did not know.

"I'm a Southern Baptist myself, Rev. Esper. I know and have known members of AME churches, of course. But I have to acknowledge that I am not very familiar with the theology or polity of your denomination."

That sounds like an invitation to enlighten him. But no, I must not lose myself in a distraction from my goal. Oh, Mr. Francis, believe me. You don't have time to hear my convoluted description of AME matters, not even a condensed elevator speech.

"Mr. Francis, the AME church is concerned when the rights of the Negro people are threatened or jeopardized anywhere in our country. Be assured that Bishop Caldwell was in telephone conversations with many AME bishops of the districts in the southern states to ensure that he wasn't speaking out of turn and that they, too, shared his concerns about the vote in Congress last week concerning the 'Southern Manifesto.' He is speaking for a lot of Negro church leaders."

"That sounds like a wise policy, Reverend. But first of all, we must be clear that there really is no such entity called the 'Southern Manifesto.' It's just a catchy name that the press came up with as shorthand for the many articles in the bill proposed by numerous senators and representatives from the southern states. The correct legal name of the legislation is 'The Declaration of Constitutional

Principles.'"

Don't fall for it, Henri. He's just trying to put you in your place as a know-less-than-nothing and that he has the upper hand in this conversation.

"To us, Mr. Francis, segregation by any other name is still segregation, which is an anathema to us and the AME church."

"With all due respect, Reverend, your church, which I am sure is very fine, does not have a monopoly on the questions of segregation or desegregation. There are many Christians, white or Negro, who are opposed to increased desegregation. Many Baptists, for example."

"You're correct, Mr. Francis, no denomination, not even the AME church nor the Southern Baptist nor anyone else possesses one hundred percent of the truth. But I am also aware that Christian churches among the Negro people, at least, are on the cusp of a revival. I don't mean the religious kind you witness in the Billy Graham crusade. No, I mean more of a massive awakening from a long sleep among the Negro population."

"That's very interesting, Reverend Esper. Can you point me in the direction of evidence of such an 'awakening'?

"There's increasing social and political ferment in Negro communities all over the country. You've noticed, I'm sure, that in the past few decades there has been a spirit of quietude and impassivity in Negro communities. That spirit has been misinterpreted by many white leaders as a sense of acquiescence by Negroes to the status quo, a reluctant acceptance of a life to which they have had to adjust and comply."

Francis was following along. "I'm not naïve enough to believe that Negroes altogether approve of their plight or are happy with the status quo."

"Wait a minute, Mr. Francis. Are you confident that the Senator would approve of your making such a statement? How would he describe the Negroes 'plight?' Your choice of the word 'plight' is very revealing. It suggests you consider the circumstances of Negroes' lives to be a predicament of some kind in which much of their daily energies need to be devoted to mere survival. If so, you are close to accurate. Your state has one of the highest concentrations of poverty in the country, Mr. Francis. Many or most of those people are Negroes...I find it incredible that you as the chief of staff of a United States Senator would think that Negroes are satisfied with such a 'plight?'"

Henri was wound up after making his point. He felt he had hit a home run. Francis wasn't certain how to respond.

"You misheard me, Reverend Esper. I never said that most or all Negroes are content with their circumstances, or the way things are. But I venture to wager that some are when thy compare their lives today with the way they were a couple of decades ago."

"Then I suggest you go over to talk with the Negroes in Phillips County. Negro folk are not accustomed to speaking their minds and telling the truth. They've lived with the fear of retribution for a long time. They have found that they and their communities are safer if they deny any displeasure with what they have, at least in the presence of white people with influence. I'm told that the Negroes of Phillips County are far beyond such fear of retribution and may just speak openly and tell the truth to people who are open to hearing it.

"There's a growing dissatisfaction among Negroes today," Henri continued. "Negroes have grown tired of Jim Crow restrictions on their freedom, their awareness that in so many ways they have been made to think of themselves as second-class Americans."

"I assure, you, Rev. Esper, that neither I nor the Senator see them as anything less than genuine citizens of the United States with full rights of citizenship as defined in the Fourteenth Amendment to the Constitution." Francis sounded defensive.

Henri felt the familiar anger brewing again. Does he really believe that? He hasn't visited the neighborhoods on the other side of the tracks for a while, has he? Has he checked to see how many Negroes are on the voter rolls? *Calm down, Henri, and speak rationally.*

"With all due respect, Mr. Francis, I think I speak for many of my people who feel that the Fourteenth Amendment has been violated so many times by whites and the governments that supposedly represent their interests. That amendment is, I'm afraid, pretty well null and void. Negroes continue to be treated as less than genuine and full citizens of this country."

"Rev. Esper, the Negroes of Arkansas are, for the most part, content with their lives here in the State of Opportunity. Sure, occasionally you'll read about a violent lynching of a Negro, but

Arkansas is not Mississippi or Alabama. Our troubles begin when outside influences try to impose their analysis and solutions on our problems when the Negroes are manipulated and, frankly, brainwashed. Like when leaders of that N.A.A.C.P. come over from Atlanta and install one of their kind as their regional representatives here in a state that is not theirs."

Henri was downright astounded by the man's barefaced, one-sided misinterpretation that bordered close to bigotry, something he was not even trying to hide. Henri wasn't at all confident how to proceed. In the vacancy, Francis continued.

"Rev. Esper, you wonder about Senator Fulbright's support of what you call the 'Southern Manifesto.' Reverend, you say that there's a growing dissatisfaction among the Negroes about Jim Crow, and so on. Well, the Senators and the other political leaders from the South, are at the point of utter frustration, too. Their resentment is growing to the breaking point at the attempts by the feds to dictate how we Southerners should live and educate our children."

The neck under Francis's collar of his dress shirt was turning a bright Razorback red now.

"I presume you are referring to the 1954 Supreme Court Ruling of *Brown v. the Board of Education*, Mr. Francis?"

"You're damn right, I am...if you'll pardon my French. What do those highfalutin judges up in Washington know about our schools in Arkansas, or Georgia, or Tennessee or any of our southern states? Don't they understand how adamantly opposed the white citizens here are to the notion of mixed-race schools? Their decree now mandates the school boards of every peaceful locality in the South and elsewhere to upset the apple cart and design plans to desegregate their public schools that we don't want. Don't they appreciate what an accursed can of worms that opens? How difficult that will be? How their Yankee ruling goes directly against our tradition here in the South, our southern way of life?"

Francis had worked up quite a passionate head of steam. He took a handkerchief and wiped the perspiration from his brow. He paused for a moment to collect himself. Next, he spoke to Henri in a more sober, pragmatic tone of voice while hardly modifying the content of his tirade.

"Anyway, Reverend, that is why the Senator supports the vow of the other southern political leaders to do all they can to undermine the requirements of *Brown v. the Board of Education*."

Henri sat looking in disbelief at the agitated Francis across from him. Henri had more he wanted to say. But would his defense of the Supreme Court's decision be welcomed at this particular juncture...or even heard?

Francis picked up a file folder from his desk and arose. "I thank you, Reverend, for your interest in the Senator's Congressional vote. I hope that my explanation has helped you understand his reasons."

Henri felt he had no choice but to rise from his chair as well. He shook Francis's extended hand, said "thank you" unenthusiastically, and hurriedly bade farewell.

Well, that was a monumental waste of time and effort, like trying to talk to the damn wind.

Chapter Seven

It comes as a great shock around the age of five, or six, or seven, to discover that the country to which you have pledged allegiance along with everyone else has not pledged allegiance to you.

James Baldwin

February 23, 1958

Henri woke up excited about the day ahead. His solo tour of the Deep South was going to metamorphose into an adventure for two. Lucius was coming from Kentucky to join him for the next legs of the journey. As such, Henri felt that he was the host and Lucius the guest.

They had settled on meeting in the waiting room in Union Station near downtown Little Rock. The venerable rail terminal landmark tall clock tower would be visible to Lucius as he drove through this unfamiliar city.

Henri arrived almost an hour early. He had gone to the breakfast room at his hotel a little after 7:30 a.m., but had forgotten that Saturday the breakfast service was delayed until 9:00 a.m.

He scouted the Union Station for a diner or at least a coffee stand where he could grab a cup of brew and a donut. When he found the coffee shop he saw the sign, now familiar to him, that they served white patrons only.

Damn! All a man wants is a humble cup of coffee to start the day. I'm not asking for much. I don't even drink it black. Damn it. I'm just going to plant myself at the door until somebody on the wait staff notices me and perhaps serves me as a take-out customer.

A well-dressed, middle-aged male traveler stepped in behind him.

"Good morning," the man greeted him in a Southern drawl. "Is this the beginning of the line?"

Initially, Henri was uncertain to what line the man was referring. "Oh no, sir. You can move right up and let them seat you. There's no line."

The man glanced at the sign just inside the door, and then the truth of the situation must have dawned on him. He turned to Henri and said, "Oh, I'm sorry. I often pop in here for breakfast at the beginning of my business trips to Memphis. I should have remembered they don't serve Nigrahs. That's an inhumane way to begin a morning. When I get seated I will order something for you and bring it out to you. What would you like?"

Henri was nonplussed by the unexpected gesture. A few frames of an imaginary film of his life in Harlem played on the screen of Henri's mind. He was on the shady side of 125th Street in order to be sheltered from the summer sun when a down-at-the-heels black man dressed in a shabby winter coat approached him and through a mouth missing a few teeth asked for the favor of a dollar and a half to get a cup of coffee and a donut. "I'm cold and it's been since Thursday when I last ate."

Since he'd come to Harlem, Henri had a personal policy not to give cash to panhandlers. "You never know how the panhandler is going to use the cash," Sylvester Plimpton, a neighboring Baptist preacher and Harlem veteran, had told him once. Henri didn't want to refuse the person's request entirely so he would ask the supplicant to accompany him to a nearby diner or donut shop where Henri would order and pay directly for a cup of coffee and a plain donut. Henri thought, at those times, that Brother Plimpton ought to be satisfied that Henri had the old parson's advice.

Now the shoe is on the other foot. I'm the indigent receiving a charitable cup of coffee and donut through the generosity of a stranger. I am glad for the coffee, but otherwise not entirely sure how I feel about the experience.

Henri received the coffee and pastry with thanks. He offered to give the man a buck and a half, but the man declined. "Just pay it forward for someone else who is in need."

Henri found an open space on one of the antique high-backed wooden benches in the waiting room and took his time with his "breakfast."

The next time he glanced at his watch, he realized that the planned 10:30 a.m. meeting time with Lucius had passed.

I've had my eyes riveted to the front door for over a half-hour to see him when he comes in. How could he possibly have escaped my notice?

He immediately got up from the bench to search for Lucius. He scouted the waiting room benches, but no sign of Lucius there. He surely wouldn't be in the coffee bar because they didn't cater to Negroes. He checked the line at the ticket window and then poked his head into the baggage room, just in case. Still no Lucius.

When he returned to his place on the waiting room bench, he heard a faint voice call out something indecipherable. Such a high-pitched voice was definitely not that of Lucius.

"You lost?" the voice asked again faintly.

The voice was so quiet that Henri wasn't certain that it had been talking to him.

"You look lost, Brother."

The question must be addressed to me. Where's that voice coming from? Who is it and what does she really want?

A Negro woman, probably in her forties, surrounded by so high a pile of suitcases on a bench that she was virtually invisible appeared like Lazarus raised from the dead. She had a tangle of hair, which might have been beautiful and neatly coiffed at some time in the past. Her red lipstick was faded from her lips. She was dressed in an elegant bluish dress that badly needed pressing.

Looking at Henri, she said, "You're looking in every corner of the station like you're searching for an exit except you don't look like you're intending to leave anytime soon."

Henri was confused by the woman's sudden appearance and by her blunt question to a stranger. "No, I was supposed to meet a friend here at 10:30. I haven't seen him yet, so I've been looking where he might be waiting for me. He's coming from Kentucky in his car, not by train."

"You don't sound like someone from these parts, Brother."

"No, I'm not. I'm a stranger here in Little Rock for just a few days."

"Honey," she said with a slight hint of flirtatious seduction in her voice. "No one is a stranger here in Little Rock. Where you from?"

"I'm from New York, actually. Harlem, to be more exact."

"Wow! A real living person from Harlem! I've never met one before."

Henri didn't want to seem rude. But he kept taking stealthy looks in the direction of the entrance door in case Lucius was running late.

"I wish I could just hop on a train going north," she said dreamily. To Harlem maybe. Anywhere as long as it's not the South. The weather is fine here, sure. But it's no place for people like us to try to make their way and get ahead."

"I've always had a romantic, starry-eyed way of thinking about the South myself."

"You've seen *Gone With the Wind* too many times."

"Margaret Mitchell didn't paint an accurate picture of the South?"

"The only important characters in the movie are white except for that clichéd housemaid, Mammy. She's the only one with the gumption to stand up to Scarlett and even criticize her."

"That part is an accurate portrayal?"

"The fine and fancy whites in these parts do all they can to avoid the truth. They're polite and sweet, alright. But all they're doin' is coverin' up the truth of the way things really are. They must be blind. The painful truth is staring them in the face but they don't see it—or want to."

"Can I ask you, what is the 'truth of how things really are' here in the South?"

"Be careful what you ask for, Brother. You're the first person who has asked me that question in years."

"As I say, I'm a stranger here. I've got a lot to learn."

"Instead of telling the truth, the white powers that be, even just ordinary white folks here, continue to live by the Big Lie."

That phrase sounded familiar to Henri, "Big Lie?"

"Damn right! The lie that God gave white folks the authority to make all the decisions and run the show in a way that in the end primarily favors them."

"You've done some serious thinking about these things, haven't you?"

"And believe it or not, a hell of a lot of reading. Ever read anything by Jimmy Baldwin?"

"As a matter of fact, Sister, I have. That's why my ears perked up when you said 'the Big Lie.' I can only read him in little bits at a time. He overwhelms you with the truth."

"That's precisely why I love to read his stuff. Nobody describes the truth of how matters stand between whites and blacks better than he does in *Go Tell It on the Mountain*. His new book of essays is even more pointed."

"Those aren't comic books you've been reading. How is it that you have time to read so much?"

"Why I'm not out working, you mean? That's what most of the white folks wonder but don't care enough to ask me. If you must know, I used to work as hard as Mammy. I also raised a little child who is not my own. She was my boss lady's daughter. All she did was buy her new fancy dresses, fawn over her princess, and brag about her to anyone who would listen. But I raised her. I taught her the numbers and the alphabet. I taught her the difference between right and wrong the way my church taught me. She was closer to me than her actual mother. She could see the color of my skin but it didn't seem to matter."

"Isn't it amazing how wise children are? But you talk of your caring for her in the past tense. You no longer work for that family?"

"No. That's a sore subject. I think the boss lady was jealous of me that little Amy loved me more than her. Besides, her husband wasn't anything but obvious about wanting to sample a piece of what he referred to as my 'nigger booty.' It got so that I never allowed myself to be in the same room with him if there was no one else nearby."

Henri felt self-conscious. He had surreptitiously admired what the bastard called her "nigger booty," plus he noticed with approval the prominent round shape of her full breasts underneath her dress. *For God's sake, Henri. Look away. You're no better than the lecherous husband of her "boss lady."*

"I think I know what happened next," Henri said.

"Yes, the boss lady fired me on the spot one afternoon after I finished with Amy's story time. Not just sacked me but called me by every bad name in the gutter dictionary. Right there in front of her precious little princess. Around here, you can't get no job without a good reference from your past employers. No way she was going to give me one."

Henri was rendered speechless. No further comment was necessary.

"Amy just cried, ran to embrace me with her tiny arms, and then yelled some similarly naughty epithets at her mother. I didn't even know that such a sheltered little girl knew that kind of language."

"'This is what I mean Hazel. Look at what a bad influence you've had on our princess. That's precisely why we have to let you go,' is all the Boss Lady said."

"It's a sad story but necessary to tell," Henri said.

"A sad story that happens down here in Dixie all the time."

"I can imagine. By the way, where are you headed with all that luggage?"

"No choice but to go live for a while with my people in

Tennessee. I ain't got a man or children anymore. Maybe I can start a new life there."

Just then Henri caught sight of Lucius approaching from the direction of the passenger platforms. The concerned look on Lucius's face melted into a happy smile when he spotted Henri.

"Oh, there he is. Will you excuse me for a moment as I go over to greet him?"

Henri stepped away to get Lucius's attention.

"Lucius, you're here! I was beginning to wonder."

"I was careful to keep the speedometer frozen at five miles less than the speed limit so that no cop can pull me over for speeding. The trip took me a little longer than I had calculated."

"But you're here safe and sound. Come on over here to meet a new friend of mine. We were just about to say goodbye."

Henri led Lucius to the woman. "Lucius, I'd like you to meet a new friend I've made this morning.... I'm sorry, Ma'am. We've been talking for a while. But I rudely neglected to ask your name."

"It's Hazel. Hazel Watson. I guess we're even. I failed to ask your name, too, Brother."

"It's Henri Esper, Hazel. I'm glad to have met you today. This is my good friend Lucius Smallwood, from Crawfordville, GA."

"How do you do, Lucius?"

"Yes, my home now is in Crawfordville, but today I came from just Shepherdsville, KY, not far from Louisville."

"That's right. Lucius has been there visiting his family. How is your dad, Lucius?"

"Better than a few days ago. Turns out it wasn't a stroke after all, but a cardiac arrest. After it's happened there's not much you can do to reverse the damage. If the patient survives the cardiac arrest itself, the doctor says, the best therapy is rest. That's what he should be doin' right now if my mother and sister can get him to cooperate. He's not accustomed to restin' on demand."

"I've noticed that among men of a certain age," Hazel commented.

"Well, Hazel. It's been great talking with you. Lucius and I are off to see how things are going in Little Rock."

"You've picked a tense time to come to my sleepy hometown, I'm afraid. I'm so proud of the courage and tenacity of those nine high schoolers at Little Rock Central. But the place is teeming with state police. Just be careful."

"WHICH DIRECTION, LUCIUS? Where'd you park your car?"

"In one of the spaces right in front of the station. It's not like New York. Here, this way."

They walked in the parking area. "Well, here she is. Our mode of transportation for this little jaunt through the south."

Lucius was obviously very proud of his car. Though he hadn't bought it new, the 1955 DeSoto Fireflight two-door sedan still looked rather newish and unspoiled. The vehicle had the appearance of a sleek military airplane in its thunder gray color accented by black framed by chrome molding.

"So, these are our wheels for the trip?" Henri asked a little skeptically.

"Better than riding the train, isn't it? Way better than being limited by schedules and timetables. Long waits at the station. No stress ahead of time about being late for the departure. Traveling through the smelly armpits of the state. Arriving at the station when everything is closed. Not on this trip, okay?"

"You make me sound like such a Luddite, Lucius. I happen to like trains, have ever since I was a kid."

"You gotta put up with the bad manners of the conductors barking at you and the potential for ignorant racial comments from fellow passengers. In the car, we're second class to nobody. We can carry on our own conversation without concern for being overheard. We ain't got room for Jim Crow in our DeSoto Fireflight. No sir. Just cruisin' on the open road."

Chapter Eight

The American triumph—in which the American tragedy has always been implicit—was to make black people despise themselves.

James Baldwin

EXITING UNION STATION, HENRI SAID, "We need to stop at the hotel to pick up *The Green Book*."

"What? You left home without it? Where's your head at?" Lucius snickered. "I knew we'd go back to the hotel before we went anywhere You don't know Little Rock any better than I do. We'll need the book to find a place for lunch and later for dinner. I've reserved the room at the same hotel again for tonight."

"Not much else we'll need, is there?"

"Today I'll have to call Delores Banks to see if our current hotel is at all handy to Central High School or if she recommends one that is closer."

"Delores Banks? That a lady you've already picked up during the few hours you've been in town?"

"She's the president of the Arkansas chapter of the N.A.A.C.P. I've never met her. But several of the Negro students who succeeded in getting through the door at Central High told me about her. She's got the responsibility of shepherding the students with whom I corresponded before I left New York, as well as others of the 'Little Rock Nine.'"

"Man, do the students' parents know you've been approaching their minor children by letter? I'm surprised no one has reported you yet to the vice squad."

"Man, your mind sure is in the gutter this morning. Wondering if I've been propositioning a married woman or lining up a harem of high school girls. Sheesh. What do you take me for?"

Lucius rolled his eyes at his earnest travel companion's solemnity and inability to go along with the innocent jesting.

"Henri, this is going to be a long trip if I can't get you to at least crack a smile. Back at seminary, you always went along with our joking and teasing."

Henri sighed his acknowledgement. "Back then, life seemed so uncomplicated and straightforward. The moral issues we debated in class or in the coffee shop were all so theoretical and easily managed. Now as I've matured, the stakes feel so much higher. Those hypothetical issues we discussed—religion, philosophy, politics—have suddenly become substantial real-life concerns for people not to debate about, but painful predicaments that they need to wrestle with and endure—usually at a dear cost."

Lucius was silent, feeling taken down a peg and slapped on the wrist by Henri's ardent admonishment. *Henri is right, but can't he loosen up a bit?*

Lucius continued, "You're right, Henri. I'm sure my poorly chosen off-color banter is offensive to a more serious-minded champion of justice like yourself. I promise that if it bothers you, I'll knock it off."

Now it was Henri's turn to feel censured. "You may have a point, Lucius. Maybe I've been taking all this civil rights controversy a little too seriously, almost personally, letting it affect me too deeply."

"You've got to take some things in life, even painful things or unjust things, with a laugh or they'll overwhelm you."

"Henri, I NEED TO ASK YOU, who was that colorful woman you introduced me to just now in the station? She was a piece of work."

"You mean Hazel?" Henri bet that Lucius's initial response to Hazel was not much different from his own. Henri chuckled. "Didn't you love that stylish evening dress and the dark hiking boots she wore to complement it?"

"I couldn't get over the huge pile of suitcases she had with her. Probably everything in this world that she owned. What did you make of her?"

"Actually, I think she's a prophet."

Lucius's face couldn't hide his surprise and skepticism.

"Not the kind you run into at the county fair that purports to predict your future or know how much change you have in your pocket," Henri continued, "but a prophet like the ones that we learned about in Jim Muilenberg's classes at Union."

"What, you think she's a chosen spokesperson for the Almighty? Come on, Henri, get real."

"As soon as I heard her voice calling me at the train station, I sensed that there was something different, unique, even otherworldly about it. When she and I chatted about race relations, she had some really perceptive things to say. She made reference to 'the Big Lie,' for instance. All kinds of insightful and, I would say, inspired things were coming out of her mouth."

"So what? Anybody who has read essays by Jimmy Baldwin would know about 'the Big Lie.' That doesn't necessarily place her in the category of prophet."

"No, not necessarily. But somehow this plain if colorful former domestic worker was inspired to read Baldwin. Makes you wonder, doesn't it?"

"What? That she was led to Baldwin by God somehow? When I picked up a copy of *Notes of a Native Son* to read, it wasn't because God suggested that I do so."

"Well, you and I have been conditioned by our education to read stuff by people like Baldwin in order to keep up with what's happening in the world. But what would move a person like her on the margins of the world without the advantage of much education to dig into the thinking of James Baldwin? Unless she feels she has been given a special mission in the area of race relations or civil rights. Make any sense to you? Or sound just like crazy talk?"

"I can just imagine the look on the face of the librarian when Hazel goes up to her and asks to be directed to the section where Baldwin's works are shelved. He or she'd have a hard time just getting past Hazel's unorthodox Sunday best."

"Well, God's prophets weren't known far and wide for their fine raiment and sleek, stylish attire. Like John in his coat of camel's hair and diet of locusts and wild honey."

Lucius had no response, not necessarily because he was conceding Henri's contention, but rather because he didn't think there was any final resolution to the discussion. Henri didn't give the impression that he considered he was the victor in a contest between old friends. He, too, felt ready to move on.

"Have you ever seen this picture?" Henri asked as he opened up a folded newspaper in his back pocket.

"I might have seen it as I flipped through the pages of the Atlanta newspaper, I don't know. It doesn't ring a bell."

"Well, ever since I saw that picture while I was still in New York it has haunted me."

"Haunted you? It's just a Negro girl surrounded by a bunch of white folks. Who is it?"

"That courageous young lady is Aliza Beckwith. She's one of the Negro students being called the 'Little Rock Nine,' although I'm sure they're called by less polite names by those who don't want them at Little Rock Central High School."

"She's one of the students you've been corresponding with?"

"Yes, she is. And I've scheduled a time to meet and talk with her this afternoon. For us both to meet her at Mrs. Delores Banks' home after school."

"By 'both,' you mean me, too? I don't know if I want to do that."

"She's just a thirteen-year-old high school freshman. She's not scary. A little shy, maybe, but no one to fear."

"But don't you think that as a shy youngster she'd be intimidated by meeting and talking with not just one but two strange men? She'd be the one who is scared."

"I discussed that with Mrs. Banks on the phone. She said the poor girl feels so isolated and alone. She would welcome any support right now after that harrowing experience captured in that photograph. She's been thrust into the limelight suddenly, unexpectedly, and against her will. Already, more than a few newspapers and even television stations have called about interviews with her. But Mrs. Banks thinks Aliza would regard us as allies who want to express our support for her and the other eight students."

DELORES BANKS ANSWERED the front door with a welcoming smile. "You must be Reverend. Esper?"

Henri was standing closer to the door when she opened it for them, Lucius a step or two behind him. "That's right, Ms. Banks. This is a close friend of mine who is my companion on this tour of the South, Reverend Lucius Smallwood of Crawfordville, Georgia."

"Well, welcome to you both. It's so good to have two preachers from beyond Little Rock show interest in our struggle here."

"It's good to be here in person finally to do what we can."

"I know that Aliza and Charissa have spoken of how much help and strength they have received from your letters to them. Admittedly at first, they were a little confused and wary, you understand, by letters from someone in New York that they didn't even know."

Henri glanced quickly in Lucius's direction. Did Lucius hear her words as affirmation of Henri's initiative in making contact with the students, or as mild criticism for sticking his nose into other people's business?

"But I think that as the struggle here has become more intense,"

Ms. Banks continued, "they appreciate your personal interest in their courageous efforts against huge odds."

"It's a personal interest, for sure, but it's based on our faith that directs us to be attentive to the plight of those who are exploited, to help carry the burden of one another. When I think of Aliza in that photograph, my heart just breaks—Christ does not just direct us but commands us."

"Yes, that's why I do the work I do. I just love these students and feel called to help them be successful and enjoy the rights they deserve."

Just then two young people, a male and a female, came in through the front door.

"Oh, here are the first of them now."

Although the two youth had completed a full day of school, enduring whatever friction being the only Negro students might have entailed, they dutifully greeted the adult guests politely.

"This is Clarence, who is a senior, and Aliza, a freshman," Delores said by way of introducing them. "Aliza knows you are here to visit with her. Clarence and I will excuse ourselves and go downstairs to the family room while you talk with her. There'll be others who will let themselves in and walk, quietly, I hope, so as not to interfere with your visit—to get a snack in the kitchen and then proceed downstairs."

Aliza sat demurely on the sofa and waited silently for the pastors to initiate the conversation.

Henri took the lead. "Aliza, we are so grateful you are willing to talk with us after a long school day. I'm the Rev. Esper with whom you've exchanged letters, and this is my friend, Rev. Smallwood."

She examined each one. "You're both preachers?"

"Does that make you uncomfortable, Aliza?" Lucius asked softly.

"No, not at all. Our pastor at Mt. Zion is a good friend of our family. Rev. Beveridge was the first person who came by to see me after the incident on September 4. That was very comforting. My parents were working that day and were unable to be there."

Lucius inquired, "September 4?"

"That's the day I thought we were scheduled to begin at Central. But the governor ordered that we not come to school that day. He said something about the white students not being ready yet to mix with several carloads of Negro students. Mrs. Banks called all of us students that morning to tell us that our first day at Central had been postponed. She tried to call me, too, but she didn't know we don't have a phone, so I never heard." Aliza spoke so softly that they could hardly hear her.

"Mrs. Banks intended to wake up early enough to drive to our house to tell us personally…"

Delores finished Aliza's sentence. "But I'm afraid I slept in. I am sorry, Aliza." She looked intently into Aliza's eyes. Then addressing Lucius, Henri added, "So, Aliza took the city bus to school on her own all by herself. She got off the bus near the school and looked for the others. But, of course, they weren't there. Aliza, you tell what happened next in your own words."

As this painfully shy student spoke her eyes were lowered to the carpet. She was about to resume the story, but then paused as though she needed to push back her tears. "So, there was a huge crowd of the white students blocking the sidewalk and shouting, 'Two, four, six eight, we don't want to integrate.' A couple of the girls moved right in beside me and chanted stuff like that. It was like I was stuck in a nightmare.

"Then I saw the National Guard troops on the other sidewalk. I reckoned they were there to protect us and to help us enter the school. I tried asking one of the guards for help, but he didn't answer at all, as though he didn't hear me. But I am sure he did. I heard on the TV later that the governor had called them to Little Rock, not to help us but to prevent us from entering the school."

Lucius and Henri were shaking their heads in disbelief as she spoke.

"That's the moment when that famous photograph was taken?" Henri asked.

"Yes, sir," she said almost apologetically. "I didn't know exactly what I should do. That's why I looked so lost and confused in the picture. I couldn't understand what was happening. The parents of the white students seemed even more angry than the students themselves."

Mrs. Banks moved beside her on the couch, put her arms around her, and allowed Aliza to cry into her shoulder.

Henri and Lucius were silent out of sympathy for the young girl's difficult predicament and respect for her tears.

Aliza wiped the tears from her cheeks and continued. "I managed to catch sight of a shelter down at the city bus stop and started to head for it to go home. All of a sudden, the bench was full of rambunctious white students. They wouldn't yield any space for me. They laughed as their prank succeeded. I could hardly hold back my tears but I remembered how my father had taught me not to let those who are tormenting me see me cry."

Lucius and Henri glanced at each other. Henri was on the verge of tears himself.

"But when an older white woman came into the shelter to wait for a bus, some of the white students must have felt self-conscious because one by one, they got up and left the bus shelter and dispersed on the street. The kind lady sat down beside me and put her arm around me. She asked if I was all right. Tearfully, I told her that I was in no physical pain, that the crowd hadn't attacked or beaten me, which I was fearing. But in my heart and spirit…

"Then the lady made the same comment as though she had overheard my father. 'Don't let them see you cry, dear.' But because now it was only her and me there, I didn't work so hard to keep myself from crying. I'm sorry that I can't stop crying now when you've come to visit me."

Silence fell over the family room except for Aliza's muffled sobbing and Mrs. Banks' quiet assurances to her. "It's all right, now, Aliza. Shedding your tears today is good for you, you have good reason to feel hurt. We're all sorry with you."

Then Aliza remembered that her story was not finished. "'Here comes the bus,' the lady had said. 'I take this same bus every day to go visit my little granddaughter.'"

"But I wasn't expecting to ride the city bus. I don't have any money to get on," I had said to her.

"She said, 'Don't you worry your little heart about that, dear. You've had enough for one day. I'll pay for two passengers.'"

"Thank God for little old ladies," Lucius commented.

"I've never been treated so nice by a white person before."

"Nice, kind white people do actually exist, Aliza," Henri said.

"Who knows? There might even be some nice kind white students at Central High, too," Lucius added. "Right now they're just too afraid of what the others might think or say to show it."

Chapter Nine

Prior to the [de]segregation of Central, there had been one high school for whites, Central High School; one high school for blacks, Dunbar. I expected that there may be something more available to me at Central that was not available at Dunbar; that there might be more courses I could pursue; that there were more options available. I was not prepared for what actually happened.

Elizabeth Eckford
(pseudonym Aliza Beckwith in novel)

"GENTLEMEN, I PREFER not to hear any more talk about your staying another night at your hotel," Delores said after Aliza left to go home. "We have a perfectly fine guest room that is vacant for the moment. L.C. and I would be honored if you stayed here for the duration of your time in Little Rock. Other civil rights advocates have stayed with us here, too."

Henri and Lucius consulted each other with glances. Civil rights advocates? "Why not?" Henri said. "Your offer of hospitality is very generous and appreciated. We've got to return to the hotel, however, before it's too late, to pick up our belongings."

"And pay up for the stay there last night," Lucius added.

"Of course," Delores agreed. "It's gotten to be a little past supper time. But while you run that errand, I'll whip up something for us to eat and it'll be ready by the time you return."

She escorted them to the door and held the screen door open for them. As she was holding the door, she peered up and down her street. Was she checking for something?

Henri jumped into the passenger seat of Lucius's DeSoto. Lucius started the engine and pulled out onto Fifteenth Street in the twilight of the evening. The Banks' home was about a mile from Central High School and equidistant to the historically Negro college, Philander Smith, where Delores taught courses in Negro history part-time.

Lucius turned left when they reached the intersection with South Chester Street, and then to the right at a busier thoroughfare.

Suddenly, Lucius noticed that a car behind him had sped up considerably and was tailing the DeSoto at too close a distance. Lucius had to raise the palm of his left hand over the rearview mirror to shield his eyes from the sharp glaring light from the car behind.

"Geez, this jackass behind us must have his high beams on. The headlights in the mirror are practically blinding me."

Henri looked back. He hadn't seen there was a car on their tail.

"When did you first notice this other car?" Henri asked, alarmed.

"I don't know exactly. I guess the moment we turned on to Fourteenth from South Chester Avenue. He pulled up out of nowhere."

"Turn onto another street when you can. If he does the same, we'll have a pretty good idea whether or not he's following us for some reason."

The tires squealed their protest as Lucius made a quick, unsignaled right turn onto South State Street. The wailing of rubber against pavement echoed through the dark street when the car behind them made the same unplanned turn. They were being followed.

It was too dark to determine by whom, but it was obvious that someone had their sights on the DeSoto and its two occupants. Lucius tightened his grip on the steering wheel. Henri felt his heart beating wildly in his chest.

"It doesn't look like a police car," Henri said. "It must be someone else. You didn't cut the guy off in traffic, did you, Lucius? Is the guy possibly ticked off by your driving?"

"He'd damn well better not be. I'd been observing the traffic laws until he pulled up behind us and started following at an unsafe distance. It's his driving you ought to be worried about, not mine."

"I'm not worried about your driving, Lucius. OK, we've got to avoid bickering and focus on the guy behind us."

"Damn!" Lucius cursed. "It looks as though we're going to have to stop at the next intersection. Look at how busy the traffic is on that cross street. I don't want the guy to keep following us, but I can't just plow through the stop sign, as much as I would like to."

"No, I guess you're right," Henri agreed, his heart feeling as though it was about to beat out of his chest now.

Lucius came to a stop at the intersection. Henri looked back. The other vehicle mimicked the DeSoto's action.

Both Lucius and Henri were eyeing the traffic in the cross street, hoping against hope that there would be enough of a gap between vehicles for Lucius to stick the nose of the DeSoto into a vacant space in the parade of cars and make their getaway from who knows whom.

Suddenly, they heard the car behind them pull up a foot or two away from their bumper. The driver turned off his ignition. Then they heard one of the car's doors open and bang shut...then a second, a third, and the fourth. Henri looked back through the rear glass and saw one male figure exit the car by one of the front doors, then at least another one if not two from the other doors.

"They're getting out of the vehicle, Lucius!"

Lucius saw them, too. Several occupants of the other car, all whites, proceeded to the window of the closed front doors of the DeSoto.

One shouted into the glass window on Lucius's side. "Open the fucking window, boy. Now!" Another male shouted a similar order angrily through the glass of the window on Henri's side. Henri feared to do so. *If I open the window, there will be nothing between me and this outraged guy.* His hesitation irritated the man at his closed window so much that he took the baseball bat in his hand and shattered the glass on the window. Small diamond-shaped shards of glass exploded into the car. Henri began sweeping the pieces of glass off his shirt, but the pieces of broken glass were all over the seat and the floor.

"Hell, boy, I told you to roll down your window. I warned you, dammit."

The other male, possibly of late high school age, addressed Lucius bitterly in the driver's seat. "What the hell were you doing at that black bitch's home? She's a fucking troublemaker, a shit-disturber, in this town. I suppose you know that. Getting you Negroes all worked up about moving in uninvited and taking over our school. If you're associating with that bitch, you must have making trouble on your mind, too. Am I right? Huh? I said, 'Am I right?' Answer me!"

"N...no, I swear we're just guests for dinner at Mr. Banks' home," Henri offered. "We're from...out of town."

"Well, we suggest you get your black asses out of our town. Right now, we've got far too many of you people in Little Rock."

"And take those trespassing Negro kids with you," the second one added. "We want our school back."

"We know where this trouble-making bitch lives. We'll have a set of eyes keeping a close surveillance on her driveway. If we see this car parked in that driveway, we'll know you're still here. Then we'll have to use other methods to undo your welcome. You wouldn't find that very pleasant, take my word for it."

"No more trouble, you hear? This is your fair warning, boys," the other man advised.

Henri and Lucius could hear rowdy laughter from the spectators in the 1952 Ford as the more vocal ones began retreating to their vehicle.

Lucius and Henri were so terror-stricken that neither said a word the rest of the way to the hotel and back to the Banks' home.

Chapter Ten

The Little Rock Crisis attracted the attention of the world. Newspapers and TV stations in places as distant from Little Rock as France, Ghana, or Australia reported how African American teens were being treated in Arkansas. People all over the world could see photos and TV footage of angry white men, women, and children assaulting not only the African American Central High students but anyone who sympathized with them.

Arkansas History Alive

PERIODICALLY, L.C. WOULD CREATE A small gap in the drapes covering his front picture window to look for Henri and Lucius's arrival. At last he saw the DeSoto approaching slowly. Only the car didn't turn in their driveway as L.C. expected. Instead, Lucius continued east past the house on West 15th Street and maneuvered into a vacant parking spot on the side of the street near Central High.

To L.C. it seemed that Henri and Lucius were ill at ease as they walked back toward the Banks'. Every few steps the pastors nervously peered back over their shoulder as though they were looking out for someone or something.

L.C. opened the front door to let them in. "It would have been ok by us if you parked your car in our driveway."

"Well, we have our reasons to park a little distance away," said Lucius.

"We had a little run-in with a carload of young white guys," Henri informed L.C. "Not a car accident, thank the Lord. No physical violence, either, though I, at least, feared we might get beaten to a pulp by these guys."

In the kitchen, Delores must have heard mention of "run-in" and "physical violence." She came out of the kitchen into the living room wiping her hands on a tea towel with concern etched on her face. "What's this? A run-in and possible physical violence with some white troublemakers?"

"Trouble for us, at least," Lucius explained. "They pulled up right behind us at an intersection. A couple of them stepped out of their car, came up to ours menacingly, and barked at us to roll down the windows. Then they asked what we had been up to at your house."

"Apparently, I was too slow to respond. One of them smashed the car window with a baseball bat and shattered the glass," Henri added.

Delores and L.C. glanced at each other with a look of both recognition and belated concern for their guests.

"Oh, my God!" Delores exclaimed. "All that shattered glass didn't injure you at all?" Delores asked.

"No, not really," Henri reported. "I tried to clean the little shards off my clothing, but there's quite a layer of glass all over the front seat and floor. I probably still have little pieces in my hair."

"These guys were convincing enough with their threats that we parked the car up the street," Lucius said.

"They said for us to get out of town immediately," Henri explained. "They threatened us if they saw our car in your driveway—that they'd keep a watch on your house."

Delores took a deep breath and slowly exhaled before she spoke. "There's been a lot of that kind of hoodlum activity around here since the summer before the kids were to begin school at Central. These guys may have been upperclassmen at Central. But we've had so many young hooligans, as I often call them, who have been recruited to Little Rock by the local white hate groups. The KKK, the White Citizens' Council, groups like that."

L.C. was silent, then chimed in. "In spite of their threats and their scaring the crap out of you tonight, this bunch seems less violent than some others, if you can believe it."

"I regret it had to happen to you," Delores lamented. "I don't mean to minimize the terror of your experience tonight. Since I've been elected as the president of the Arkansas branch of the N.A.A.C.P., we have had burning crosses thrown into our backyard. Everybody knows who's responsible for that. On the base of one of the crosses was scrawled, 'GO BACK TO AFRICA. KKK.' One night, a rock was thrown through that window and nearly hit me. A few nights later, a volley of shots was fired at our home. We jumped and lay face-down on the floor." She pointed her index finger in the direction of the living room wall. "Take a look at that spot on the wall there. See the bullet lodged there? L.C. and I began to have the horrifying feeling that here in our own hometown there were people who actually wanted us dead." Her voice was cracking.

L.C. came over and put a comforting arm around his wife.

"I didn't know that the resistance to the Negro kids at Central

High was still so violent," Henri said. "We get the news up in New York, of course. We hear about the protests against the students. But you have to be here to appreciate the cruelty of some people and the extent of hatred and violence in the air in Little Rock."

"Living in rural Georgia as I do," Lucius continued, "I have some idea of the kind of resistance by the white community, and the tensions between whites and Negroes that can arise at times. And the whites always get their way."

"Then you have a notion of the many shapes that resistance can take," said L.C. "Delores and I lost our business that we spent sixteen years building up."

"Yes, the *Arkansas State Press* was our baby," Delores added. "People in town called it 'the Negro newspaper,' but we tried to make it the alternative paper. Yes, it was owned by Negro proprietors and supported by Negro businesses. But we wanted all folks in Little Rock to hear the truth of events—the decisions of the city council, school board, public works department—things like that, which affect white people as much if not more than the Negro community."

"As townsfolk learned to know us and trust us, the white people would express their gratitude for what we were doing—things that the mainstream press like the *Democrat-Gazette* wasn't paying attention to. But…"

Henri was listening sympathetically, Lucius with ears that had stories like this before.

"But one day in the winter of '57, a middle-aged white woman I didn't know stopped by our office and asked for me specifically," Delores amplified L.C.'s summary. "She told me that she had come as a representative of a new group called 'Southern Women' who had delegated her to appeal to me as a fellow 'Southern woman.'"

Lucius interrupted to ask, "Appeal to you?"

"That's how she put it, yes. Her appeal was that 'for the sake of the common good of the children of Little Rock,' I use my influence with the nine Negro students attending Central High to persuade them to withdraw from the school."

"To withdraw?" Henri asked, scandalized. "To give up their place so hard fought for?"

"That's what she asked, as baldly as that. She tried to soften the request by explaining. 'You know, Mrs. Banks, that the school board is committed to desegregating Central High School. And not only

Central but all the schools in the district eventually. We know it's going to happen. But having the Negro students at Central withdraw will give us time to prepare the community for integration. We need time.'"

"I've heard that phrase back in Kentucky, too," Lucius said.

"Progress for us Negroes will always come, but eventually," Henri added with a definite note of sarcasm.

Delores seconded Henri's point vigorously. "And women were promised the right to vote eventually when 'the nation is ready' but the nation was slower getting ready than molasses in January."

For the first time that evening, a smile came over Delores's face. "You got it! Anyway, this woman suggested that I call a press conference the next day to announce that 'for the good of the community, especially the children, I would withdraw my support from the Negro students and advise them to return to Negro schools.'"

"I wonder what kind of weak-kneed person she took my wife to be?" L.C. said as he chuckled caustically.

"As the woman was speaking," Delores admitted, "I was reliving the afternoon back in September when Aliza ran into our house in tears after being terrorized by the white students. I was thinking also of the other eight Negro students. The woman was talking but I don't think I was able to hear a word she said through my anger and sadness. I just thought about Brother Thurgood and his team as they stood up and advocated for the rights of students like Aliza and all the nameless ones in towns and cities all over the South to go to a decent school. The more she talked, the more I grew in the conviction that there was less than a snowball's chance in hell that I would ask the Negro students to withdraw from Little Rock Central. God in heaven, it would amount to such a cowardly betrayal of the hopes of these nine students, but also of all the children and their parents of the years to come and efforts of those heroes arguing before the Supreme Court in '54. I wouldn't be able to live with myself."

Henri was totally enraptured by Delores's love for the students and commitment to the just cause of equality in education. Mentally, he vowed a renewal of his own commitment.

"The woman was in my office at least an hour. Finally, I asked her, 'You told me that if I withdrew my support from the Negro students, you will assure me of the support of the Southern Women.

But what would happen if I didn't?'"

"Oh, boy." Lucius interjected before Delores continued. "I can imagine her answer."

"The woman looked at me straight in the eye. 'Why, Mrs. Banks, you'd be destroyed. You'd lose your newspaper, your reputation, everything."

Delores was breathless after finishing the story. Henri and Lucius looked exhausted, too, having heard the sad tale.

L.C. took over from his wife. "Delores didn't sleep a wink the next few nights. When I finally asked her what was troubling her, she related the encounter with the woman. She hadn't told me because she suspected how angrily I would respond. I cannot stomach bigots parading behind the banner of Christianity."

"L.C. told me almost right away, 'You did the right thing, babe, by refusing her preposterous suggestion.' He said nothing more, but I think I know what was going through his mind."

"But in the next few weeks" L.C. added, "we started noticing letters from some of our best advertisers that they were pulling their advertising in the *State Press*."

"That was hard," Delores said. "We had worked so diligently to build strong bonds with all our advertisers, Negro and white. We used all our resources to save the paper. However, it soon became apparent to us that we were fighting a losing battle."

"I'm sorry to hear that," Henri remarked.

"But God is good. We did receive hundreds of letters of support and encouragement in the midst of all those cancellations. I was so moved when the mail arrived one morning. The return address on the envelope was McComb, Mississippi…" Delores had to pause to collect herself before she went on. "Two quarters were Scotch taped onto the back of a piece of crumpled cardboard. The message inside was printed in a child's hand on lined notebook paper. 'Dear Miss Delores. I am ten years old but this is all I have.' Delores could no longer hold back her tears. 'I was saving it to buy my mom a birthday present. But I want you to have it. I know she won't mind. I want to help' The letter was signed simply 'Larry.'"

Spontaneously, Lucius let out a heartfelt whoop. Henri, his eyes soaked with tears, reached over and embraced Delores. Lucius did the same with L.C.

"Indeed, God is good!" Henri managed to say.

"Mighty good," Lucius agreed.

Chapter Eleven

The hunger for justice among the Little Rock Nine sparked a change that would affect America greatly. Little Rock Nine inspired many African Americans to stand up for themselves and stand against racism. They also helped desegregate schools, which later led to the desegregation of other public areas. Little Rock Nine was an inspiration to the 1960s as seen through their background, impact, and contributions.

High school senior essay

May 1958

"I see you parked your DeSoto in our driveway this time, Lucius," L.C. said on another evening when they were about to enjoy dinner again together at the Banks'. "I'd say that's progress."

"Having heard your story the other night about losing your newspaper as a consequence of refusing to withdraw your support of the nine Negro students at Central," Lucius responded, "how could we even think of allowing a few bombastic threats from a bunch of rowdy ruffians to cause us to live in fear?"

"Not when we remember what Aliza Beckwith had to endure," Henri said.

"And conquer," Lucius added.

"There's no guarantee, of course, that they wouldn't follow through on their threats," L.C. said, "but chances are they were just trying to impress you with their muscles like seventh grade boys, and intimidate you with their bravado."

"The meaningless showing off of youth," Delores said.

"Thank you for another delectable dinner," Henri said.

"And inviting us to observe the school board's public summit to discuss what they should do now when the new academic year begins this fall," Lucius

"No, I'm the one who should be doing the thanking," said Delores. "I am grateful that you decided to accompany me to the meeting. It was reassuring for me to look out from the stage at a mostly hostile crowd in the auditorium and see at least two supporters there from out of town."

"The opponents of desegregation had stacked the speakers in the meeting and the crowd with segregationists from Georgia, Alabama, and Louisiana," L.C. lamented. "The opponents came with reinforcements."

"It was a grossly unfair contest," Henri said. "I would grade your remarks and responses to the uptight segregationists with an 'A,' Delores. Even an 'A plus.' You didn't stand a chance of really being heard, much less understood."

"The representative of the Klan and the guy from the White Citizens' Council must have been reading from the same script," Lucius said.

Henri pulled out a small writing pad. "I jotted down some notes during the meeting. Let's see...I couldn't believe the openly racist remarks by that Elsie Johnson of the Women's League. The woman practically characterized any male Negro student admitted to a Little Rock school, even in the lower grades, as some kind of horny sexual pervert. Other mothers, she said, had expressed to her their fear of allowing their little princesses to attend desegregated schools because they might conceivably be physically overcome by much bigger Negro male students."

"God forbid that we end up with a society of mixed-race children," Lucius joked and broke out in slightly mischievous laughter.

"What an up and down contentious arm-wrestling match between the two sides," Delores commented. "The Mothers' League having convinced the Chancery Court to hand down a temporary injunction against continued integration of Central and all the other schools in Little Rock? My heart sank when the injunction was announced. But then it was revived again when the school superintendent announced that Brother Thurgood had convinced federal judge Davies to overrule the Chancery Court's decision and order the school board to proceed with immediate integration. I was transported to heaven when I heard that."

"Until we heard from our illustrious vacillating Governor Faubus, that is," L.C. corrected his wife. L.C. quoted Faubus mockingly. 'I ask you, good people of Little Rock, what in God's name is happening to this country? Given the lack of consensus among the citizens of Little Rock, I, the duly elected governor of the sovereign state of Arkansas, decree that all public high schools in Little Rock shall be closed for the academic year 1958-9.' "The chicken-livered namby-pamby will actually cause the students to miss a whole year of school so that he doesn't have to be remembered as a governor who complied with the federal courts to desegregate the schools."

All four sat around the dinner table in mournful silence as though at a funeral.

"So, what will happen to the nine Negro students at Central?" Henri broke the solemn stillness and ventured to ask.

"I guess they'll need to disperse to other schools," Delores answered dejectedly. "One or two plan to move into their grandparents' homes out of town and try to squeeze themselves into formerly white schools in those districts as they did here. After all, they're seasoned veterans of fighting the system now. I suppose several others are so exhausted from the struggle at Central that, for the time being at least, they'll return to their previous Negro high school here in Little Rock. Clarence White is hoping to graduate from Central this Friday if all goes well. I'm so proud of him. The first-ever Negro graduate of Little Rock Central."

"I don't know the young man, of course, but graduating under the circumstances he had to undergo ought to make every Negro in Little Rock proud," Lucius said.

"Would you like to come on Friday evening and witness Little Rock history being made? I'll check with Clarence if he still has a couple of tickets left to the ceremony. It'll be held in the football stadium."

"I know I'd like to be there," Lucius volunteered.

"You going alone, my travel companion? If Clarence can get a ticket, I want to go, too."

THE EVENING OF FRIDAY, May 27, 1958, was an exquisite clear-sky herald of the coming summer. Henri and Lucius managed to find two bleacher seats where they could get an unobstructed view of the stage where the graduates would be presented. Delores and L.C. sat not far away with a small group of other N.A.A.C.P. leaders.

During the week, Delores had filled in some details about Clarence's life before Central High. His father had died when he just turned ten years old. His mother Thelma was in the office secretarial pool at the Little Rock school board. She had serious misgivings about Clarence's physical safety when he first announced to her and his younger sister that he was close to committing to register at Central for his senior year. Although his parents had vowed not to interfere with their children's choices regarding their education and career, Thelma initially expressed her parental concern in the form of probing questions: "Are you sure that you want to be in an academic environment where you will be among the minority? Will you find friends at Central who share your values? Will the potential for tensions with the white students be a distraction from your studies?"

Henri and Lucius heard from Delores that the week before graduation had been a difficult one for Clarence. He had told her that two days before graduation a collection of white male seniors conspired to push him down the stairs. 'You didn't really want to come to graduation, did you Clarence?' was their only excuse for an apology.

"This was by no means the first instance of this kind of threat," Delores said. "Clarence had learned how to maintain his balance on the stairwell, and the ploy failed. But he knew that two nights later the same gang of toughs would be at the graduation ceremony possibly with a new plot to humiliate their classmate further.

"While Clarence's academic excellence, achievement, and perseverance in the face of such intimidation had won him the favor, or at least the respect, of many members of the Central faculty, even of some who had originally been against the integration of the school. The principal called him down to his office one morning and made him an offer that might alleviate much of Clarence and his family's anxiety about potential mischief against him, and at the same time assuage his own growing apprehension of violence marring the celebratory event on Friday night.

"'Clarence, you could opt to skip the ceremony. The school board would gladly send you your diploma through the mail.'"

"'I am grateful, Mr. McKinney, for your concern for my safety at the graduation,' Clarence had responded to the principal's offer. 'However, I didn't go through all the trials I've had to endure this year to get to this point in order to miss the celebration.'"

"What do I know? A bunch of uninvited white supremacists is putting on their own show to compete with ours."

Henri and Lucius strained to peer over the crowd in the seats to the street adjoining the stadium. They could see a parade of young people maybe a little older than the graduates marching and chanting something indecipherable. When the group was parallel to where they were seated, they could begin to make out the words of the chant: "Arkansas, obey the law, open our public schools to all; after Brown, segregation's against the law."

"Did I hear that right?" Henri asked Lucius. "Is that a pro-integration protest?"

Before they could decide for sure, the lights atop police cruisers were bathing the street in streaks of blue. The parading group wasn't disbanding as Henri and Lucius suspected they had been ordered to do by the police. But within a few short minutes the chanting was silenced and members of the group escorted roughly into the Little Rock police department vehicles. The attention of the people in the stands returned to the stage in the middle of the football field. Mr. McKinney received surveillance reports on his walkie-talkie regularly from his assistant principals who had spread out in the stadium to monitor people's behavior. All the dispatches to him were favorable.

"What was all the hubbub out on the street?" McKinney asked the assistant principals.

"Just a bunch of strangers I couldn't recognize chanting something about the Brown decision. They might have been U of A students, come to think of it. Many of them were wearing the Razorback jackets."

When the ruckus outside the stadium had been quelled, the faculty marshals signaled for the senior class to rise and form a line in alphabetical order as they had rehearsed earlier that morning. Henri and Lucius saw that with a surname beginning with "w," Clarence had positioned himself near the rear of the procession.

As the names of the graduates were read, small clusters of family members joined together to applaud their son or daughter.

The pastors saw Clarence looking up into the stands to where his mother and sister were sitting. "Clarence can probably tell that with the long wait until his name would be called and the short commotion outside the stadium, his mother had grown increasingly anxious."

Finally, some seven hundred names later, the guests heard the master of ceremonies announce "Clarence Gideon White." Henri and Lucius wondered that before he took the four or five wooden steps up to the stage, Clarence seemed to pause. Later he intimated that he had been saying a short prayer of thanksgiving to God for empowering him to succeed at Central and for allowing him to enjoy a graduation that was free of difficult and potentially embarrassing hitches.

Mr. McKinney invited the crowd to stand and sing a rendition of *God Bless America*, and then dismissed the graduates to join their families and well-wishers indoors in the gymnasium for cool refreshments and a time of celebration.

In the gymnasium, Henri and Lucius were pleased to notice how many of his fellow graduates, including some white classmates, greeted him in the gym with congratulations.

"Maybe no one is more surprised than Clarence himself," Lucius said.

They followed a few steps behind Clarence as they saw him winding his way through the crowd until he caught sight of his family.

There were a couple of others standing with Clarence's mother and sister. It grew to four others when Delores and L.C. Banks joined them.

As soon as she saw Clarence, a female student not wearing a graduation robe ran out to embrace Clarence triumphantly and led him in an impromptu dance.

L.C. and Delores put their arms around the couple, too, and they all danced to a melody only they could hear.

"Hey, distinguished graduate, I want to introduce you to someone whom I invited to come as a guest to this historic event this evening," Delores said to Clarence. "He has come all the way from Atlanta, but this afternoon he was the speaker at the graduation at the University of Arkansas at Pine Bluff."

She took Clarence by his arm and guided him to a handsomely dressed distinguished-looking Negro gentleman who was standing and carrying on a polite conversation with L.C. "Clarence and Charissa, I'd like to introduce a good colleague of mine in the N.A.A.C.P., Rev. Dr. Martin Luther King, Jr."

Clarence looked totally astonished by Delores's introduction. *The illustrious Dr. Martin Luther King, Jr.? Here, in Little Rock, at my graduation?*

Henri and Lucius looked at each other when they overheard.

Henri said, "Travel companion, this is actually the leader of the Montgomery Bus Boycott in person. Can you believe it?"

"Congratulations are in order, Clarence," the guest said in his sonorous preacher's voice. "Mrs. Banks has told me of your accomplishments as one of the brave Negro trailblazers this year at Little Rock Central High School. Negro youth and adults alike marvel at your courage and fortitude. Nothing short of miraculous, Clarence."

"Thank you, Dr. King. What an honor to have you here for this occasion. I am overwhelmed. I had no idea that you would be here. Please, allow me to introduce you to my mother and younger sister, and to Charissa Sands, an eleventh grader who started here at Central the same time in September as I did."

Recognition dawned on Charissa's face. "THE Doctor King? Wow! Welcome to Little Rock, Dr. King," Charissa effused as though she were in the presence of a movie star. "What an unexpected pleasure to have you at our school."

Delores didn't overlook her house guests. She introduced them to King. "These are two traveling clergy visiting many of the sites of the struggle in the South. They've stopped here in Little Rock to lend their moral support for the Negro students."

The pastors shook King's hand. Looking at Lucius, King asked, "Crawfordville, you say? I'm sure you know my colleague in Crawfordville, Dr. Ezekiel Kirkland?"

"At First Baptist? Sure. We see each other for lunch at ministerial association meetings every month."

"Well, you say hello to old Zeke from Martin, won't you, Lucius? He's a respected veteran of the Movement. He's been leading the fight for equal rights in southeast Georgia for a long time, years before I first saw the light of day."

"I'll be sure to bring him your greetings, Dr. King."

"Tell me, fellas. You're visiting sites of the struggle in the South? Where have you been so far?"

"Our trip has just started, Dr. King," Henri reported. "I stopped in D.C. and met Dr. Bayard Rustin at the N.A.A.C.P. office. At the same time I enjoyed some time with a local Negro barber who was an advocate for Negro high school students. I was humbled by his selfless activism."

"So, you've met the incomparably colorful Bayard? He's hands-down the best organizer of our mass events like protests and demonstrations and the like. That barber you talk about sounds like one of the invaluable but often nameless foot soldiers of the Movement. We'd be nothing without them. Where are you heading to from Little Rock, gentlemen?"

Lucius said, "We'll have to see which way the breeze is blowing when we awake, then we'll follow it."

"Well, let me say, if you have no definite plans, then point your car in the direction of Alabama. You can't bypass the Heart of the Confederacy. I'd love to show you around Montgomery, and I think I can speak for Rev. Shuttlesworth in Birmingham, the most segregated city in America, although knowing him, I'm sure Fred Shuttlesworth will do something dramatic to change that designation."

Chapter Twelve

Ain't gonna let nobody turn me 'round,
Turn me 'round, turn me 'round;
Ain't gonna let nobody turn me 'round,
Keep on a-walking, keep on a-talking
Marching up to Freedom's Land.

May 29, 1958

The next morning, Lucius and Henri talked about the surprise they felt when they met Dr. Martin Luther King, Jr., at Clarence's graduation. Dr. King had a presence that made two thirty-something preachers, no less than an eleventh-grader like Charissa and the precocious high school graduate, feel that they were in the singular company of a new kind of royalty. The man's handsome physical bearing was complemented by a dignified demeanor, which hinted at the aristocratic without sacrificing the common touch.

"Did you hear Alabama beckoning when he talked with us?" Lucius asked.

"No," Henri answered. "I heard God calling us to come to Alabama."

"Well, in that case, we're under a divine imperative. I guess the wind is blowing in the direction of the Cotton State."

Delores went all out to prepare a farewell breakfast for her two guests. "So, you are intent on leaving today to explore the Heart of Dixie?"

"Dr. King made a strong case for it," Henri said.

"Personally, I draw a firm line at the border of Mississippi. The Mississippians have a deserved reputation for their own unique style of "southern hospitality," Lucius said with his typical irony. "But I have no interest in being lynched."

"Thanks again for inviting us to Clarence's graduation last night," Henri remarked.

"Isn't he a peach?" Delores commented rhetorically.

"That young man is exceptional. I predict he's going to go far in this world," Henri said.

"Clarence's mother telephoned me this morning. She kept a careful list of Clarence's cards and gifts. Dr. King enclosed a check for $15.00 in his card. That's a lot of money to give to someone you've never met before. That's very humbling. I hope Clarence feels it, too. I'm sure he'll want to keep the check uncashed and frame it as a memento. What a gracious gesture."

Henri remembered that he and Lucius had stuffed a $10.00 bill in their card for Clarence. He reluctantly skipped to another topic. "There are all kinds of surprises this morning. I skimmed the morning copy of the *Democrat-Gazette* that I found on your stoop, Delores. I'm sure you heard the protesters who made their brief appearance outside the stadium last night. When I first heard them, I assumed they were local segregationists trying to disrupt the celebration. But they fooled me. They were actually chanting praise for the *Brown v. Board of Education*. From our seats we could see Little Rock's finest rounding up the demonstrators into the backs of their cruisers. Not at all surprising."

"A predictable response," Lucius interjected.

Henri nodded in agreement and continued, "But what is a total surprise to me is the name of the leader of the protest, according to the newspaper. The name won't mean much to the two of you. It's Wallace Vandorf. I met him when I arrived on the train in Fayetteville. He's a University of Arkansas undergraduate who came to my rescue when I couldn't find a place to eat at the station. He had a car and offered me a ride to a diner, and we shared a meal together, then he drove me to the hotel where I had reserved a room for the night. He seemed very pleased that the next morning I was going to the office of Senator William Fulbright to register my dissatisfaction with his favorable vote in Congress for the Southern Manifesto.

"He didn't say much to me about his own political leanings. Frankly, I was almost afraid to ask a stranger in Arkansas about them but it seems that he had come by car to Little Rock all the way from Fayetteville yesterday to protest the segregationist policies of the current Arkansas administration, and to express his support for Clarence and the other Little Rock Nine."

Making a strategic rhetorical pause, Henri then added, "The punchline of the story is that Wallace is white."

AFTER THE MORE THAN AMPLE breakfast prepared by Delores, Henri and Lucius put on their black clergy shirts with a clerical collar.

"I don't think I've seen you look so ministerial, Henri, since our graduation from Union. Is that how you dress up on Halloween?"

"Very funny, Lucius. Don't you ever wear the traditional uniform of the clergy?"

"No, usually just what we've been wearing: an open collared sport shirt. Especially on hot summer days as this one is predicted to be. Hotter than hell, they say."

"You're probably right about that. I don't suppose a clerical collar has the same reassuring effect on folks here in the South as it does with all those Catholics and lapsed Catholics up north."

"No, that's about right. But I figure that a collar might serve as an extra layer of protection against a segregationist with a hankering to inflict some hurt on two ordinary Negro dudes driving around on their highways. Maybe some of them have a vestige of reverence for men of the cloth and will leave us alone."

They headed southeast out of Little Rock for the almost four-hundred-and-fifty-mile drive to Alabama's capital. Delores had sent along a handsome picnic basket filled with chicken salad sandwiches, Oreo cookies, several apples and oranges, and two thermos bottles of iced tea so that they could keep moving and not have to spend time looking for a diner or restaurant that served Negro customers.

After a couple of hours on Arkansas Highway 65, Henri suddenly exclaimed, "Uh-oh! I forgot."

Lucius was startled. "What? What did you forget? Don't tell me we have to go back to Little Rock to get something."

"There's no direct route from Arkansas to middle Alabama without crossing Mississippi. We'll have to cross the Arkansas-Mississippi border in about...I'd estimate an hour or so. I'm sorry, Lucius."

"Let me see that!" Lucius, a look of panic on this face, grabbed the roadmap in Henri's hand, tearing it in half.

"Hey, partner. Take it easy. I would have given the map to you if you'd asked."

"Well then, give it to me."

"I will. Just as soon as you pull over on the side of the highway."

After Lucius did so, Henri took the half of the map puzzle that included Arkansas and placed his index finger at a spot on Highway 65 where he estimated they were presently located. "See, look here, Lucius. We're not far south of Dumas. We've got to keep going this way till we reach Route 82, turn left, and we'll be headed toward the bridge over the Arkansas River..."

Having reached the end of his piece of a map, Henri picked up Lucius's half and struggled to turn it once or twice so that it was right side-up, then found the bridge over the river.

"See that? That'll put us on the route through Greenville and Indianola to Columbus—not Columbus, Ohio or Columbus Georgia, but Columbus, Mississippi."

"Geez, look at that," Lucius said, pointing at the map. "We're gonna have to drive all this distance through Mississippi just to get out of this God-forsaken state. Geez."

"If it makes you feel any better, we can stop here somewhere on the Arkansas side and have our picnic lunch."

"Assuming we can find a gas station to fill up before we have to look for a station in damned Mississippi. A gas station that has an unlocked can where Negroes are allowed to empty their bladder."

Lucius seemed to hold the steering wheel more tightly after they crossed the bridge and drove through Greenville. "Wait a minute," he said as though he had just realized something. "Greenville? I've heard of it sometime in the past. Greenville is in what they call the Mississippi Delta, isn't it?"

Henri pondered Lucius's question. "I think so. My sense of the geography down here is pretty rusty."

"I remember where I've come across Greenville in my reading," Lucius said, self-satisfied. "Man, Money, Mississippi isn't far away from here. You know what transpired in that shining metropolis, don't you?"

"Of course. It was where Emmett Till's relatives lived."

"And where he was lynched," Lucius made a point of adding. "He wasn't the first Negro who was seized there and strung up by a rope from a tree. I'm sure he wasn't the last either."

"Lucius, I don't think we're going to be lynched and our beaten bodies thrown into the river. For one thing, we haven't hooted suggestively or flirted with any white women recently. Besides, Money is up here near Greenwood, not back in Greenville."

"Show off! I thought you said your knowledge of the geography down here is rusty. Greenwood, Greenville, it's hard not to get them mixed up."

To Make Matters Even more confusing for Lucius, they

ended up driving through Greenwood as well as Greenville. They noticed the home-painted sign attached to a metal fence at the point of entry into the Greenwood city limits: Colored folks: Don't Let the Sun Go Down on you in Greenwood.

"Just think, buddy. Only another half-hour or so and we'll be fixin' to cross the border into Alabama. We haven't been lynched yet."

"Didn't you see that sign as we entered Greenwood? God Almighty! We are in a Sundown Town. You get discovered here after sunset, you're asking to be lynched," Lucius said apprehensively. "Or at least thrown in jail."

"Surely, we have more protections from such things today than back in the 1930s."

"Go ahead and make fun of me. For God's sake, Henri, don't be so naïve. Were you born just yesterday? We wouldn't be the first two Negro males cruising down the open road minding our own business who become the quarry for a carload of Ku Klux Klan hooligan predators looking for a pair of unsuspecting victims to spirit away and send prematurely to meet their Maker. Who do you think put up that sign?"

They continued on past Greenwood. "I wonder if all the highways down here are so dark at night," Henri asked. "God, I can barely see ten feet ahead. How is the visibility for you?"

"About the same as you."

Suddenly, the light shining on the DeSoto's rearview mirror stabbed Lucius's vision. A vehicle had sped up behind them, and its piercing headlights were aimed right at the DeSoto.

Henri noticed Lucius's difficulty in propelling the car forward. "What's going on, Lucius?"

"I'm not sure, but I think we have company just as we did that evening in Little Rock."

Suddenly, the light in the mirror turned blue and strobed on and off.

"Now I'm sure we have company. Damn! It's a police car on our tail."

The police vehicle pulled up beside the DeSoto. One of its occupants turned on the interior light, rolled down his window, and ordered Lucius to slow down and pull over on the shoulder of the highway.

Lucius obeyed, although the shoulder of soft, loose gravel made it hard to handle the car. "How fast was I going?" he asked Henri nervously.

"You haven't exceeded forty-five mph since we crossed the river."

"Then why the hell are they pulling me over?"

"I haven't got a clue but I think we're about to find out."

The driver of the cruiser stepped out of the vehicle, placing his right hand on the revolver at his hip. The other occupant of the cruiser got out, too, and stood back holding an industrial strength flashlight aimed in the direction of the Lucius's door. The first trooper shone a smaller but barely less intense flashlight directly into his eyes.

"What are you boys doin' here?"

"We're traveling toward Montgomery," Lucius responded nervously. That was all he managed to get out of his tightened throat.

"You've got a valid license?"

Carefully, avoiding anything that might look like a jerking motion, Lucius reached into his pants rear pocket and pulled out his wallet. He fumbled through the collection of cards in the wallet, accidentally dropping one.

"Leave it, boy. Out of the car. Stand up straight. No funny business. Just show me the license."

"Yes, sir." Lucius found the license and handed it over to the trooper.

"From Georgia, eh?"

"Yes, I am. My traveling companion here is visiting from New York."

Henri handed the man his business card that showed his address.

"All the way from New York! What business do you have way down here in Mississippi?"

"Well, sir. None at all in Mississippi. We're expected in Montgomery, Alabama, tonight."

"And what will you do in Montgomery?"

"We're intending to have a reunion with a clergy colleague, that's all."

The trooper shone the small flashlight into Lucius's face. "Boy, you drove through Greenwood?"

"Yes, sir, we did, just a few minutes ago."

"A few minutes ago was still after sunset. Couldn't you read the big sign by the road when you entered Greenwood?"

"Yes, sir, we did."

"And what did it say?"

"That Negroes were not welcome in Greenwood after sundown."

"You read right, boy. Then let me ask you, what the hell were you doin' poking around a Sundown Town in the dark?"

Henri's ire was provoked. "We weren't poking around at all. We were simply driving through to get to Montgomery. We didn't stop at all in Greenwood." Henri was trying not to sound too defiant even though he felt that way.

"Well, seeing that you two fellahs are priests, I'll just write you a warning. The people of Greenwood don't want no vagrants to be cruisin' down their streets. I don't ever want to see you or this car in Greenwood after dark. You got that, boy?"

"You can be sure, Sir, that we won't be here anytime soon."

"Better not, boy. We'll have our eyes lookin' out for you. Good night." He turned off the flashlight, handed Lucius the warning. and made his way back to the cruiser.

"Damn arrogant son of a bitch," Lucius muttered under his breath. "Welcome to Mississippi."

IT WAS DARK WHEN THE PASTORS pulled into Montgomery. At a traffic light, they asked the Negro driver of an adjacent car for directions to Dexter Avenue Baptist Church.

"You mean that little church near the state capitol? The one with that good preacher? Why, sure. But there's a bunch of confusing turns to the right and the left to get there. Finding it can be a bit of a challenge, especially in the dark. Let me lead the way to Dexter Avenue to make sure you find it."

"We don't want to make you go out of your way," Lucius said apologetically. "You've probably got things you have to do."

"Nonsense, brother. You always have to have time to lend a hand to a stranger in need. Follow me."

"That's awfully kind of the chap," Lucius remarked as they endeavored to keep the man's car in view lest they miss one of those right or left turns. "My answer to the man's generous offer sounded like a New Yorker's, didn't it? In New York nobody's going to take the time and go out of their way to offer to accompany a stranger personally to their destination. But my experience living in Crawfordville should have taught me that in the South, the guy is right. People in the deep South, especially Negroes, make time for others."

Henri thought again of young Wallace in Fayetteville, and he and Lucius made a point of being generous with their thanks when the man's Chevrolet pulled over in front of Dexter Avenue Baptist Church. Lucius's DeSoto followed right behind.

They got out to find that the front doors into the church were closed and locked. They proceeded to walk together around the building to the back, trying every door along the way to see if one had been left unlocked for them. Finally, they found an unlocked door and entered the building.

At this hour of the night, they weren't surprised to find themselves in an eerily silent hallway with just a little night-light on to show the way. In the ambient light, Lucius found a sign that read "Pastor's Study" and an arrow pointing downstairs. On a wooden door that anyone familiar with the layout of southern churches would be safe in assuming it was the Pastor's Study, they spied a white paper sign.

"Dear Colleagues. Welcome to Montgomery and Dexter Avenue Baptist Church. I apologize if you are arriving when the building is vacated. I and the rest of the staff have gone home to be with our families and get our beauty sleep. I have made a reservation for you at the Ben Moore Hotel on Highland Avenue in the black business district known as Centennial Hill. Mr. Moore is part of the Movement and allowed us to use his hotel's parking lot as a pick-up and drop-off location for riders during our bus boycott. He will treat you really fine. I'll meet you here tomorrow morning. I generally arrive at the office by 8 a.m."

THEY DIDN'T ARRIVE TO MEET Dr. King at his office at 8 a.m. but almost an hour and a half later. The late arrival at their hotel the night before caused them to sleep in.

"Good morning, gentlemen," King said by way of greeting. "I trust that you found the accommodation to your satisfaction and that after your sojourn from Little Rock you got some sleep to recuperate."

"Yes, very much to our satisfaction, thank you, Dr. King," Henri said.

"Just Martin would be just fine. After all, we're colleagues."

"And you can call us by our names Lucius and Henri," Lucius

responded.

"I want to show off my church. Would you like a brief tour?"

"By all means," Henri said enthusiastically. "I remember reading about Dexter Avenue Church in Dr. Vernon John's memoir. It would be a thrill to see it with my own eyes."

"Yes, Vernon did a lot to loosen up the leadership of the church when he was pastor here. Vernon paid a price for his outspoken, combative style. The cautious, conservative board at the time pretty well made life so difficult for him that he had little choice but to resign. But I don't think they'd put up with me if he hadn't blazed the trail.... What are your plans this morning?"

"We're free and easy. Do you have a suggestion?"

"I'd like to introduce you to some members of our Montgomery Improvement Association who worked so hard to guide our bus boycott. I especially would like you to meet the secretary of the board. He's an exceptional fellow. I am sure you will see what I mean once you meet him. His name is Pastor Otto Grau. That name sound Lutheran enough for you? He's the relatively new pastor of Trinity Lutheran Church, a neighbor of Rosa Parks and her husband."

Chapter Thirteen

People always say that I didn't give up my seat because I was tired, but that isn't true. I was not tired physically.... No, the only tired I was, was tired of giving in.

Rosa Parks

June 1, 1958

No one can rightly say that Dr. King wasn't persuasive. He had a commanding presence without being an autocrat. It was clear to Henri and Lucius that King strongly preferred that they meet the secretary of the Montgomery Improvement Association board, so they agreed dutifully and did so.

"Yes, we would like to meet him and talk with him, Dr. King," Henri said before they left King's office. "But first things first. If you look down at the shoes on my feet, I'm sure you'd agree that they are in no condition to be worn when we meet the board secretary. I need to go to a shoe store and buy a new pair. Perhaps you can recommend a good shoe business in Montgomery?"

"Certainly, Henri. If you had asked back in 1956, I would have advised you to go to the shoe department at the Montgomery Fair department store downtown. But unfortunately, in 1956 Montgomery Fair fired Rosa Parks from her assistant tailor job. So even though the bus boycott is over, the MIA is recommending the Negro community avoid giving their business to that particular department store."

"Then, by no means do we want to go there," Lucius said. "Right, Henri?"

"Yes," Henri agreed, "by no means."

"There's a good shoe store on Montgomery Street not far from the courthouse. It's called H&M Shoes."

"Can we get there with the city bus?" Henri asked. "We're in Montgomery, Alabama, now, after all. Home of the successful first scrimmage of the Civil Rights Movement. I want to ride one of those buses that gave such trouble to Mrs. Parks and other Negro riders and gave rise to the boycott."

"Sure. Just catch the bus southbound on Dexter Avenue at Decatur Street. After the state capitol, Dexter becomes Vaughn

Street. Stay on the bus until Taylor Avenue, then walk a few blocks north to Montgomery Avenue. You'll have your choice of shoe stores there."

The pastors followed the instructions. When they stepped on the bus they had the feeling that they were relieving history. They deposited a dime each in the fare box. Almost all the seats in the front of the bus were occupied, but not exclusively by white passengers, as it would have been before Rosa Parks' stand and the successful boycott by Negro riders.

"Whenever I have to go up to Atlanta, I drive, of course," Lucius said to Henri. "That's because taking a bus in the city involves a lot of inconvenience and downright humiliation. There's a sizeable group of clergy brethren who were inspired by the bus boycott here to begin applying some significant pressure on the Atlanta city bus system. The matter is before the courts as I speak. But for now, if you and I were taking the bus downtown there, we would have paid our fare up here in the front, then had to step down the stairs, go around the bus on the outside, reenter by the back door, and sit only in the back rows of seats. Depending on the whim of the driver, the bus might take off without you while you're still making your way around the bus. I'm done with crap like that. Getting on the bus this way feels like we have left the first half of the twentieth century and entered the second. But I still prefer the comforts of my own car."

"We owe a huge debt of gratitude to Rosa Parks."

"Not to mention Rev. King."

"Right, you are," Henri responded. "I remember reading in *The Times* about the bus boycott. About ten years ago, a Negro veteran of World War II came back home to Montgomery. After riding the buses in London and Paris, he forgot the antiquated routine on the buses back home and paid his fare, then plopped his behind down on a vacant seat in the front of the bus. Of course, the driver ordered the man to get up and walk to the seats in the back. Well, the veteran was emboldened by a few beers and didn't move from his seat in the front. He told the driver that he couldn't see any reason why he should have to move to another seat. There were empty seats in the front, and the ones in the back were full of passengers.

The driver scuffled with the passenger in an effort to make him move by force, but the ex-soldier was too strong and adept at handling himself. The driver returned to his seat and called on his radio for intervention by the men in blue. A few minutes later, two cops entered the bus and managed to wrestle the G.I. down the aisle and toss him out the door to the pavement. To make sure their errand was completed, one of the cops jumped out the door and put a couple of bullets into the man's chest."

"Ironic. He had made it safely and in one piece all the way home to Montgomery alive, but wasn't so fortunate in racist Alabama," Lucius commented darkly. "Of course, the authorities never even questioned the cop, right?"

"You got it right, Lucius. Are we near Taylor Avenue yet?"

"You're asking me? I'm as new to this town as you are, friend," Lucius said good-naturedly. "I'll go ask the driver."

Henri watched as Lucius walked up the aisle. When the driver had come to a stop at an intersection, he carefully asked the driver about Taylor Avenue. Henri was surprised that the driver was a Negro; he felt more relaxed.

Lucius returned from his errand to report that the driver promised to call out the stop for Taylor Avenue. "I had forgotten that one of the conditions that King and the bus boycotters had put forward before they would call off the boycott was that the company hire Negro bus drivers."

The driver was true to his word. After he called out Taylor Avenue, Henri and Lucius stepped off the bus and walked the few blocks south to Montgomery Avenue. They saw a row of shoe stores along the busy street and walked until they came upon a vintage storefront. The door had an elegant classic, almost antique handle that suggested that this business had stood at that location for a while.

When they entered, they were greeted by a middle-aged male salesman who asked if he could help them find the kind of shoes they were looking for.

"Something plain and simple, comfortable, and cheap," Henri said, chuckling good-naturedly.

The salesman either didn't find humor in Henri's answer or chose to ignore it. He didn't even crack a smile.

"Of course, I can find you shoes that are plain, simple, and comfortable. I think you are the best judge if the shoes are inexpensive enough for your budget," he said mockingly.

He left to go into an area of the store that was out of view of the customers. He returned balancing four or five shoe boxes and placed them down on the floor at Henri's feet.

Henri tried on a couple of the pairs the salesman had fetched for him. Each pair seemed to Henri to have some flaw or shortcoming.

The salesman returned to check on his prospective customer. He was interrupted, however, by an impatient white customer with a question about the shoes he had been shown. "I can come right away to show you the difference between the different pairs of shoes, sir, and help you choose the ones that are best for you."

Henri was left sitting with several shoes in the seat beside him. "Sure, Mac," he uttered in a hushed but angry tone meant for only Lucius to hear. "Go ahead and satisfy the white customer before you answer the Negro's question and help him find a pair of shoes that is best for him."

"Hurry up, Henri. I don't get the impression that this salesman likes Negro customers, at least not us," Lucius observed.

"Tough. If I'm going to spend some of my hard-earned money on a pair of shoes that I consider to be much too expensive, I want them to be right. I'm not leaving here until I get a pair that I like," Henri said in a defiant voice that Lucius hadn't heard come out of Henri's voice before.

They stood and waited for the salesman to finish with the rude white customer. When it looked as though he was satisfied and had what he wanted in a shoe box under his arm, yet another white customer impeded the salesman's route to Henri and asked for service. The salesman gave her his attention.

"Didn't he notice that I was waiting to ask him a question, too?" Henri asked Lucius. "I guess you have to be white to get service here."

"I guess Jim Crow is still the way of life at this joint," Lucius said.

"I suspect at a lot of the joints here in Montgomery," Henri added. "I've just about had it with this place. Let's go."

HENRI PUT THE SHOES IN HIS HAND back on the floor but didn't bother to place them back in the boxes. They left H&H shoes wordlessly and without a new pair of shoes to replace Henri's old worn-out ones.

Back out on Montgomery Avenue, they headed back to Taylor Avenue to catch the bus back to Dexter Avenue Church to retrieve Lucius's car. They also hoped to catch Dr. King back at his office to continue their conversation of this morning, which had felt much too brief.

They had trouble finding Dr. King when they arrived at Dexter Avenue Baptist Church. They knocked on a few doors in the vicinity of the pastor's study, but there was no reply. The building was totally silent except for the humming of an air conditioner emanating from behind the door to Dr. King's study.

"He's probably gone to do what eminent preachers do on afternoons," Lucius remarked.

"Of course, since we're such pedestrian preachers, we wouldn't have any idea of how the upper tier of proclaimers of the gospel spend their afternoons," Henri responded.

"Speak for yourself, Rev. I bet that we less-learned preachers spend as much time preparing our sermons as do the Martin Luther Kings. They're just more adept in preaching off the cuff than you and me."

"But the smooth ones also make more money."

Lucius turned more earnest after Henri's remarks. "Although I hear from King's colleague back in Crawfordville that King only keeps a small portion of his salary for his own needs and those of his family. The rest he donates to the new civil rights collective that he is forming, the Southern Christian Leadership Conference. I was humbled when I heard that."

They heard footsteps on the stairs; Dr. King was descending to the first floor where Henri and Lucius were waiting.

"Gentlemen, back from your bus excursion into downtown Montgomery, are you? I'd like to see your new shoes, Henri."

"The bus excursion was fine, but our luck ran out at the shoe store," Henri reported. "We waited to be served there by the sales staff, but they were more interested in the white customers who came later than we did but received attention sooner."

"That sounds like the old Montgomery. I'm disappointed that you were made to feel like second-class citizens. I have to give credit to the proprietors and staff of H&M Shoes who have always given me first-class treatment. Perhaps I should give the manager a friendly call to encourage his staff to treat you more congenially tomorrow?"

"Dr. King, I hate to have you pull strings, but then again, it might be the only way I can get a new pair of shoes," Henri agreed.

"Come on into my study, gentlemen, and take a seat. I'll go to the kitchen and fetch us a cup of coffee. Let's take a moment to chat."

"If you can spare the time, Dr. King, I think we would like that," Henri said.

Henri and Lucius waited and scrutinized the books in the shelves that lined King's study.

"Get a load of the titles of some of these books," Lucius pronounced. "Some are about philosophers that not only have I never heard of, but also whose names I can't even begin to pronounce."

"I at least know of Simone de Beauvoir and Henri Bergson," Henri said and chuckled. "But when is a pastor going to have the occasion to quote Luce Irigaray or Julia Kristeva in a sermon?"

They tried to keep their voices low and were glad they had when King entered the study with a tray carrying China coffee cups. "I'm sorry to keep waiting, gentlemen, but now that the Montgomery Improvement Association uses our building for its meetings, things tend to find their own unique resting places where I can't find them when I need them. We need some orderly, tidy woman like Coretta to come over some afternoon and reorganize the whole kitchen. But she's got her hands full at home getting the kids to put things back where they found them."

"We were admiring your collection of books," Henry said.

"Far be it for me to boast, but I have to humbly acknowledge that I have actually read at least a part of each book. But since I got here to Montgomery, I haven't been very disciplined in making the time in my weekly schedule for study and reading."

"Isn't that a problem for most conscientious clergy who want to love the Lord with all their mind as well as all their other faculties?" Lucius asked.

"It's true at least in my case. But someday I will receive a call to a church in another city where there aren't as many demands on my time and energy. I keep promising the Lord that I'll get back to my studying then."

"Montgomery has been a busy place for you, Dr. King?" Henri asked.

"Getting selected as the first president of the Montgomery Improvement Association within a few short months of arriving here suddenly added to my workload and breadth of my leadership responsibilities."

"Many of us wonder how you manage to balance all the various balls you have in the air without dropping any of them," Henri said admiringly.

"There have been days, in fact, when I fear that I may have dropped too many of them and racked my brain to invent ways to hand the juggling act to someone else. I am becoming a much more spiritual pastor since I came to Montgomery."

"How so, Dr. King?" Lucius inquired genuinely.

"In fact, one reason I wasn't here when you arrived from your shoe shopping expedition was I was upstairs in my private sanctuary having my regular visit with my Father."

"Daddy King is here now and not back in Atlanta?" Lucius asked, confused.

"No, Lucius. I mean *our* Father from whom all blessings flow."

"Oh, yes," Lucius acknowledged, embarrassed of his literalistic misinterpretation.

"Many of us religious professionals have taken our familiarity with the ways of God for granted, assuming that our service to Him somehow exempts us from the responsibility of fostering a healthy relationship with our Higher Power. We do so to our own peril and that of the people we serve."

"I acknowledge your point, Dr. King," Henri said. "It's a professional hazard, isn't it?"

"It certainly was for me. But not so much that I neglected to cultivate my relationship with God. It's more that I was going about it in a rather dangerous, one-dimensional way. Perhaps even to the wrong God."

"I'm sure, Dr. King, that many people would find your statement to be totally unexpected, confounding, maybe even borderline heretical," Lucius remarked.

"As a matter of fact, Lucius, I confessed my spiritual challenges in a sermon to my congregation a few weeks ago in the same way I'm confessing it you now. And you're right. The initial response by many was just as you predicted. But thank the Lord that with time most came around to understand what I was telling them.

"I told them that I had returned to the parsonage late one evening, after midnight actually, after a particularly difficult and strained meeting of the MIA executive council. I call what followed as my "kitchen table conversion." I asked the congregation, 'You know how sometimes at midnight strange things happen?'

"I came home overtired but couldn't fall asleep. I got up out of bed and went down into the kitchen for a cup of warm milk, thinking that would help. I sat down at the kitchen table to sip my milk. I couldn't calm my brain, much less turn it off.

"It didn't help that while I sat there, the telephone on the wall rang. I got up and answered it after the first ring so that Coretta wouldn't wake up. On the other end was an extremely ugly voice like ones I had heard many times before around town and in my dreams. 'Nigger, we're mighty tired of the mess you've created here,' the gin-soaked voice said. 'If you don't get out of Montgomery in three days' time, you'll be sorry you ever came here. We're gonna hang you from a tree and bomb your house again.'

"I had heard threatening words such as those plenty of times during the boycott before. But this time, at midnight, my endurance was weak, and suddenly I was overcome by fear as never before. The white supremacists had succeeded in bombing our house before. Why not this time? I sat at the table and thought of our first-born daughter, not even a toddler yet. *How easily we could lose her.* I thought of my devoted wife, Coretta. *How impoverished I would be were they to take her from me.*

"Out there in the night, I imagined someone was loading a twenty-gauge pump action shotgun to take me down, pouring gasoline into a glass jar to blow the limbs off our baby. In the darkness, I paced the kitchen floor. Both of my hands clenched into fists, my stomach turned into lead. I turned over every metaphorical rock in search of some way out of my now impossible duties with the MIA. I felt caged like an animal, bound in chains.

"With each thought I grew increasingly and uncontrollably afraid. Without my leadership, the boycott might unravel. Nothing will have been accomplished.

"You mention Daddy King, Lucius. As if out of nowhere Daddy King's deep voice spoke to me. 'Why don't you kneel down and pray to God for strength?' But I couldn't do that. The God of all my doctoral study and books was an impersonal, philosophical God who didn't intervene in human affairs. 'I've been trying,' 'No,' Daddy King countered, 'I mean pray to the God I taught you about and your upbringing in the church inculcated in you.'

"I told the congregation that suddenly, at the sound of my father's loving but insistent voice, my eyes filled with tears. I cried openly sitting alone at the kitchen table. I even knelt down on my knees beside the table."

"'Dear Lord,' I said to God, 'you make a path for us when there is no way. You see me tonight weak and powerless. I want to feel and rely on your power. I can't let the people of Dexter Avenue Church or the Negroes of Montgomery see me like this. If they see me losing hope and strength, they will, too. I'm trying to do what's right. But I need you to guide me, Lord. I need you to show me the way.'"

King paused to allow the power of his confession sink in. It was clearly as fresh and compelling to him as on the late night when he had been overcome by the transcendent experience.

"I sat in the darkness of the kitchen in silence for what seemed like a long time. I realized then that I needed to keep the personal God I had avoided facing for so long close to my heart, to make space for God's Holy Spirit to infuse me with strength the way my Daddy had always encouraged me to. I couldn't continue leading the boycott without that inner assurance. Neither could the foot soldiers who walked the miles to get to their job persevere if this movement was not a spiritual one.

"At that point, I heard another voice within me, a stern yet somehow reassuring one. 'Martin Luther. Stand up. Stand up for righteousness. Stand up for Truth. Stand up for Justice. Preach the Gospel. And lo, I will be with you till the end.'"

When King was finished Lucius sat at the table in absolute silence. Henri wiped tears from his cheeks.

Chapter Fourteen

As the white minister of an African American congregation in Montgomery, Alabama, Graetz's [Grau's] home was bombed several times and he was harassed by white residents for his participation in the Montgomery bus boycott. In Martin Luther King, Jr.'s memoir of the boycott, Stride Toward Freedom, King recalled that Graetz served to remind those who were boycotting that "many white people as well as Negroes were applying the 'love-thy-neighbor-as-thyself' teachings of Christianity in their daily lives."

Brian Lyman
Montgomery Advertiser, September 21, 2020

June 3, 1958

It was time to meet Rev. Grau, the secretary of the board of the Montgomery Improvement Association, as they had promised Dr. King. Lucius drove the DeSoto slowly from Dexter Avenue into a residential neighborhood of small one-story bungalows made of concrete blocks erected a few decades earlier in the Great Depression. They located Trinity Lutheran Church at the corner of Decatur Avenue. It was a handsome structure, though very small. It was clear that at its founding in the mid-1940s, its builders had intentions to build a larger building at a later time since the existing one had an expansive front yard that would provide sufficient room.

Lucius parked the DeSoto underneath some shade trees in a small lot at the rear of the church. The front door of the church was unlocked and led them into a small empty anteroom. They waited when they heard the clip-clop of female footsteps in heels on the basic concrete floor. A pudgy, large-bosomed, late middle-aged Negro woman entered from the corridor. She caught her breath after coming promptly from her office to see who had entered the building. She smiled and introduced herself as the part-time secretary-receptionist, Mrs. Williams.

"We've come unannounced to meet with Rev. Grau. We were sent by Rev. Martin Luther King. We are two clergymen touring various sites in the South."

"I'm sure Pastor Grau would be happy to meet with you. I saw his car pull into the parsonage driveway just a half-hour ago. I can call him and tell him you're here. Unless he's in the middle of

something important, I'm sure he will be over in a few minutes."
While she was talking, she led them to her small office. "He uses a
room in the parsonage as his office," she added, pointing out the
picture window to a white stucco bungalow adjacent to the church
and much like others in the neighborhood. There were several untidy
piles of bits and pieces of lumber of various lengths and halved
concrete blocks thrown up beside the house as though left over after
a construction project had been commenced but not completely
finished.

Mrs. Williams noticed that the curiosity of the visitors was
piqued.

"Oh, I see you're wondering about all the lumber and blocks.
Everybody who doesn't know what happened wonders about those.
That project is to repair some of the damage from the bomb last year.
I'll let him tell you the story."

At the word "bomb" spoken so nonchalantly by Mrs. Williams,
Henri and Lucius regarded each other with subdued alarm and asked,
"Did she say 'bomb?'"

Mrs. Williams took her keys from a drawer on her desk and
unlocked the door into an adjacent room. The room was almost
empty. The bookshelves built into the walls were a dead giveaway
that this room must have served at an earlier time as the pastor's
study. The wooden desk in the center of the room was empty save
for several outdated issues of a denominational magazine. Henri and
Lucius each picked up one to serve as reading material as they
waited.

They heard Mrs. Williams say, "They're waiting in the spare
office." The pastors figured that Rev. Grau had arrived in the
building. They rose up and stood dutifully in preparation to greet the
pastor loci. A thirtyish man in a clerical collar entered the spare
office.

"Good afternoon, gentlemen. I'm sorry to keep you waiting."

"No apologies needed," Henri said. "We came unannounced,
and you probably weren't expecting two visitors. I'm Henri Esper, a
UCC pastor in New York. My colleague here is the Rev. Lucius
Blackwood, a Baptist preacher from Crawfordville in Georgia."

The three shook hands and shared some niceties.

"I'm Otto Grau, pastor here at Trinity Church. Welcome."

Henry and Lucius were rendered speechless by the surprise.
This Rev. Grau whom King recommended that they make a point of

meeting was white.

"Your reaction is not at all unfamiliar to me. You aren't the first visitors to be confused when it dawns on them that the secretary of the board of directors of the Montgomery Improvement Association is as white as a fresh piece of writing paper."

"Well, Pastor Grau, to be honest we are surprised," Lucius said. "We shouldn't be, I suppose. Why shouldn't a white pastor serve on the board of the organization that oversaw the bus boycott?"

"That's evidently how the rest of the board felt when they elected me to their number. It's also how Rev. King felt when he nominated me in the first place. I was both very humbled and flattered."

"You must tell us how it came about," Henri inquired, "that the white pastor of what appears to be a small Lutheran congregation in a southern city is selected to the board of directors of an organization charged with calling the shots in a boycott to further the rights of Negroes? That's astounding."

"Aren't the ways of God often that way?" Grau countered. "It was partly the result of timing. Providentially, I had just received and accepted the call as pastor of Trinity in the late spring of 1955, just five months before Rosa Parks was arrested. The local Negro pastors noted that I was called as the white pastor of a congregation that was almost a hundred percent Negro. At first, that was a source of curiosity to those Negro pastors and thankfully, in time, a source of respect and trust."

"You list the timing as one factor in your being selected to the board," Henri said. "What is the second factor?"

"Dr. King himself. He's a unique kind of leader. His vision for the MIA was that it be an inclusive multiracial, or at least biracial, group that joins both black and white hands together to work for equal justice for all people, black and white and red and brown."

"That's an admirable vision," Henri commented. "How do you feel you have been received by the fifty-five thousand Negro residents of Montgomery?"

"Honestly, you'd have to ask them. But I don't think that my commitment to the Negro community is questioned at all. When I graduated from seminary, I asked the district executives that they assign me to a biracial or Negro congregation. We moved into the parsonage in this predominantly Negro neighborhood. My wife, Dianne, and I tried from day one to participate in cultural and social events in this and other Negro neighborhoods. Rosa and Raymond Parks lived just a few houses over from us before they moved out of town. A truly humble and committed couple, they spoke well of us to their neighbors. A major turning point came with the two bombings of the parsonage."

"Two bombings?" Lucius asked, startled. "Not just one? But two?"

"Separated by almost a year, thank the Lord. My wife and kids and I were away on vacation in Ohio in July 1956. The bombers were not aware of that. And they didn't do a thorough job of setting the small bombs so that the damage to our home was minimal. More like a cruel warning perhaps from the bombers—most likely white supremacists, the neighbors figure. The second bombing occurred just after the boycott ended in January 1957. That was on another order of danger. The bomb was simply sticks of dynamite tied together, pure TNT. One bundle landed just feet from our front door. We had a nine-day-old baby asleep in the house, as well as four other school-age children. The TNT did a lot of structural damage. You can still see evidence of it in our side yard. But thank God, we suffered no loss of limb or human life.

"Our church board encouraged us strongly to move out of Montgomery. I asked, 'What? And let the white supremacists think that they had won?'

"It might have been worse, we learned later. Our children playing outside found one of the bundles of dynamite in the backyard. It had not been ignited. But Diane and I tremble to think of it. What if our children had been more curious to learn what might happen if they lit the wick? The local fire chief said that the explosion would have been enough to damage the whole neighborhood."

"God Almighty!" Lucius uttered.

"But we didn't feel alone. Dr. King's home had been bombed several times during the boycott. On the night our home was hit, it turns out that four other Negro pastors' homes were bombed. And several occupied homes of residents in the neighborhood were set ablaze." Grau continued. "It was a wild night; the Negro community came together to cook meals and help us rebuild. Nothing works like disaster or calamity to one of their own to unify a people. 'Whenever one suffers, all suffer together.'

"It was here in Montgomery that Dr. King was arrested for the first time. He hated the inside of jail cells and feared being confined in one. When he was released and returned to our meetings, he said quite plainly that if any of us being installed that evening onto the board were not prepared to endure what he had for the sake of the boycott, we had better not accept. My decision to accept his invitation to serve on the board was affirmed a thousandfold that night and thereafter by his challenging words."

Feeling both challenged and their spirits renewed, Henri and Lucius rose, shook Grau's hand, and thanked him for his hospitality, then said a short parting prayer for Grau's continued service for the Movement and for God's abiding with Martin Luther King in his efforts to maintain leadership in Montgomery in the wake of the boycott. Grau opened the glass door and escorted his two colleagues out into the impromptu parking lot under the trees behind the church.

As they walked around the church building, Lucius uttered, "Uh oh," and stopped in his tracks.

"Did you forget something back in the church, Lucius?" Henri asked.

"No. But geez, look at our car."

The DeSoto was sitting unusually low to the ground. The tires were flat, all four of them. On closer examination, they didn't see any slash marks in the tires depleted of air.

"Well, that's something to be thankful for," Henri said, relieved. "Four new tires would have set us back a few bucks."

"Don't talk too soon," Grau warned. He knelt on the concrete surface and reached his hand underneath one tire. "Just as I thought," he said as he stood up again.

"What did you think?" Lucius asked.

"This same thing has happened to my car several times here in Montgomery. The tires are slashed all right, but in places on the tires you can't easily see."

"If they're intent on slashing them, why do it in a part of the tire that we don't see? I don't get it," Lucius asked, bewildered.

"Because the slashers hope it's more deadly this way. If they slashed them openly where you can see the damage, they know you would just take it to a local shop and pay them to put on four new tires. But if you don't know the tires are slashed, you'd just stop and refill them with air. The tires would hold the air for a half-hour or so, and by then you'd be speeding along on empty tires and possibly lose control of the vehicle. The results could be fatal. The family and

I took off for vacation in Ohio last summer thinking the tires might have looked down a little. But after a few miles on the open road I was pushing sixty miles per hour when steering our car felt next to impossible because it turned out the tires were flat."

Henri and Lucius looked at each other, possibly out of begrudging admiration for the ingenuity of the slashers, or confusion about why someone would want to perpetrate such a menacing subterfuge with a vulnerable car full of five kids.

"Some of the white supremacists down here hate not only Negroes," Grau said matter-of-factly, "but more than that, they hate *white* people who are sympathetic to Negroes. They've done things like this to me periodically for over a year. But I don't heed their message. I haven't taken their suggestion that we get the heck out of 'their' town. They've given up on me. But someone must have spied your car pulling in at the 'nigger loving preacher's church' and called their yahoo friends—probably Klansmen—to come and send you a message so that you wouldn't come back."

Chapter Fifteen

According to Young, northern whites were more reluctant to accept change because they had yet to confront their own racism. Ultimately, Young believes that race relations were slower to change in the North than in the South because the North was segregated geographically, whereas the South was primarily segregated legally. Because southern whites had lived with African Americans in their midst for generations.

Andrew Young

June 4, 1958

Henri and Lucius's departure from Montgomery was delayed until later in the day. Reverend Grau gave his visitors the name of a trusted member of Trinity, a car repair shop where they could get the flat tires replaced. As they sat in the congested waiting room, Henri and Lucius compared notes about their recent unpleasant experience in the Trinity Lutheran Church parking area.

"Man, I thought that Mississippi was an unwelcoming place," Lucius said. "Four new damn tires all because some local yahoos didn't want us here. I wish I could send the buzzards the bill to them to pay the damages."

"Good thing that we were at Grau's church when it happened. We might never have located the slashes in the tires," Henri replied. "Rack the experience up to learning what it's like to be black living in the Deep South."

Lucius did a quick inspection on the new tires. When he was satisfied by the quality of the tires and the labor, he jumped into the driver's seat to begin the next leg of the trip. He jockeyed the DeSoto through Montgomery.

"Where to next, boss?" he asked Henri before they had proceeded very far.

"We'll have to pay a visit to the biggest city of the Old Confederacy sometime soon. But not yet, I think. I feel the need to take a sabbatical from my sabbatical and go back to Harlem to check in on my mother to see if she's saved a place for me to live when this adventure is over."

"I've been thinking the same thing, now that you mention it. I have a church to tend to. I tend to forget that. I should get back to

Crawfordville to see if I still have a job."

"St. James gave you this sabbatical time so that you can tag along on my southern sojourn. I'm grateful, buddy. How long of a sabbatical did they agree to?"

"No agreement was formally presented or signed. They originally talked in terms of a month or two. Maybe another couple if I felt I needed it."

"A month or two? That's it? It was late February of '57 when we met up at the train station in Little Rock. By my reckoning, that's over four months ago, Lucius. Haven't you been keeping track of the passage of time?"

"Not really. I've been having such a good time on the road. These stops at some of the civil rights hotspots have been utterly fascinating."

"I agree, brother. But, Lucius, good Lord, you can't just abandon your church like this without being in communication with them."

"Has it really been almost a half-year that we've been traveling?"

"Yes, sir. Just add them up. Little Rock. Traveling here to Montgomery. It all took time."

"I told you, Henri. I need to go back for a visit." Lucius spoke angrily but Henri knew he was only embarrassed by his irresponsibility.

"Yes, you most certainly do."

Crawfordville, GA
June 8, 1958

Henri, my dear travel companion.

I trust that this letter finds you safe in the Big Apple and happily reunited with Emile and your mother. How was the train journey?

My drive across Alabama to Georgia was without incident, not even a single flat tire or a stop by Alabama state troopers. I was pleasantly surprised by the short distance from Birmingham to the outskirts of Atlanta. Whenever I arrive on a trip of any length in the bright suburbs of the Peachtree City, my body feels that it is almost home in Taliaferro County.

I have to say that I felt like a different man on my drive from the one who arrived in Little Rock to begin our tour. The towns somehow looked different to me. As if for the very first time, I noted the obvious economic disparities between the sections of the towns where the Negroes chose or were forced by economic circumstances (or most likely zoning laws and real estate practices) to live, and the well-manicured zones chosen by their white counterparts. I had noted such things before, of course, in my travels from Crawfordville to Atlanta or Savannah, but only out of the corner of my eye. Our drive through Arkansas, Mississippi, and Alabama opened my eyes to conditions in my home state. Did you have a similar experience on the train ride back to New York?

I've got to tell you about my stop in Forsyth County just south of Atlanta. I needed to relieve myself. I remembered from a pastoral visit I made to an older lady from St. James, who had been relocated from Crawfordville by her adult children to Forsyth to be closer to them, that there was a public restroom in the town library (the only place in town, I was told, where Negroes were allowed to use the facilities).

I located the library again, used the restroom, and decided that since I was so close to home, I could take an hour or so to explore the library's holdings. I picked up a small book in a display of books for local interest. The little volume featured an article about Forsyth County that I had never heard before (but now that I've heard and seen some of the events in our people's struggle, I am not at all surprised by the event).

The event goes like this. In 1912, it seems that the mutilated and bloody corpse of an eighteen-year-old white woman was discovered partially buried in a field out in the county.

Does this sound vaguely familiar? Don't all incidents of racial violence begin with a question of sex with a white woman like the story your teacher told in eighth grade, the one about the massacre of Rosewood, Florida? Or the destruction of the Greenwood district of Tulsa in 1921?

Actually, the identity of the real felon has never been ascertained, and the case remains unresolved even to this day. But—predictably—some local white know-it-alls were certain that only a Negro male could do such a dastardly deed. Two teenage Negro boys were lynched, and their corpses carried and put on display in the town square. Thousands of the majority white citizens showed up to watch the lynching. Some of the men and teenage boys joined in and fired bullets into the helpless corpses.

Apparently, the book says the two teenaged boys joined the ranks of hundreds of other Negro males who were lynched in the general area of Forsyth between 1901 and 1951.

After the public lynching, white vigilante gangs rounded up every Negro person they could find and drove them out of Forsyth. Some 1,098 Negroes—about ten percent of the known population of the county—were forced out of their homes and communities. The result is that Forsyth's current population is only about 3.5 percent Negro, unusually low for Georgia.

I placed the book back in the display case and left the library. I drove the remaining ninety or so miles to Crawfordville with tears of both anger and sadness in my eyes.

Well, I've got some surprising news to share with you, some good, some bad. Let me tell you the bad news first. I felt more than a little self-conscious coming back to St. James after so many months away. The congregation had visibly diminished since I left. Some people kept referring to a Reverend Buford. I finally asked who Reverend Buford was. I was told that he was a semi-retired elderly preacher who drove down from Washington, GA, every Sunday morning while I was gone to take the worship service. The next part of the sentence, though, caught my attention. "While the board of St. James makes a decision about searching for a new pastor."

A new pastor, they said, because their "former pastor was cruising free and easy around Arkansas, Alabama, and Mississippi and wherever the wind would blow him next."

To put it bluntly, I was fired from St. James. I wasn't really surprised. I would have fired me, too.

I met with the board the next evening to try to make my case for keeping the job, but I don't think I was very persuasive. I knew when I left for Little Rock in 1957 that there were some members who thought my being granted a sabbatical of several months was a risky, unorthodox practice. But Henri, I should have been in touch with the board sooner. You know what? As I think about it, I didn't really want to preserve my job as pastor of St. James.

When I got home from the meeting with the board, I got a telephone call from Ernest Caldwell. He's not on the board any longer, but the real power in the congregation still rests with him because as the owner and operator of the successful Chevy dealership in Crawfordville so no one dares to oppose him and cause him to withdraw his annual pledge. Without Ernest, there would be a lot of unpaid bills.

Ernest was still on the board in 1957 and was a hundred percent convinced that a sabbatical would help improve my preaching, which I admit had grown kind of old and tired. I'm sure that St. James kept paying me a small monthly salary all these months I was gone because Ernest saw to it that it happened, probably with his own money. It turns out that sermons like the one I gave when I got back are just what Ernest Caldwell has been hungering and thirsting for.

"I can see, son, the difference this sabbatical has made in your preaching," he whispered in my ear as he put a supportive around me, "and I'm sure in your life attitudes and values. Now, I can't get you your job back at St. James, unfortunately. But I want to keep sponsoring your development as a pastor of the church, evidently not ours here in Crawfordville but somewhere else. In return, I ask only that you give me an estimate of what amount of financial support you will need to continue your educational tour with your colleague.

He called me after the meeting not to chastise me for constantly extending the sabbatical unilaterally without the board's agreement. Rather, he called to congratulate me on my sermon that morning. "Man, there's been a drastic change in your preaching if today's sermon is any indication. It felt like a gust of fresh air. In these revolutionary times, it was just what the congregation needed to hear, though I suspect they don't realize it. It shook us out of our complacency. It aroused us out of our slumber. You weren't afraid to describe the desperate political and economic condition of our people."

"Henri, I myself wouldn't describe my homily this morning as particularly outstanding or relevant. But as I think about it now, it was different from what I had been preaching before I joined you on this discovery tour of the civil rights movement. I adopted Jesus' parable of the Good Samaritan as my starting point. After commending the Samaritan for dressing the woeful traveler's wounds and paying the innkeeper to care for the victimized man's physical needs, I posed a question: What do you predict, friends, would occur on the road to Jericho the next time a lone traveler were to happen along? Don't you reckon that the same gang of ruthless brigands would attack the lonesome traveler the same way they assaulted and robbed the ill-fated traveler in Jesus' story? Someone

would have to keep on applying salve and wrapping bandages on the man's near-fatal wounds until there weren't enough salve and bandages to be found in the whole county to suffice...until and unless, that is, some bright, enterprising compassionate person or group of persons were to raise the issue of the lack of public safety on this particular road and petition the powers that be to address the situation and promote public policies and practices to protect the safety and welfare of travelers on the Jericho road.

I related to the congregation stories of wise, compassionate people I met or heard about in the course of our trip so far who are working diligently to promote the rights of people like us who have been "robbed" as it were, by the white majority, and left unprotected by laws that were meant to protect us.

I didn't speak those words for any other reason but that I have been filled with admiration for people like Delores Banks, Rosa Parks, Reverend Grau, and, of course, Dr. King.

"Just give me your solemn word, son, that once this sabbatical of yours is over, you consider accepting a pulpit in a church that needs to hear what you preach and is open to how the gospel can guide their lives in these turbulent times," Evidently not here at St. James, but somewhere else here in the South. Also, that you write to me about your discoveries and experiences from time to time and even come back to Crawfordville some time to be my wife's and my guest for dinner and conversation. All I need from you before you leave town again is for you to give me an estimate of how much financial support you will need from us to continue your travels with your friend to these hot spots in the struggle."

Isn't it William Shakespeare, Henri, who named one of his plays, "All's Well That Ends Well?"

Write back soon to describe your homecoming to Harlem. I'm eager to get back on the road again as soon as we can arrange it.

As you can see, Henri, my trip back to Crawfordville ended up better than I had reason to expect, probably much better than I deserve. We call that grace, don't we?

Chapter Sixteen

My mother wrote me a letter, and she said "Dear Robert, I thought you went to school to get an education; you need to get out of that mess. You're gonna get hurt." I wrote her a letter back and said, "Dear Mother, I've acted according to the dictates of my conscience." I don't think she knew what I was talking about. This is something that I have to do.

John Lewis
Walking With the Wind

June 6, 1958

Henri and Lucius decided to extend their visits at their homes for another month or two.

Lucius took the opportunity of his new status as unemployed to drive to the small town near Louisville where his mother was still living after the death of her husband earlier in 1958. He suspected his long absence and limited communication with his mother and siblings would be a source of irritation for them. They were sure to remind him several times over during his stay with them, but they received him with open arms, nonetheless.

Henri, back in New York, familiarized himself again with Harlem, which he judged had begun crumbling and taken a step or two down economically and culturally in his absence. At street corners, menacing groups of young adult males congregated, though Henri was sure they should be working. He made mention of these collections of healthy-looking young men and was told by his family that they would be working if only there were jobs available and business enterprises to hire them.

"I don't remember seeing so many unemployed young Negroes on the streets of Harlem in the past."

His brother Emile answered the implied question. "It's not just Negroes, Henri, although it is mainly. There's a lack of opportunity for all young people in Harlem. We're not just 'drifting around' aimlessly as you make it sound, Henri," Emile said defensively.

"This nation as we knew it for generations has begun to undergo a transformation of monumental proportions," Henri said. "That transformation is most dramatic among our own people, and no more so than in the southern states. I felt a call to see this historic transformation of southern society for myself up close. No, more than that, a call to find some way to *participate myself* in this transformation."

"Son, I don't understand what you mean by a 'transformation.' You sound like a highfalutin doctor of politics or something from New York, not a plain speakin' preacher from Dixie."

It didn't dawn on his mama that Henri considered that a compliment, a badge of honor, not a criticism.

"MAMA, THIS TRANSFORMATION is historic, and I want to be exposed to it. This reformation in the way Americans are living is being brought about by smart and courageous Negro leaders like the Rev. Dr. Martin Luther King, Jr. I emphasize the title *Rev. Dr.* to impress upon you the roots in the Christian faith of the Civil Rights Movement that they lead."

"But I hear that these rebellious and restless leaders of the Civil Rights Movement only preach about political matters, not the true gospel of the forgiveness of our sins in Jesus and the promise of eternal life in heaven. I'm not against political matters. They can make some difference in how we live. But, son, not the profound enduring, immortal difference that Jesus wants to make in our hearts."

Henri realized his mother was both angry and mournful because he had grown in a spiritual direction different from hers.

"Mama, isn't the God we are inviting our people to worship and serve the One who became incarnate in Jesus supremely concerned about what the people he was talking to would eat and how they would be able to feed their children and how to keep the wolf from the door? That's how the Son of God is depicted in Scripture, Mama. Why then is the Jesus I hear about in many if not most churches I visit sound like a pale, colorless distant cousin of that Jesus of Scripture? I stopped going to church some time ago on my vacation because when I do go, I go hungering and thirsting to hear the Truth. But what I hear too often is a poor counterfeit of the Truth. Yes, Jesus promised eternal life in heaven. But that day is in the distant future far away. I want to know what difference that promise makes in the difficult lives of our people *here and now*."

Perhaps ceding a little ground, she said, "I hope for you, son, that day will be in the distant future. But for Daddy, it was unannounced and immediate. It will be that way for me, too, soon and all other older people."

A reflective silence fell over both mother and son in the wake of her sober reminder of their mortality. Henri regretted that he might have used his learning as a cudgel against his own mother.

Then his mother injected into the stillness: "You've been thinking about this a long time, haven't you, son? And you sound like you're really convinced of what you say."

"Yes, Mama. A long time. All the years in seminary at Union. Every year since. I swear I won't become the preacher in a church again until I can be sure that the people of that church are hungry to hear the truth and that I am ready to be bold and strong enough to speak it."

"I see," his mother conceded. "I pray that day comes."

She was drained after hearing his passionate diatribe and was ready to let it go for now.

"I'm sorry for the fire and brimstone sermon of mine, but remember, you brought up the subject."

She rose with some significant effort from her deep rocking chair and walked over silently to where Henri was sitting, put her arms around him and, holding the arm of his chair for balance, whispered into his ear, "I love your sermons, son."

"You may be old, Mama, and a little out of touch with the modern world, but I love you lots, too."

Chapter Seventeen

It was clear to me that if we allowed the Freedom Ride to stop at that point, just after so much violence had been inflicted, the message would have been sent that all you have to do to stop a nonviolent campaign is inflict massive violence.

Diane Nash

April 1961

"Hello?"

"Henri, buddy, I'm about ready to get on the road again and be your travel companion. Are you ready to pick up where we left off?" Lucius, as usual, didn't bother to identify himself on the phone. He just picked up the conversation as if nothing had happened since the last time they had talked a few months ago.

"I'm still in Harlem. Where are you?"

"I got a group of old friends to help me pack up and move me to Atlanta. There aren't enough women in Crawfordville who are looking for a man from Union Theological Seminary in New York City."

"I haven't run into one like that even here in New York...not that I've been looking for one."

"Well, it's been a long time since we left Montgomery. Still got the bug to travel the civil rights highway through the South?"

"Haven't shaken the bug yet. The civil rights struggle has only become more intense since we rode the Montgomery city bus together."

"I'm actually being recruited as a civil rights missionary of sorts. My generous benefactor, Ernest Caldwell, who has kept me above the financial waters for these intervening years, has made a request."

"If he's paying the bills, you'd better consider it."

"His brother's daughter, Lucretia Caldwell, twenty-three years old, has been accepted by Jim Farmer, the director of CORE —the Congress for Racial Equality—to participate in the so-called 'Freedom Rides' beginning next month. Ernest is a little nervous about sending his niece on a bus alone through the South among any sex-starved males who may be going along for the ride. He wants me to apply to CORE as well to watch out for Lucretia's well-being and safety."

"What is he thinking? Sending the fox along to guard the chicken coop?"

"Lucretia is already taken. By a theology student at Candler. But Ernest also figures it's time for the likes of me to get committed to the struggle instead of sitting around reading about it. So I agreed. But I'd rather have my travel companion along with me to watch out for my safety and well-being."

"But are you sure you're ready to leave the car in Atlanta and travel all those miles on a public Greyhound?

"For Ernest Caldwell, yes."

"I'm definitely interested in joining you, Lucius, but I have to admit that I don't know much about the notion of 'Freedom Rides.'"

"What's there to know? They are just what their title suggests."

"A ride into freedom? Or a ride on behalf of freedom? What?"

"Come on, Henri. You're the one who knows about writing. You know about using certain words or images as summaries or shorthand for longer, wordier concepts. Even I understand that. Everything we are struggling for in this movement is summed up in the image or vocabulary of freedom. We were an enslaved people, Henri. The Civil War granted us freedom from forced labor and all that, but we aren't really free, are we? Because of Rosa's defiance and courage and Dr. King's brilliant leadership, you and I were free to sit anywhere we chose on the bus to downtown Montgomery, remember? Freedom."

"So we will be crisscrossing the South in a bus to see whether or not Negroes are or are not free?"

"Well, yes, specifically free to travel from place to place in a desegregated bus. Free to sit and wait for their next bus in a waiting room in which both whites and Negroes are equally welcome."

"And I hope free to use the restrooms designated for customers of both races."

"I knew you would catch on. Those old white guys on the United States Supreme Court up in Washington have helped us in that regard. Last year, in the case Boynton Virginia, they reaffirmed the unconstitutionality of bus companies' or political jurisdictions' schemes of refusing our riding on buses on which whites are riding as well or relieving ourselves in bus station restrooms that are arbitrarily assigned to 'Colored' patrons only. That's where freedom meets the road."

"But weren't Negroes free to do all those things before last year?"

"Technically and in terms of the law of the land as defined by those same justices in Washington, yes, we were. But you know how this nation works. Many of the forty-eight states dragged their feet or totally defied the Court's ruling, many of those are among states that we are touring."

"You mean fifty states, don't you, Lucius?"

"Yes, you know what I mean. It's only been a year. I'll eventually get accustomed to remembering that Alaska and Hawaii are states now."

"As I recall from my reading, these Freedom Rides are not the very first ones."

"No, but the first ones in fourteen years and the first to venture into the deep South. In 1947, the Congress on Racial Equality sponsored the Journey of Reconciliation to try to draw the nation's attention to the change in laws that a ruling of the Supreme Court in 1946 banned segregation on interstate buses. CORE gathered and trained sixteen individuals, both white and Negro, to travel on buses to see if Greyhound and Trailways were heeding the new law."

"So the Freedom Ride is the Journey of Reconciliation Redux?"

"Sure, the same principle, but otherwise I hope that the Freedom Rides are more enduring and successful."

"The Journey of Reconciliation didn't succeed in its mission?"

"It was planned and designed on the back of an envelope, as it were. James Farmer, the leader of CORE, might have been a civil rights pioneer, but he was no Martin Luther King, Jr. King wasn't even twenty years old then. The Journey of Reconciliation ended with a whimper and ironically when twelve of the riders, including Bernard Rustin, another leader of the project, were arrested in North Carolina for violating the segregation laws still in the books there and in those other states in defiance of the Supreme Court's ruling. The twelve riders wound up serving twenty-two days in a chain gang."

"My Lord! A real chain gang? The kind Sam Cooke sang about? You know the one. 'Ho. Ha. That's the sound of the men working on the chain gang.'"

"That's how the ill-fated Journey of Reconciliation came to an unceremonious end.

"Fourteen years of the federal authorities' ambivalence toward the Supreme Court's ruling and the states' outright open defiance of it followed. But Farmer and Rustin are back to give it another try. They plan to provide training for a group of chosen volunteers to ride the buses and inspect the practices and policies of the bus lines to verify if the rate of compliance has improved to the now-fourteen-year-old ban on segregation on interstate buses and trains and facilities in the terminals."

"So Farmer and Rustin are either fools or gluttons for punishment."

"I choose to hope they are paragons of grit and patient perseverance," Lucius said to counter Henri's skeptical outlook.

THE RIDERS WOULD NOT LIMIT their expeditions to the border states alone but venture into the deep South, places like Alabama, Mississippi, and Louisiana, generally known as the "belly of the segregation beast." The Freedom Rides would end in New Orleans on May 17 to celebrate the anniversary of the *Brown v. Boad of Education* ruling—if the virulent segregationists, of whom there would be many surely along the route, found a way to cause the plan to finish in New Orleans to be altered or aborted.

Lucius took a plane from Atlanta where the training program would kick off on May 4. Henri hadn't received confirmation that he had been accepted as a Freedom Rider until just before that date. Finally, the letter from CORE arrived with instructions to meet the others at the Friends' Fellowship House in Atlanta. Henri rode the rails to Atlanta.

Among the participants gathered for training were a sixty-year-old University of Michigan professor Walter Bergman and his wife, Frances, a New York journalist; folksinger Jimmy McDonald; a white field secretary for CORE, Genevieve Hughes; and one Jim Peck, a veteran of the 1947 Journey of Reconciliation. The Negro participants were visibly younger, like John Lewis of Pike County, Alabama, the first president of the Student Nonviolence Co-coordinating Committee (SNCC); Hank Thomas, a student leader at Howard University in Washington, D.C.; and Lucius's friend, the stunningly beautiful Lucretia Caldwell.

Much of the riders' training was in the principles and practice of Gandhian nonviolent resistance taught by James Lawson. Director James Farmer struck Lucius particularly as ambitious and fervently too protective of CORE's reputation and authority as the principal organizational support for the Freedom Rides. Farmer handed out waiver forms for all Freedom Riders to absolve CORE of any responsibility for any possible physical injury that might be endured by the Riders.

"But you probably won't encounter very much such danger, I assure you," Farmer added as the members of the group rose from the floor to board the buses.

As they were filing out of the Fellowship House, Lewis gave Lucius a knowing look and wink of his eye that seemed to say, "A likely prediction, I'm sure."

Half the group lined up to buy a ticket on the Greyhound while the other half went across the street to the Trailways terminal to procure a ticket to Rock Hill, SC.

When they stopped in Fredericksburg, an hour south of Washington, they were pleased that the "whites only" and "colored" signs had been removed from the terminal.

"Looks like they knew we were coming, friends," Lewis shouted out. "Maybe they've baked us a cake."

No signs in the Richmond terminal either, nor in Petersburg. Farmville, VA, was a different matter. Farmville was the county seat of Prince Edward County where the school board had closed the public schools two years earlier rather than obey the *Brown v. Board of Education* order to integrate. Most of the county's white children had transferred to private schools while the Negro pupils had gone two wasted years without education. So no one on the Freedom Ride was surprised that not only had the "whites only" and "colored" signs remained in the terminal but were freshly repainted to provoke the riders.

After quick stops in Lynchburg and Danville, the Freedom Bus rolled across the border into the rougher territory of the less welcoming states of the Carolinas where the Ku Klux Klan had been first organized in the wake of the Civil War. When the Greyhound pulled into the terminal at Rock Hill, SC, abutting the border with North Carolina, John Lewis said quietly to Lucius, "There's trouble awaiting us here. I can sense it in my bones."

Perhaps Lewis had heard or read about the lunch counter sit-ins by college students in downtown Rock Hill in the previous year, which had roiled the white citizenry. Not many of them objected in January when nine Negro students from Friendship Junior College were arrested at a McCrory's department store downtown, nor when the students were sentenced to thirty days on a road gang.

Lewis and the physically imposing Al Bigelow needed to use the bathroom after the long ride though Virginia and North Carolina. With a hint of defiance, they entered the bathroom designated for "whites only." Around the pinball machines in the terminal near the entrance into the bathroom stood a leather-jacketed, duck-tailed gang of young white men.

"Other side, Niggers," one of the men said gruffly to Lewis and Bigelow, pointing to a door down the way with a sign that read "Colored."

Bigelow stepped away from the urinal and looked at the man with threats of his own written all over his face.

Lewis, as always, appealed to the man's reason. "We have the right to use this bathroom on the grounds of the United States Supreme Court in the Boynton case."

The man looked a little confused but was not impressed. "And we have the right to kick your asses out of here on the grounds of a long-held and sacred tradition of our southern way of life. Shit on your Supreme Court."

With that, the man's fist smashed the right side of Lewis's head. Bigelow stepped in, inserting his substantial body between Lewis and the man. The man and one of his fellows by the pinball machine ran into the restroom and began to pummel Bigelow, whose hands were hanging limply at his side, not raised Cassius Clay like to protect his face or inflict a blow on the attackers. Lewis lay on the floor in a fetal position. The man who had warned Lewis and Bigelow to leave the whites only bathroom, delivered his foot viciously against Lewis's undefended head.

Taking no heed of the gender or racial designation on the signs, the diminutive Genevieve Hughes, followed by Lucretia, stepped into the bathroom as the white attackers were exiting and were shoved to the floor.

That caught the attention of the solitary policeman on duty at the terminal who had witnessed the whole altercation. He helped Genevieve and Lucretia back to their feet. "Are you alright, ladies? This is the men's bathroom."

Then he approached Lewis, took his handkerchief from his pocket, and pressed it against Lewis's bleeding scalp. "Do you wish to press charges against these local punks?"

Without so much as a glance toward either Bigelow or Hughes

for their assent, Lewis replied, "Thank you for your intervention, sir, and concern for us. But no. Our struggle is not against one person or even a small group of men like this. They're just victims, too, of a much larger problem. To focus just on them would be a massive distraction, a sideshow that would draw people's attention from the larger, deeper issue of state sanctioned segregation in the South."

The policeman was stunned by Lewis's unorthodox response. "If that is your decision, I will not try to talk you into an alternative one. Just know that white people in these parts don't take too kindly to Negroes or radical college students being brought in here from the outside and trying to overturn our traditional, cordial way of life."

News of Bigelow and Lewis's unfortunate violent encounter at the Rock Hill bus terminal made its way to Atlanta and Negro communities elsewhere in the South. Lewis and Bigelow were afraid of what Martin Luther King's reaction would be to two Freedom Riders getting into a scrap including physical violence on a journey dedicated to peace and justice. They related the events of the late afternoon in Rock Hill to Farmer and the nonviolence instructor James Lawson.

Lawson had a more magnanimous attitude toward his two star pupils' actions. "This probably won't be the last time on this journey when you will need to counter violence with nonviolence. You did very well today, fellows."

On the other hand, Farmer grew nervous and agitated as he listened to Bigelow and Lewis's reconstruction of events, "This kind of thing is exactly what we in CORE wanted to avoid. You were injured badly enough. The last thing we need is the notoriety of our Freedom Riders' involvement in violent encounters with locals."

Lawson looked as though he couldn't believe that Farmer could be thinking only of CORE's aversion to "notoriety."

Lewis took a cue from the look of disbelief on Lawson's face. "With all due respect to your concern for CORE, Mr. Farmer, surely, you can't think that we went looking for such a fight when all we wanted was to take a whiz."

Just then, the telephone at the CORE office rang. Farmer answered. "Yes, Martin. You heard correctly. This was the first occasion on the Freedom Ride when we encountered violence. Yes, just a moment, Martin. They are both right here with James Lawson and me. I'll put him on."

He handed the receiver to Lewis. Farmer pressed a button on the telephone, which enabled everyone in the room to hear both sides of the conversation,

Dr. King spoke first. "Actually John, Rev. Lawson called me and outlined the sequence of events in the bathroom in the bus terminal in Rock Hill. Were you badly hurt, John?"

"I have a bandage on my skull, and the bleeding has stopped presumably. My neck is a little sore. But I grew up in a small household of six other boys. I've been injured more seriously in brotherly scraps in the barn than I was today."

King chuckled at Lewis's remark. "I've been in a few scraps like that myself, even though I had only the one brother, A.D. I still have the marks of a wound he inflicted in anger on my head one day with an axe handle even though the steel head was missing."

Lewis had a hard time imagining that.

"But John, judging from the short article in the *Atlanta Constitution* this morning, it sounds as though the attack in the bathroom yesterday did exactly what we in the Movement wanted it to do. It drew attention. We can't know how many white people saw or read the short article, what with all the news this morning of astronaut Alan Shepherd's being shot into space on NASA's first manned rocket. But I would hope that the ones who did read about you being attacked so brutally by two white men would perhaps see white supremacy as in a mirror and begin to think about the racial violence in this country in a fresh, new way."

Chapter Eighteen

Oh we, shall not, we shall not be moved
we shall not, we shall not be moved
Just like a tree planted by the water
we shall not be moved.

African Slave Spiritual

May 8, 1961

Word came to Farmer and the riders on Greyhound that the Trailways bus group had arrived in Rock Hill two hours later. The Trailways riders were greeted by locked doors when they tried to enter the terminal. They missed all the excitement in the men's washroom.

"But they also missed the opportunity to use a bathroom and freshen up," Lucius remarked to Henri. "They had to go through the humiliating experience of looking for an establishment along the highway that would allow them to use the facilities. I, for one, am tired of that."

Both buses rolled on through the rest of South Carolina and into Georgia without any further incidents. The riders were happy to limit the excitement and danger to the Rock Hill incident.

Dr. King's voice crackled over the walkie-talkie when he checked in again with Farmer about the condition of Henri and Lucius. He congratulated Farmer and the whole group for their success in traveling so many miles safely. Before King signed off the call, he said directly to Farmer, "I'm afraid you may not have such indisputable success in Alabama."

In Atlanta, nine new volunteer Freedom Riders, white and black, joined the original thirteen and almost filled a second Greyhound. All three buses found a place to park adjacent to the terminal in Anniston, Alabama, while the tired passengers proceeded into the terminal to order food for dinner.

Lucius and Henri were pleasantly surprised that the snack bar staff was obeying the Supreme Court order to serve all customers, white or Negro. When all had their dinner plate in front of them on the counter, Farmer signaled to Lewis that they were ready for a prayer of thanksgiving for the food and the safe travel to Anniston.

No sooner had Lewis concluded the brief prayer with an

"Amen" than the riders heard a loud explosive sound from the direction of the parking lot and saw the sky lit up brighter than the midday Alabama sunshine.

"What the hell was that?" Lucius asked Henri, not really expecting an answer.

Since Lewis was still on his feet to speak the prayer, he raced out the glass doors that opened to the parking lot. The others shot up from their seats and followed Lewis. What they beheld was one of the Greyhound buses in burgeoning flames that poured out of each exploded passenger window followed by columns of pitch-black smoke billowing toward the sky. Those of the Freedom Riders who could put two thoughts together under the circumstances thought the scene looked like the photos in *Life* magazine in the aftermath of a tank battle in World War II.

Farmer and Lawson agreed that the bus was a total loss. They shouted at the Freedom Riders to take seats in the remaining two buses.

"What about our stuff in the burning Greyhound?" one rider asked Farmer.

"Do not lay up for yourselves treasures on earth, where moth and rust destroy and where thieves break in and steal, and fires consume," was Farmer's clever impromptu response. "Just get your bodies on the buses so we can get out of here."

The bus drivers turned on the ignitions, gunned the engines, and rushed the behemoth vehicles from the spaces where they were parked.

In the confusion of switching buses, Henri and Lucius ended up in different vehicles. Henri chose one of the few remaining vacant seats in the second Greyhound. He sat sharing a bench seat with a petite, impish white woman who Henri guessed was probably in her mid-twenties.

"Hello. Is anyone else sitting in this seat?" Henri asked.

The new rider inspected the seat over Henri's shoulders as though she were searching for something, or someone. When she was satisfied that what or whom she was looking for wasn't there, she smiled at Henri innocently and said, "I looked, but I don't see anyone else in the seat. I guess that means it's yours."

"Well, that's good, because there aren't very many other open seats elsewhere on this bus."

"Do you have a name?"

"I'm Henri Esper, which is short for Esperance."

"That sounds exotic. French, right?"

"Close. French Canadian. My family moved from Canada to the Northland of New York state when I began elementary school. How about you? Now that we're sharing a bench seat, it's appropriate that I know your name just as you now know mine, don't you think?"

"Sure. I'm Priscilla Lawton, not short for anything. I'm from Ardmore, Pennsylvania, just outside Philadelphia. Is the Freedom Ride always this crammed with danger and excitement?"

"This is really just the first episode of this kind of danger and breathtaking, red-hot drama in our four days since the buses left Washington."

Priscilla winced unabashedly at his attempt at humor. "I'd been forewarned of the potential risks of volunteering on the Freedom Rides, but I didn't expect an explosion and burning bus so soon."

"Well, Miss Lawton, let me say I'm glad you have joined us, even though your welcome to the Freedom Ride today has been less than pleasant."

The buses' initial forward progress was impeded almost immediately. Someone from among the cursing crowd of men that had gathered in the lot got to the rear tires and slashed them.

Lucius thought of his own car with deviously slashed tires in a church parking area in Montgomery. But this was worse, much worse. The lives of all the Freedom Riders were at stake.

Even with the huge rear tires flattened, the drivers gunned the engines violently again and darted out into Highway 76 heading west toward Birmingham, their next scheduled stop. The mob, which had swollen by now to several hundred, ran back to their vehicles in the parking lot. The buses rumbled on flat tires with fifty or so pickup trucks and souped-up cars in hot pursuit.

"This is a scene from a bad B movie," Lucretia said to her seatmate.

"The worst kind of B movie," Lucius added when he had overheard Lucretia's remark.

The buses had to roll to a stop some six miles later, their tires worn down to the rim. Henri saw the driver of the Trailways bus jerk the handle to open the door and jump to the pavement. Henri thought the escaping driver looked like a scared rabbit. The fire on the other bus must have spooked him.

The first of the mob of several hundred rioters arrived and poked their heads in the open door. They screamed obscenities at the riders, who were sprawled on the floor to avoid the glass flying from the smashing of the windows.

Then someone threw in a Molotov cocktail through the broken rear window. As the smoke and flames began to fill the bus, the riders flattened themselves on the floor and crawled as well as they could to the door in the front. But they couldn't pull it open. The mob was pushing the lever forcefully to keep the door shut. The riders were trapped inside. Suddenly, in the front seat, an unfamiliar white passenger pulled out a pistol and waved it at the pushing crowd.

"Who the hell is this guy, does anybody know? What's he doing on our Freedom Ride?" Farmer tried to make his voice heard above the screams of the female riders.

Lucius didn't remember having seen the stowaway.

"I chatted with him at the snack bar back in Anniston," Jim Peck responded. "He says his name is Eli Cowling from Montgomery. I don't think he was supposed to tell me. But he's an Alabama state investigator traveling undercover to keep his eyes on us for Patterson."

"One of that racist governor's boys, eh?" asked Hank Thomas. "I doubt it's a high priority right now to keep his identity secret. His life is on the line just like the rest of us now."

"Welcome to the Freedom Ride, Mr. Cowling!" Lucretia called out with a mixture of gratitude and biting sarcasm.

The mob backed off. Al Bigelow rammed the exit door open. Riders were coughing and choking as one by one they tumbled out the door onto the grass on the roadside. Just as the last rider managed to spill out, the ground was rocked violently as the bus's gas tank exploded.

The mob moved in while the riders were disoriented and deafened by the blast and blinded by the piercing flash of the explosion. Al Bigelow, whose gargantuan size was usually a deterrent, was smacked on the side of the head by a steel pipe. Lucretia knelt down to comfort him, but a member of the mob pulled Lucretia away from Al by her face, which left her with a bloody split lip. Rocks and sticks were heaved by people in the mob too afraid of Cowling's pistol to come any closer.

Almost out of nowhere, four Alabama state police cruisers filled with troopers sped into the area and squealed their tires as they came to a hurried stop. The officers had their weapons drawn as they stepped out of their vehicles.

"Are they here to rescue and protect us?" Lucius asked no one in particular, "Or kill us?"

The mob dispersed faster than a colony of ants discovered under a rotting log. No arrests were made. The troopers ordered ambulances, and twelve of the riders, most suffering from smoke inhalation, were taken to hospitals. But of the twelve, only Genevieve Hughes, because she was white, was admitted.

THE RIDERS AND THEIR LEADERS were taken in for the night in the home of an elderly Negro couple. When a small party of the riders knocked on the door of the tiny cabin in the woods outside Anniston, the frail old man of the house answered cautiously, suspiciously. As soon as he heard Hank Thomas give the briefest summary of their plight and ask to stay in the cabin for the night, the man wordlessly closed the door.

A tiny Negro woman's voice could be heard asking the man who was at the door and received an answer said to her husband, "Oh Victor, open the door again. Those are our young people working faithfully for the good future of all our people."

"But Mildred, if the state troopers or the Klan learn we took them in, think of what they could do. Burn down the house or even kill us."

"Victor, I'm tired of living in fear of the Klan and the police. That's not living. That's a kind of death. Does it make any difference if they murder a couple of old folks like us? Our time is coming to an end. But these young people's time is just beginning. Let them in!"

Early the next morning, Henri heard the telephone ringing in some other room of the cabin.

The old husband answered it. "Who do you say you are looking for? I am having trouble hearing you."

"James Farmer, the director of the Congress on Racial Equality. I believe he is there at your home with a group of Freedom Riders."

"Oh, the boss man? I think I know who you are talking about."

Meanwhile, Henri had figured out what was happening and found his way to the room in which Farmer was sleeping. "James, there's a telephone call for you. In the old couple's bedroom, I think."

Thinking the call was about an emergency, Farmer shot up off his bed, put on the light in the other room, and stepped over several sleeping bodies.

He took the receiver from the old man. "Hello, this is Jim Farmer. Who is this?"

"Floyd McKissick, Jim. You probably haven't seen the morning papers yet. There's a big photo on the front page of the burning Freedom bus in Anniston yesterday. Are you all right? Were any of the Freedom Riders injured? I knew this was a bad idea. The board knew it, too, but deferred to you."

"A few of the riders were taken to the hospital in Anniston. I'm a little shaken by it all but otherwise unhurt."

"I called some of the board members this morning. Jim, they want you to call off the rest of the Freedom Ride."

FARMER RECEIVED ANOTHER REPORT that the Trailways bus, once they caught sight of the burned and charred remains of the first bus, had not dared to stop at the Anniston terminal. The driver immediately kept the buses pointed resolutely west toward Birmingham. Farmer soberly informed the riders that the welcome at Birmingham had not been any more friendly than the one in Anniston. Dr. Bergman, already bloodied from the ambush in Anniston, was beaten to the terminal floor and kicked repeatedly in the head.

All the riders agreed that Dr. Bergman's bravery matched anyone else's on the ride. But his sixty-something old body was not up to the beatings he received that day. Farmer reported that in the attack, Bergman had also suffered a stroke and sustained brain damage.

When the bus stopped strategically two blocks away from the Birmingham bus station, the riders were ready and made their way without hesitation into the waiting cars of Fred Shuttlesworth, pastor of Bethel Baptist Church, and some of his more intrepid men of his congregation who drove the riders to Shuttlesworth's residence for safety. Shuttlesworth had the previous evening led the same convoy of volunteer drivers to Anniston to search for the Greyhound riders who had been separated from the group and to bring them back to Birmingham.

The riders spent the rest of the evening in a rap session in Shuttlesworth's crowded living room. Well into the night they took an inventory of their drastic situation. The discussion became more urgent when James Farmer announced that given the growing danger to riders' life and limb, the CORE board had directed him to cancel the rest of the ride. Plans were being finalized for the riders to be flown from Birmingham to New Orleans.

Farmer's unexpected announcement cast a pall over the group. There arose a deep groan of bitter disappointment from the group.

Henri was the first to speak. "Certainly, given what's happened to Dr. Bergman and almost to the rest of us, the thinking behind CORE's decision is understandable. But…"

Lewis completed Henri's sentence. "But this decision defies one of the most basic tenets of nonviolent action."

Many of the others broke into spontaneous applause at Lewis's remarks.

Lewis added, "Truth and justice cannot be abandoned, even in the face of pain and injury, even in the face of death."

In his head, Lucius agreed wholeheartedly with Lewis's sentiment, but in his gut he was less sure. "Pain, injury, death?"

Hank Thomas asked the group, "Haven't we come too far on this ride to turn back now?" To which the majority chanted, "Yes! Too far!"

Farmer also informed the group that in the White House were President Kennedy, his brother Bobby, the Attorney-General, and the Attorney-General's new assistant for civil rights matters. Burke Marshall had conferred and decided in light of the incredible violence of the white backlash to ask CORE to call off the rest of the Freedom ride to protect the riders.

Another groan of protest came from the eager riders.

James Lawson had been noticeably quiet during the discussion, but asked now, "But does the President or anybody else in the administration really understand the strategies and principles of nonviolent resistance? Do they really see the inestimable value of the violence of the opposition to the Movement? Do they appreciate how the photos of burning buses in their newspapers and news clips of white hoodlums beating up on and paralyzing sixty-year-old professors are contributing to the success of the Movement? I doubt they do."

"No, no, they surely don't," the riders recited in unison as though singing a spiritual.

Meanwhile, Lewis reached Diane Nash by telephone at Fisk

University in Nashville. Diane served as student co-leader alongside John of the Nashville Student Movement in the successful lunch counter sit-ins in the previous several years.

Diane told Lewis on the phone that as they spoke, she and James Bevel, Marion Barry, and Lewis's seminary classmate Bernard Lafayette were meeting to discuss the aborting of the Freedom ride by CORE. "John, we are unanimous in offering to sponsor a continuation of the ride into Mississippi as planned. Not just unanimous. But adamant."

"God bless you, Diane. God bless the Nashville Student Movement. We can't rename these the SNCC Freedom Rides, but we can rebaptize them the Nashville Student movement Freedom Rides. Have you told Farmer?"

"That's the next step that I'm not looking forward to. But for now, we've got Marion out working already to raise the funds that will be needed."

The next morning, May 17, Lewis, Lucius, Henri, Lucretia, Priscilla, and the others found themselves back on the buses again, this Greyhound bound for Birmingham, Alabama.

Henri, an old chorister from his days as a youth in Cape Vincent, led the group in the resolute singing of a civil rights spiritual.

"We're taking a ride on the Greyhound Bus Line
We're sittin' in the front seat to B'ham this time
Hallelujah, we're a-travelin'
Hallelujah, ain't it fine?
Hallelujah, we're a-travelin'
Down freedom's main line."

Chapter Nineteen

We will have to repent in this generation not merely for the hateful words and actions of the bad people but for the appalling silence of the good people.

Martin Luther King, Jr.

May 12, 1961

The ride was supposed to go to Birmingham next. But that plan was quickly altered when just as the Freedom buses were about to depart from Montgomery for Birmingham, Reverend Fred Shuttlesworth called the bus terminal and asked to speak to a member of the Freedom Riders team. The communications officer at the bus terminal had no idea of who was in charge of the ride. He saw Henri paying for his breakfast in the coffee shop and motioned for him to come to the telephone. Henri was a little confused about whose attention the man was trying to catch. When he realized that it was no one other than himself, he headed like a man on a mission to the front counter and picked up the phone receiver, curious about what all this was about.

"Hello. This is Reverend Henri Esper. May I inquire whom I am talking with?"

"Yes. This is Fred Shuttlesworth, Reverend Shuttlesworth. I met you, didn't I?, the other night when all you Freedom Riders crowded into my living room?"

"Yes, you did."

"I didn't know who to ask to speak to. I know Jim Farmer is no longer in charge of the ride, but I didn't know who's el hombre principal."

"Yes, Mr. Farmer has returned to New York. The Nashville Student Movement has assumed leadership until we get to New Orleans. I think that either John Lewis or Diane Nash is keeping it all together."

"Diane Nash? A woman in charge? That's a first for the Movement. El mujer a cargo? In any case, we need to postpone the arrival of the Freedom Ride in Birmingham. Bethel Baptist suffered some significant fire damage last night."

"I'm sorry to hear that. I gather Bethel Baptist is your

congregation?"

"That's the one. Been pastor there since 1953."

"How bad was the damage from the fire?"

"Bad enough that we can't have you riders sleep here overnight as we planned and turn it over to you as the Freedom Ride HQ."

"Any idea what or who's responsible for the fire?"

"We've got a few ideas. We didn't call the fire department or police for help. Can't trust them. They're too beholden to the Klan. I'm not sure, in fact, that there's any meaningful difference between the Birmingham Police Department and the local klavern."

"So it's the Klan behind the arson?"

"At the least whoever set the fire would have the Klan's explicit or implicit approval and encouragement. There are numerous gangs of local young white nationalist yahoos here in Birmingham who have perfected the setting of fires to Negro churches into an art form. So it's not just the mess of the detritus from the fire in parts of the building that make it impossible for us to host you at Bethel. There's a certain level of danger in having a group of almost thirty Negroes and friends of Negroes sleeping like sitting ducks in our church."

"Should we postpone our ride into Birmingham until enough time has passed to allow repairs to be made?"

"I don't know how long that will be. Around here, it's very difficult to find a building supply merchant who would risk selling to a Negro congregation, especially if they know it's Fred Shuttlesworth's church."

"I'm not authorized to make any unilateral decisions for the group on my own. What alternatives for us do you see?"

"I'll talk to some of my close colleagues in the ACMHR—I'm sorry, the Alabama Christian Movement for Human Rights—but I hate to put any of them or their churches in a vulnerable position. I'll spread the word among our most committed congregants and recruit someone to organize a program of assigning Freedom Riders to private homes. But I have to add that some of my members are scared to death that the yahoos or the Klan will find some way to make them pay for giving shelter to the Freedom Riders. That's life, I'm afraid, in today's 'Bombingham.'"

THE NASHVILLE LEADERS DECIDED to proceed directly to Jackson, Mississippi, and detour around Birmingham for the time being. The Freedom Riders should have been apprehensive as they neared Jackson, the state capital. Jackson was more a symbolic place for many of the Negro riders than an actual location on a map.

Henri shifted into "tour guide" mode. "Up in Pennsylvania, you probably don't hear much about Jackson, Mississippi. Let me tell you a little about it. In the previous century, Jackson was in the heart of the most productive cotton-growing region of the country. Owners of some of the largest cotton plantations in the South were a common sight on the streets of Jackson; they came to town to purchase slaves, a sighting that a hundred years after the Emancipation Proclamation would induce fear in the hearts of even free Negroes."

"We're stopping at Jackson and skipping Birmingham?" Priscilla asked, a little confused.

"I just got off the telephone with Reverend Shuttlesworth. He says his church suffered significant damage from a fire last night and that we'll have to postpone our stop in 'Bombingham' as he called it. He figures that, directly or indirectly, our friends in the Ku Klux Klan are responsible for the arson."

"Maybe it's Birmingham we should fear rather than Jackson," Priscilla intimated to Henri. "Don't come to a final decision about that just yet. I doubt we'll be welcomed with a ticker tape parade here by the civic leaders and citizens. Neither place is exactly Ardmore or Cape Vincent."

Priscilla shared with Henri the experience of disgust in the pit of her stomach more than apprehension as they regarded the mainly white shoppers and businesspeople in the state capital through their window, a feeling shared by the Negro riders particularly.

The first contingent arrived at the Jackson bus station about ten minutes before the second. The first arrivals were greeted by a party of Jackson's finest who wasted no time in arresting the Freedom Riders, shackling them in handcuffs and loading them in cruisers, then delivering them to the Hinds County Jail and charging them with "a breach of the peace."

When the Greyhound arrived, the riders, including Henri and Priscilla, walked resignedly and in an orderly fashion like kindergartners with their teacher on a field trip to the vacant benches in the waiting room. They knew what was awaiting them. They waited calmly and compliantly for the police squad cars to return and gather them up and take them also to the county jail.

Jim Farmer had flown back to New York when the Nashville

Student Movement assumed responsibility for completing the ride. The Nashville student leaders, Diane Nash, Jim Bevel, and Marion Barry flew down to join the party of riders for the last leg to New Orleans. Counting them, now there were twenty-seven Freedom Riders confined in the crowded Hinds County Jail, and all of them refused bail.

THE NEXT STEAMY MORNING, SEVERAL jail guards came to the cells to separate the female riders from the male and the white ones from the Negro. They were escorted silently by guards armed with rifles to Mississippi Department of Corrections passenger vans and transported for what seemed like hours to an ominous-looking state penitentiary at Parchman out in the middle of nowhere. A state judge had levied a $200 fine on each rider and sentenced each to sixty days of labor at the farm in the Parchman prison.

A few of the riders, like Henri, were familiar with the reputation of the Parchman farm. Lucius in the other bus had heard about Parchman in the same way he'd heard about Mississippi as a whole—in tones of horror and brutality. In a South filled with nightmarishly inhumane prisons, Parchman was notorious for being the worst.

"So this is the infamous Parchman, folks." Henri called out. "People say that it is a twentieth-century slave plantation, owned by none other than the illumined State of Mississippi and worked by hundreds of these stripe-suited mostly black convicts like these out your window. Do you see them? That's a portrait of us for the next sixty days."

At that, Priscilla lowered her head onto Henri's shoulder for comfort and reassurance.

John Lewis added, "Look at that barbed wire around the whole complex. And the snarly guards holding their shotguns at the ready. Don't even think of trying to escape. The barbed wire will slice you into pork chops if you try to climb the fence. Or else the guards will fill you with lead."

"That's a reassuring thought," Priscilla said loudly enough for everyone in the van to hear.

The van stopped in front of a complex of boxy, concrete buildings to allow an officer to step on board at the front of the bus. "Listen up, folks. I don't have a clue what you've done to deserve being here at Parchman, but you are here, and I hope you make the best of your time here," he said as he chewed on a fat unlit cigar. "We've got some bad niggers here on death row. They'll eat you up or cut you to pieces as soon as they look at you. I warn you: Just mind your own business and stay out of their way. Anyway," pointing to the squarish huts, "these will be your accommodations until your sentence is finished."

The men were led into one of the huts, the women into another. In the men's hut, guards with cattle prods stood by while men obeyed the order to strip naked. They were commanded to stand up straight and face the empty concrete wall. The guard nearest to Hank Thomas extended his cattle prod and playfully inserted it in the crack between the two cheeks of his rump.

"Hey, Fisher. We've got a good one here. Maybe we can come back later when the lights are out and invite our handsome friend here to play with us."

"Alright, all you guys. Go into the rooms and choose a bunk. Two to a room. But no niggers with whites. And no roommate for Pretty Boy here," he said, pointing at Thomas with his cattle prod. "We've got plans for him later."

"You're in luck today. The illustrious Governor Barnett of our state has called Superintendent Jones and ordered him to take it easy on you. It seems that some fuckin' meddlesome newspaper from up north knows you're here as our guests. The governor wants no news of 'cruel' treatment of our guests to be broadcast all over New York City or whatever damn place the newspaper is from. So you will be in our protective custody. Good night."

A small breakfast of cereal and milk was available to the group of riders in another rectangular concrete building almost identical to the others. Henri observed the long faces among the group so he tried to loosen the mood.

"Come on, folks. We don't have to strain and grunt out there under the blazing sun. I certainly wasn't expecting that grace. It might get a little boring just hanging around our room all day, but I would vote for that any day over breaking rocks with a heavy sledgehammer. I've been singin' Sammy Cooke's 'Chain Gang' silently in my mind since we saw those poor guys out there in the hot sun yesterday. I think we should all join in and sing it together. What do you say?"

"If you start us off, Henri," one of the women responded.

"Surely, Miss. Here we go."

"Hoh. Hah. Hoh, Hah."

Henri glanced at Big Al Bigelow who took the cue to add his deep bass voice, "Well, don't you know that's the sound of the men working on the chain gang…"

Henri was all smiles as the whole group played a part. Instinctively, the women knew to continue and took up the song.

The group laughed joyously as they finished the song.

Henri said, "Thank you, friends. You've got some real potential. We gotta ask Dr. King to put in a good word for us and ask someone from Chicago with Chess Records to come down and hear us. Maybe we've got the stuff for a record."

The group howled with laughter.

Priscilla spoke softly to Henri after the singing and when the laughter subsided. "Speaking of having real potential, Henri, I swear you sounded like a slightly older version of Sam Cooke himself. Where'd you learn to sing like that?"

"Well, thanks for the compliment. I don't think I'm ready to be called the King of Soul, however. That's reserved for Sam. But from what I hear, he and I both learned to sing in a church choir. Only Sam was good enough to be asked to sing solo."

"Women love a man who can sing."

"Are you speaking about women in general, or about a certain woman I know in particular?"

Priscilla responded with her pseudo-innocent smile, but she couldn't hide that she was blushing.

THE SIXTY-DAY WORK GANG sentence at Parchman and the monotony brought on by inactivity were punctuated by such joyful and audacious group singing. Sometimes they joined their voices in familiar spirituals and often, when they marched back at the end of the day to their huts, they sang the civil rights anthem, "We Shall Overcome." On other days, one of the riders would shout out the name of a popular song as a request, "Ain't That a Shame" by Fats Domino, "Banana Boat Song" by Harry Bellafonte, and more. Invariably, someone would know the lyrics of the song by heart, lead off, and be joined spontaneously by the others in the group.

Superintendent Jones came by to announce their pending release and to bid farewell. "Okay, you've done your time. Now get out of here and go back to New York or Pennsylvania or wherever you've mistakenly come from to our beautiful Magnolia State, and don't ever come back, you hear?"

After release from Parchman, the whole group squeezed into the modest bungalow home of Medgar Evers and his wife, Myrlie, in Jackson. Medgar was the Mississippi field secretary for the N.A.A.C.P. and an energetic and ambitious civil rights organizer throughout the state.

The riders sat cross-legged on the living room floor even though some of them were very stiff from the cramped ride on the bus. They ate a fried chicken dinner. Medgar turned on the television to his habitual station, WJTV, CBS channel 12 in Jackson, which was more sympathetic to civil rights events than the more popular NBC affiliate across town.

Mostly oblivious to the sound and images being broadcast on the television, the riders were engaged in good-natured casual conversations, comparing their experiences at Parchman. Gradually, they found it necessary to raise the volume of their voices so that they could hear one another over the babble of the television. Hank Thomas sat in an overstuffed easy chair off to the side, maintaining his shy reticence even more firmly than usual. He tried to pretend that the humiliating incident with the guard's cattle prod never happened. Still, his eyes averted those of his peers but were focused on the images on the television.

Suddenly, Hank saw part of a news clip that he recognized immediately. Raising his voice above the din of his fellow riders' discussions with one another, he tried to get their attention. "Hey guys. Look at this on the television."

The happy exchanges of words among the riders were quickly muffled. "Hey look. That's our Greyhound bus burning," Lucretia remarked. "That's at the Anniston bus terminal. God, the flames and smoke pouring out of the windows look hellishly menacing. How did we ever survive that incident?"

The eyes of everyone in the living room were glued in wonder to the black and white CBS Evening News broadcast. With the waiting room of the Montgomery bus terminal as a backdrop, the familiar figure of Roger Mudd appeared.

"By now, just about every American has seen scenes like this one from the so-called Freedom Rides in various locales across the South, roughly evenly mixed teams of white and Negro passengers riding in commercial buses from city to city to draw Americans' attention to the gradually receding and disappearing of some of the familiar traditional ways of segregation of the races on buses and in bus terminals. The waning of many of those practices based on segregation is the result of the United States Supreme Court's watershed ruling in the case named *Boynton v. Virginia* last year that effectively rendered the practice of racial segregation illegal in vehicles and buildings used in the course of traveling from one state to another. The so-called Freedom Riders have been testing the effectiveness of the new laws passed to comply with the Supreme Court's decision. They have found mixed results in the South, many of the states maintaining the status quo and a few changing the laws on their books to adhere to the Court's decree.

"The first Freedom Ride bus departed with thirteen volunteers from Washington, D.C., on May 4 and is still on the road as we speak. That bus has endured demonstrations of the opposition and resistance of the largely white crowds that have come to bus terminals to express their strong displeasure with the Freedom Rides' purpose and actions. No Freedom Rider has been killed in these clashes to date, but several have suffered serious injuries at the hands of white resistors that have forced them to withdraw from the project.

"Yet, the stamina and endurance of the Freedom Riders seem remarkable. For every one Freedom Rider who has found it necessary to abandon the project, it seems that at least five new volunteers come forward to take their place. The leaders of the Freedom Rides predict that later this summer, the number of Freedom Ride buses dispatched across the South will have mushroomed to over sixty and the number of volunteer participants swollen to over four hundred. There are clearly many people dissatisfied with the way things have always been in the Jim Crow South."

For this part of Mudd's report, the camera was aimed at the "Whites Only' and "Colored" signs near the restrooms.

With the news that there would be more than sixty Freedom Ride buses, the group of riders burst into victorious cheers. Medgar and Myrlie added their voices. Seeing their parents' elation, their three little children joined the general festive mood of celebration.

The next image was of Mudd standing outside the front of the Montgomery bus terminal. "There is an almost miraculous mood of jubilation amid the Freedom Riders about their victories in spite of the dangers and threats to their safety they have encountered. Yet, the segregationists have not raised the white flag of surrender. They have devised new and ingenious methods of sabotaging the Freedom Rides.

"CBS News has learned of one such furtive stratagem for hindering, and perhaps exacting revenge on the Freedom Riders. The segregationists have no hesitation to exploit and victimize innocent Negroes in their scheme."

Hank's ears perked up. "Hey guys. Hush for just a minute and listen to this," he called out to the energetically chatting riders.

Mudd continued. "I spoke yesterday with Ella Mae Williams who had been enticed to participate unknowingly in what are beginning to be called 'Reverse Freedom Rides.' A fellow Negro here in Montgomery had promised her a steady and comfortable job as a domestic with the family of President Kennedy no less at their summer home in Hyannisport, Massachusetts.

"The promise from a total stranger at first seemed too good to be true," Ella told me. "But when I thought about the offer, I began to see it as a once-in-a-lifetime opportunity to escape the Jim Crow South and make a new life for myself and my nine children in the freedom of the North. The stranger handed me money to pay the fare for all of us from Montgomery to Hyannis. I was told that a representative of the Kennedy family would be at the bus station to meet us and drive us to the Kennedy compound. So, full of hope, I packed the nine children onto the bus with me and headed for Massachusetts."

Mudd inserted a pregnant pause before he continued his report. The riders were totally hushed now, some with their mouths agape as they concentrated on the woman's story. The camera showed an immaculately dressed Ella Mae Williams shepherding her brood of children, all dressed in their Sunday best to meet the President, on the hot pavement of the parking lot of the Hyannis bus station. She herself was wearing an elegant black dress accented by a triple string of pearls and a white Sunday hat—appropriate dress, she was confident, to start a new life of freedom.

"But, of course," Mudd resumed his report, "there was no one from the Kennedy family there to meet them. There was no job with the Kennedys. There was no housing for her and her children as she had been promised. She had been a pawn in a segregationist game.

"We've learned that more than two hundred desperate African

Americans from the South have been duped to follow their dreams to the North. When, like Ella Mae, these African Americans wake up to the sad reality that their dream for a better life has been exploited, all they can do is scrape for the funds to buy a bus ticket back home.

"Thankfully, the Interstate Commerce Commission has caught wind of the Reverse Freedom Ride schemes and has been empowered to aggressively assign stringent fines to individuals or groups engaged in the practice. Consequently, the Reverse Freedom Rides are largely disappearing from the Civil Rights landscape.

"This is Roger Mudd reporting for CBS News from Montgomery, Alabama."

In contrast to the energetic hubbub of the riders' conversations earlier, a funereal silence descended upon all in the living room. Even the fidgeting Evers children became mum, sensing that the group had witnessed something of a holy significance.

Some of the riders wept openly; others, including Lucius, surreptitiously wiped their cheeks and eyes privately of tears.

"Isn't that the damnedest, cruelest, most inhumane thing you've ever heard?" Lucius asked. "I had never heard a word about these brutal, hateful things called 'Reverse Freedom Rides,' have any of you? This is the lowest the segregationists have stooped. Somehow the angry epithets, the threats, the rocks and bricks thrown at us, the slashed tires, the punches and blows to the head, I can understand. More than once, I've been so filled with rage and hate that I've had the urge to fetch an iron pipe and smash in the head of one of those segregationist cretins myself. I know it's not right or our chosen way. But I've had to struggle mightily to stop my bitter self from retaliating. But I would hope that the Prince of Peace would never allow us to stoop to the level of duping some poor, innocent mother of nine and dashing her hopes."

Chapter Twenty

Carry me
Home to Birmingham…

Traditional, adapted by the Stampeders

JIM BEVEL WAS MORE THAN ANXIOUS to propel the Birmingham Campaign forward yesterday if not sooner.

"I'm more than a little sick and tired of all these fricking delays, discussions about the same old topics every time, and the futile negotiations with the white business leaders who have shown over and over again that they want only one thing, and it's not justice and progress for the Negro."

Diane Nash was accustomed to his irritability and impatience whenever events were not moving along as quickly as his nimble mind preferred. Fresh in her mind was Jim at their wedding just a few months ago when the Methodist officiant, James Lawson, had led Jim and the groom's party to the front of the nave but had to excuse himself and go back to the vestry to fetch his homily. Even though Lawson had been the couple's esteemed teacher and trainer in the Gandhian philosophy of nonviolence, Bevel didn't hide his irritation for the last second delay in their wedding. He was ready to proceed; why wasn't everyone else?

Diane giggled as she related this story to Henri and Lucius. They had met her when the Nashville Student Movement, of which she was co-leader with John Lewis, took charge of the Freedom Ride once the riders arrived in Jackson. Henri and Lucius took to Diane almost immediately. Her stunning appearance seemed to command the attention of both men. Intellectually, she was a cut above the others, including the male riders. As the bus returned to Birmingham from Jackson, Henri and Lucius agreed that the trials and tribulations of the ride since Rock Hill had taken their toll on their energy. Anticipating that the stop in Birmingham would quite likely be at least as turbulent and emotionally tumultuous as Anniston and Montgomery had been, they agreed to stick around but hopefully sit in the back row and not be called upon to assume taxing leadership responsibilities.

They recognized that Diane would be in the middle of the action. Since Henri and Lucius intended to sit this one out, they asked Diane to be their eyes and ears so that the two clergymen would miss as little as possible of what they sensed was going to be an eventful campaign in the biggest city in Alabama.

Dr. King had anointed Jim as the primary architect of the participation of the children and youth in the Birmingham campaign. Now he was preparing to present the idea to Dr. King that, in the absence of much adult presence and support, the youth and children should not just have an adjunct part in the campaign but would essentially be the heart and soul of the campaign.

"Well, Jim," Diane said, "you are the SCLC's Director of Direct Action and Nonviolent Education. What do you plan to do to spur on the elders and motivate them to get on with what we were called here to Birmingham to do?"

"I've got an idea or two. It's just that I'm not sure that the SCLC board or even Dr. King would go along with it. Some of those sticks-in-the-mud aren't sure what to do about me and whatever I suggest.

Henri and Lucius intuited the conflict between them. But they were impressed by Diane's ability to look past her differences with Bevel and to get back to listening to her husband supportively.

"Well, I don't particularly care if that pipsqueak Shuttlesworth or Andrew Young or Julian Bond or even John Lewis approve of my plan, as long as Dr. King does...and you do."

"That's very flattering, Jim, but I have difficulty picturing you as a hen-pecked husband like my father."

"No, I'm not a hen-pecked husband. Just one who has learned that in these matters you are usually right...Well, look. Before he invited Dr. King and the SCLC to come here and give him a hand with this campaign, Shuttlesworth was able to raise the issue of segregation of the retail businesses downtown and the dearth of jobs in their stores for Negroes, and that's good. But too many potential volunteers for the marches and demonstrations were turned off and fed up with his shrill, irritating preaching at them to sacrifice and join the movement. Now the same comfortable middle class are suspicious and resentful of Dr. King as an outsider. When he tells them of the inestimable value to the success of the campaign to be willing to be imprisoned for the cause, they retreat back to their safe fortress. Good Lord! Only Shuttlesworth, Abernathy, and King himself had the courage to go to the Birmingham jail. Even Dr. King couldn't inspire and persuade these frickin' bumps-on-a-log to accompany him in jail. Not for him, but for themselves and their children so that they could go to better schools."

"Jim, I've talked with some of these 'bumps-on-a-log' as you call them. They're not lazy or lacking commitment to the cause. It's just that they've witnessed so many of their friends being let go from their jobs if they do join the movement, getting beat up by the Klan's flunkeys, having their house burned down, or bullets shot into their living room. that they're scared, Jim, terrified of what would happen to them or their children. You've got to cut these brothers and sisters some slack."

Henri and Lucius noticed that Bevel was silent and looked admonished. He seemed to know better than to debate his wife point by point.

Instead, he said, "I told you that in these matters you're right more often than you're wrong. Here's a case in point."

"You still haven't told me of your plan."

"Neither Shuttlesworth nor Dr. King have been able to rustle up enough brave volunteers to get arrested. But think of those kids we work with over at Sixteenth Street Baptist. Sometimes I think the youth and the children understand what's at stake in this campaign better than their parents and elders. All we have to do is tell them that today is the time to march and show the whites our gumption and courage, and they'd be ready to form a huge army, unarmed, of course, of eager, idealistic young people hungry for real change."

"You're proposing that the youth and children form the front line in the confrontation between the Negroes and the white powers that be?"

Lucius and Henri looked at each other in astonished disbelief.

"That's pretty unorthodox, Jim," Diane said in a tone that sounded as though despite her surprise she hadn't dismissed the idea completely.

"You know me, Sweetie. Some of my best ideas often border on the unorthodox and unproven."

Bevel chuckled at that.

"Well, Jim. We'll soon see whether the SCLC board and Dr. King consider the idea to be totally bonkers and out of the question...or a stroke of genius."

HENRI OVERHEARD BEVEL approaching Dr. King the next morning at Shuttlesworth's church.

"Dr. King, I have a few thoughts about the campaign I'd like to run past you."

"That's great, Jim. The rest of us have run out of thoughts. I'd welcome a new thought or two. The board of SCLC isn't here in its entirety, but let me alert Ralph, Andrew, Fred, John, Bernard, Jesse, and Bayard to call them to a meeting ASAP at the Gaston Hotel. Make sure your better half comes, too."

Diane indeed attended the meeting that was called at 9 p.m. later that evening. Neither Henri nor Lucius was included among the inner circle of Dr. King's associates; they depended on Diane's report of the proceedings.

She told them that Fred Shuttlesworth had some other church business to attend to and couldn't be present at Gaston's for the meeting. The others were relieved because since the SCLC leaders had arrived, Shuttlesworth had been rather combative and critical of Dr. King's leadership of the campaign. The group wouldn't miss the tension in the room. But they noticed that Dr. King remarked that he would miss Shuttlesworth's ideas at the meeting, and that he sounded sincere when he said that.

"Jim, what do you have for us?" King asked.

Bevel was unusually nervous, Diane said, as he looked at her across the room for reassurance. She nodded at her husband almost imperfectively as a signal to go ahead with confidence in his plan.

"I'm thinking that many of the adult Negroes in Birmingham have jobs in businesses that may not take too kindly to their employees' participating in our campaign or hold mortgages from banks that might revoke them for much the same reasons. But the youth and children that Diane and I have teaching and training every day at Sixteenth Street Baptist, they don't have jobs to lose or mortgages to been pay or protect. They are the most attentive and enthusiastic students Diane and I have ever had the pleasure to teach and train."

The attendees looked on with indifferent stony faces and signs of droopiness at the end of the day. No one read the mood in a room better than Dr. King did. He didn't know yet what kind of plan Bevel had concocted. In fact, he was almost afraid to hear. But he'd learned to appreciate Jim Bevel for his ability to think outside the box and his courage to propose bold, innovative solutions. King wanted to support the young firebrand preacher.

Bevel took a breathing break from his talk to strategize on the fly how to proceed next with his presentation. Everyone in the room understood that they weren't finished with the matter yet. But they agreed eagerly with Dr. King when he suggested that it would be nonproductive to continue that evening because of their exhaustion and difficulty focusing so they would return to this agenda item first thing after breakfast.

Jim was amenable to that. He felt that he had introduced the solid reasoning behind the plan he had in mind. Maybe, he thought, they'd wake up refreshed in the morning and more favorable to the possibility of the unconventional and seemingly counterintuitive plan he would propose to them.

Chapter Twenty-One

"Do you hear what these children are saying?" they asked him. "Yes," replied Jesus, "have you never read, 'From the lips of children and infants you, Lord, have called forth your justice?'"

Matthew 21:16

JIM BEVEL AND DIANE NASH did indeed convince Priscilla to join their forces in preparing for the Birmingham Children's March, or Crusade, as Bevel preferred to call his pet project. Whether it was by way of Priscilla's request or suggestion or not, they did not leave Henri and Lucius as mere interested bystanders. Bevel sought them out and recruited them as marshals for the children's march. They were among a group of adults enlisted to help maintain order among the school children, to line up on the pavement along the edge of the sidewalk, and to assist the police by stretching out their arms to prevent the adults in Kelly Ingram Park and along the march route from leaving their places and inserting themselves into the march.

Henri and Lucius debated between themselves about the wisdom of agreeing to serve as marshals. By serving in that capacity, were they endorsing Bevel's bold and unorthodox proposal of making the children and youth the primary participants in this phase of the campaign? Bevel's idea elicited significant bewilderment and perplexity even before Bevel had had the opportunity to present the idea of a children's march to the SCLC leaders and Dr. King. Many of the local Negro clergy voiced their opposition to a plan that put innocent children in harm's way. Caucuses of parents of the children protested that defenseless children and youth would be no match for Eugene "Bull" Connor, the Commissioner of Public Safety whose control of the police force and fire companies was unrivaled. Everyone knew that he was an avowed white supremacist who displayed no sympathy whatsoever for the Negroes' plight in Jim Crow Alabama.

Henri and Lucius appreciated the wisdom expressed by much of the opposition to the whole idea of a march by children. They agreed in their skepticism about Bevel's vision. They almost turned down the invitation to serve as marshals. They probably would have refused it had it not dawned on Henri that serving in that way was the best opportunity to keep a protective eye on Priscilla.

"How do you predict that Dr. King will respond to Bevel's strategy?" Henri asked his travel companion.

"If he still feels the same way about it as he was feeling yesterday, I venture to wager that he gives the 'thumbs down.' You don't think that either the SCLC or Dr. King himself want to risk their reputation as a rock-solid source of prudent leadership of the Movement by supporting such a perilous strategy, do you?"

"No, Lucius, I think you're right. But then again, I've been surprised before by Dr. King's tactics. I would be ready to reconsider my hesitation to help with the march as a marshal if Dr. King chooses to support and endorse Bevel's plan. Are you with me on that?"

TO THE EXASPERATION OF MANY of the children's march dissenters, Dr. King did indeed lend his support to Jim Bevel and his detailed plan for the Children's Crusade. A smaller crowd than usual gathered for a mass rally at Bethel Baptist on the eve of D-Day when the organizers declared that the march would begin.

Dr. King announced his decision succinctly and straight-forwardly. "Brothers and sisters, it's become apparent to me that the commitment on the part of Negro adults to the program of demonstrations, boycotts, sit-ins, and the strategy of being imprisoned that have characterized the present campaign for justice in Birmingham to date has been diminishing with each passing week. At the same time, however, the children and youth who have been instructed by Reverend and Mrs. Bevel at Sixteenth Street Church have exhibited increased enthusiasm for making a positive difference in Birmingham, and a growing sophisticated understanding of the dynamics of the age-old inequities in opportunity for the black and white children and youth of Alabama. There comes a time—and I devoutly and genuinely believe that the time has arrived now—for a bold new initiative for justice led by a whole new generation."

That short statement by a man whom they could trust was sufficient for Henri and Lucius. Just as they had been trained to be marshals by a couple of senior high school students, Henri and Lucius showed up in the nave of the Sixteenth Street Baptist Church more than a half-hour early, but already the worship space was hopping. Bevel walked back and forth at the chancel speaking in his upper register voice into a microphone in his left hand.

"What are we here for, children?" Bevel bellowed in the microphone.

In the typical Negro call and response liturgical format, the children and youth chanted their response in near unison, "To march!"

Bevel continued the ritual. "To what end?"

Without a moment's pause, the juvenile congregation chimed in, "To break the chains of injustice!"

The piano in the rear of the room launched into a melodic introduction to a song. The children roared their approval for the pianist's selection of one of their favorite freedom songs that the children had known since the early grades of Sunday school:

This little light of mine,
I'm gonna let it shine.
This little light of mine,
I'm gonna let it shine.
Let it shine, let it shine, let it shine.

We won't let them blow it out,
We're gonna let it ring.
We won't let them blow it out,
We're gonna let it ring.
Let it ring, let it ring, let it ring.

The children were more animated with each verse: "Shine all over Birmingham." "Let it ring on every street." The children ran out of traditional verses, but still the pianist continued playing, and the children put their hands together and clapped to the beat.

Henri caught a glimpse of Priscilla sitting with her back to him in one of the forward pews, singing along and encouraging the children near her to keep the song going. Henri longed to will her from across the room to turn around so that he could see her handsome face, one of the very few Caucasian faces in the assembled congregation. But as he imagined the broad smile on her face as the church was filled with the joyful singing of Birmingham's Negro children, Henri was satisfied and proud.

Finally, Bevel waved his arms to quiet the voices and punctuate the singing with a deep "Amen."

"Okay, God's precious children, the time is approaching for

marching. I ask those of you in the congregation serving as marshals to leave the rally at this time and take up your assigned positions along the route."

Henri obeyed the command and joined about forty or fifty men and a few tall college students dressed in identical dark rain jackets with bright orange piping and the word "Marshal" printed on the back. The men rose from their seats and proceeded toward the front doors to exit the church.

"Mrs. Watson," Bevel resumed while the marshals progressed down the aisles, "I wonder if you'd kindly play the intro to another freedom song that we can all belt out together while we wait for the marshals to be ready out on the street. How about 'Blowing in the Wind'?"

Again, the children cheered their approval.

During the singing, two marshals lined up the children in pairs and signaled for the front pair to proceed through the doors and down the stone steps to the sidewalk on Sixteenth Street. There must have been fifty children pouring out through the doors. They kept on uninterrupted, repeating the lyrics of Bob Dylan's popular folk song even though they could no longer hear the accompaniment of the piano.

Their instructions from Bevel and Nash were that they were to march from Sixteenth Street Baptist to Birmingham city hall. When the first children stepped off the stairs onto the sidewalk, their approval was clear.

However, they needed to cease singing for the time being when a couple of police deputies spoke directly to them. "You are guilty of violating the city's injunction against public demonstrations. I'm afraid you'll have to march right on over there," said one deputy, pointing with his hand to one of the white police paddy wagons parked along Sixteenth Street. Without any hesitation or sign of confusion, the children complied, resuming their singing and laughing at the novelty of being inside a paddy wagon.

"Look at that. I can't believe they're going to pile these unsuspecting kids into the filthy city jail," Lucius commented to Henri as he shook his head in disbelief.

The first group of marchers filled several paddy wagons. As the vehicle pulled away from the curb, another disciplined, orderly clump of children, almost identical to the first, marched down the steps and onto the sidewalk along the street, Again, the police deputies cut short the forward movement of the young marchers and diverted them into two more paddy wagons.

"That's two groups of fifty each, I'd say," Henri said. "Do they have enough cells in the jail for all these kids?"

"Or if they do, they'll have to pile four or five in each cell, or even more. Will there be ample room in each cell for that many kids to be able to stretch their limbs and have sufficient space to lie down and sleep tonight?" Lucius asked.

The second wave of marchers was followed by another, and then another. Henri overheard one of the police deputies calling a dispatcher on his walkie-talkie requesting more paddy wagons ASAP.

"Also, we've shipped several hundred kids already. They just keep on coming. There seems to be an endless supply of them in the church. The jail is approaching its limit."

Then the deputy signed off and shouted to another, "Central says to take the kids to the county fairgrounds and house them there."

While the police waited for additional paddy wagons to arrive, groups of children continued apace to march down the stairs. By noon, the police force felt overwhelmed and outnumbered by kids. Bull Connor's staff called the school board and requisitioned a fleet of school buses. They were told by school board officials that on that day they could make them available only because so many school children were playing hooky in order to be at Sixteenth Street Church that not as many buses would be needed to transport children home.

With no more paddy wagons to fill, the police directed kids to the idling school buses. The children became giddy with glee because it felt as if they were going on a school outing. When some of the kids caught wind that they were being carted to the county fairgrounds, their delight turned to exaltation. Most of them had never been to the fairgrounds because Negro customers were admitted to the county fair only on Saturday nights after 9 p.m., too late, parents thought, for them to take their children to the fair. This unplanned and unscheduled detour to the fairgrounds was a treat the children hadn't been expecting to enjoy.

May 2, 1963, D-Day, was coming to a close. Henri and Lucius heard reports emanating from city hall that more than six hundred children had been arrested by the Birmingham Police Force without the marchers' provocation or retaliation.

Lucius chuckled and said to Henri, "You know, before this unique Children's Crusade, the largest group of adult demonstrators that's been arrested in any one day is a dozen or so, on Good Friday when two of that number consisted of Dr. King and Ralph Abernathy for leading demonstrations in defiance of the city's injunction against them. Henri, I am beginning to acknowledge that by supporting Bevel in this project, Dr. King knew what he was doing. I'm glad that we were asked to be marshals. I wouldn't have missed this spectacle for the world."

Among the things that the civic leaders and even Bull Connor had not anticipated was the fact that Dr. King had urged James Bevel to alert the news directors of the television networks and editors of newspapers, including *The New York Times* and *Time* magazine, of the pending Children's Crusade. Consequently, no one was more overjoyed than Dr. King that not only had not a single child been injured by the police, but also that reporters and photographers from television stations and the morning papers had been in Birmingham to document the events, interview some of the children, and display photographs and film footage of the police escorting eight- and nine-year-old school children to crammed paddy wagons. The nation was beginning to have its moral conscience pricked.

In faraway Washington, D.C., President John F. Kennedy had also seen the television news film footage and heard the news reports about Birmingham. Kennedy was alarmed that the earlier rumors that children and youth would be the shock troops had been true, and angry at Dr. King that he would even entertain and approve such a plan. He ordered his brother Robert, the Attorney-General, to place a call to King, strongly pleading with him to withdraw the children from the march.

King refused in his usual diplomatic but firm way.

Chapter Twenty-Two

The Civil Rights Movement ought to thank Bull Connor. He's helped it as much as Abraham Lincoln.

President John F. Kennedy

May 3, 1963

The second day of the Crusade turned out to be even more dramatic and heartrending, and thus more emblematic of the transforming power of nonviolence. Already on the previous day, Henri and Lucius thought they had seen signs in Bull Connor's face and demeanor that the Children's Crusade was getting under his skin. When Henri and Lucius arrived the next morning at Kelly Ingram Park, where they had been posted, directly across Sixteenth Street from the church, they remarked that it appeared that even more school pupils were skipping school than on D-Day. In addition, they estimated that more parents had been intrigued enough by the previous day's events to come to the park to get a personal eyewitness view of the second day's events.

Bull Connor was visibly perturbed that the police action of arresting their children hadn't had the effect of disheartening and frightening their parents to make them stay away and keep their children away. So many Negroes tried shoehorning themselves into the usual mass meeting at Bethel Church the night of D-Day that organizers had to disperse the crowd to an additional three churches. Obviously, Connor concluded, more drastic means would have to be employed to disperse these persistent pests.

Overnight, Connor had ordered the canine unit to arrive the next morning with their German shepherd dogs and the city's fire companies to come prepared to attach their high-powered hose to the hydrants to force the crowds back.

Connor stationed several armed officers and a few others with German shepherds on a leash at a strategic street corner to prevent marchers or spectators from wandering off the route and going to demonstrate at city hall or the department stores downtown.

First thing in the afternoon, a line of youth marchers like the ones the day before descended the front steps of Sixteenth Street Baptist Church. Spontaneously, the line turned left as if to head downtown.

Connor barked into a megaphone, "Get your sweet little behinds back into the church."

The marchers persisted in singing their freedom songs and paid Connor no heed. This aroused Connor to a new level of anger and contempt. He shouted to the canine unit to release the fulminating dogs and the firemen to aim their hoses at the marchers.

The mighty jets of water knocked several of the children off their feet and their helpless bodies down onto the pavement. The force of the jet from the hoses tore the pretty white dress of one female student to shreds. She screamed in terror of the violent torrent of water, and many other girls added their horrified screams. One young boy, perhaps a ten-year-old, tried to stand up off the pavement when there was a brief respite from the rush of high-pressure water. As soon as he managed to get up on his feet a mighty gush of water tore the pant leg from his jeans and exposed his naked skin.

After some twenty minutes of the high-powered jet, even Connor had had enough for the time being. He barked an order to the firemen to cease and desist.

"I want to see these dogs work," Henri heard Connor exclaim. "I want to see these nettlesome niggers run for their lives."

One angry dog rushed toward a little girl of possibly six or seven years. Instinctively, she backed up as far as there was room against the pane of the showcase window of a small store. The dog stopped suddenly in its tracks as though it ran over an invisible electric fence. It then stood erect on its hind legs, nearly the same height as the girl who had her spindly arms raised to protect her face from the threatening teeth of the dog rushing off its leash and barely three feet away from her.

The girl and dog were directly in front of Lucius. Without a further thought, Lucius ran forward and jumped into the diminishing space between the girl and the incensed dog. At his place on the edge of the park, Henri felt a shot of panic course through his body when he saw the frenzied animal resume its position and dart toward Lucius with its fangs exposed.

"Lucius! Lucius, watch out!!" Henri cried out.

Several women from the adjacent park shouted frantic but futile orders to the girl to move and slip over quickly to the safety of the park while the dog's attention was focused on Lucius. But the diminutive girl was too terrified of the barking dog to move even an inch to one side or the other. She was paralyzed with abject terror.

The cur's barking transmuted into a sinister, deep growl. Suddenly, it leapt through the air at Lucius. Instinctively, Lucius turned his face from the dog. Like the girl before him, he raised his arms for protection, then flailed blindly at the attacking animal with his fists, striking its face once. The dog let out a high-pitched howl, and again stopped in its tracks, then lowered its head toward the pavement to nurse its pain.

Henri seized the opportunity to grab a thin branch of a tree from the floor of the park. He raised the hunk of wood above his head and ran wildly onto the street toward the dog, the defenseless girl, and the staggering Lucius. The dog caught sight of Henri rushing toward them with the makeshift weapon and resumed its loud protest. It pivoted on its hind quarters, preparing to spring at Henri.

Henri swung the stubby limb at the leaping dog like a baseball slugger. The dog managed to evade the hunk of wood. Henri recovered and took another vicious swing only to miss the animal a second time. Henri shouted frantically at the crowd in the park, "One of you men come here and carry the girl in your arms to the safety of the park while I try to divert the dog."

The sleeve of Lucius' shirt was saturated with fresh red blood within seconds. The animal was intent, it seemed, on tearing Lucius's arm right off its socket. But still clutching to the stubby limb of the tree, Henri took one more swing at the dog. This time the limb struck the dog squarely in its face. The dazed dog was rendered a humbled, docile pet. It was still alive as it laid its bloody head placidly on the hot pavement in defeat and emitted a series of anguished wails

A woman stepped forward from the park and wrapped a kerchief from her head around the bleeding bite wound on Lucius's arm to absorb the blood and to try to staunch the flow. As she raised Lucius's arm to complete applying the makeshift tourniquet, he cried out sharply in pain.

One of the other marshals for the march, taller and visibly older than the high school students. stepped in and began to lead Lucius gently from the street by the shoulder. "This man needs to get to a hospital right away, to treat the wound, test for rabies, and so on. I have a car a few blocks away."

Suddenly, there was a lot of angry commotion on the street and spilling over into the park.

"What in the name of hell happened here?" It was Bull Connor demanding an answer, his head and neck above his collar as bright red as crimson. He looked to his right and noticed the wounded German shepherd lying helplessly on the pavement.

"Who the hell did this? This dog is the property of the Birmingham Police Department." Taking the injured dog by its snout, Connor examined the animal. "Thank God this dog is still alive. But our veterinarians will have to judge if it's still capable of serving as one of our guard dogs. If it can't, shit, someone of you niggers is gonna have to pay for medical restitution and a fine for animal cruelty. I'll make damn sure that the judge levies a high one."

Chapter Twenty-Three

We have also come to this hallowed spot to remind America of the fierce urgency of Now. This is no time to engage in the luxury of cooling off or to take the tranquilizing drug of gradualism. Now is the time to make real the promises of democracy.

""" Have A Dream" speech in Washington, D.C.
August 28, 1963

June 9, 1963 – The Streets of Birmingham, Alabama

The sun was slow in setting on that early June evening. It was as though it was determined to extend this bloody day as long as possible and delay dusk and the darkness of night indefinitely. Bull Connor's German shepherds were thirsty and exhausted by the day's vicious events and were ready to be taken back to their kennel for the night. The sidewalks were emptied of canines, as were the paths in Kelly Ingram Park. All that remained were a few straggling marchers stunned by the force of the water hoses and a few pedestrians not yet taken to the hospital to have their wounds, lesions, and lacerations left by the teeth of the dogs checked out and salved and bandaged by the medical volunteers.

June 12, 1949 – Holy Family Hospital, Birmingham, Alabama

Observing the way his friend was joking with the nurses, Henri could tell that Lucius was regaining his strength and overcoming the pain of his wounds.

"Your hand and arm look so much healthier today, Lucius, best we've seen them since your encounter with the German shepherd over a month ago," Henri said, his voice and expression reassuring Lucius he meant what he said. "Isn't that right, Priscilla?"

"Yes, much better," Priscilla agreed.

"Well, if it isn't the Congregational preacher from Harlem and his much prettier woman. I'm surprised frankly that you've dared to come back and visit me after my shameful behavior on your last visit. I'm truly sorry, I didn't mean to be so grumpy and negative."

Priscilla put her hand tenderly on Lucius' left shoulder, careful to avoid applying any pressure on his right one she feared might still have been acutely sensitive from the dog attack that just about separated his arm from its socket. "No need to apologize, brother Lucius. You're allowed some grumpiness when the pain medication wore off our last visit."

"Well, thank you, Miss Laughton. You're being very magnanimous. Thankfully, I feel better today even though the doctor said he was going to lower my dosage of painkiller."

"When do they intend to burden the rest of the world with your presence?" Henri asked.

"If you mean when will I be discharged, the patient is always the last to hear. Since I'm feeling better, I hope it's relatively soon."

"I wonder if you'll be able to come to Washington with us in August," Priscilla said.

"Washington in August? It'll be hotter even than Hotlanta in August. More like hell."

"We thought you'd seen on the television about the big march." Henri added.

"It's called 'The March on Washington for Jobs and Freedom,'" Priscilla explained. "Dr. King and others like Randolph have been envisioning it quietly for a couple of years. Now, after the gains for the Movement in Birmingham, they figured that the forward momentum makes this the right time for a mass rally at the Lincoln Memorial."

"Dr. King said to us after the Children's Crusade, 'You'll be there, of course.'" Henri reported a little boastfully. "We were flattered that he'd give us a personal invitation. But we explained that we'd have to see how you recover by then before we commit to being there."

"That's my gallant travel partner," Lucius said to Priscilla and winked at her. "I'll be able to drive the car and go, I'm sure. But if for some reason I can't, you two go. You don't need a chaperone. I'm sure, Henri, you would be a perfect gentleman with as attractive a companion as Priscilla here." This time he winked slyly at Henri.

Henri was relieved to see Lucius energetic and talkative.

Pointing at the TV with his good hand, Lucius said, "I don't know how to change the channels on this television. It's stuck permanently on Romper Room and Bozo The Clown. I can't change the channel so that I can get some news."

"You're missing a lot. CBS just expanded their evening news

from a quarter hour to thirty minutes. NBC and ABC will follow soon, I bet," Henri informed him.

"They can fill a whole half-hour with news?"

"Sure," Priscilla assured him. "For example, over a half of Walter Cronkite's broadcast last night was taken up by what they're calling George Wallace's 'Stand at the Schoolhouse Door.'"

"That racist governor of Alabama, the 'segregation now, segregation tomorrow, segregation forever' guy?" Lucius inquired. "What's he up to now?"

"No good, I assure you," Henri responded. "A standoff between the feds and Wallace has been brewing for months. The University of Alabama informed two Negro applicants that they were to be admitted to the school. Needless to say, Wallace and his segregationists vowed, 'Over my dead body.'"

"So someone advanced the desegregation cause by killing him? Wow."

"No, unfortunately, or so I guess," Henri said, unsure of how a Christian minister committed to nonviolence should be responding. "But Cronkite reported on another murder on the same broadcast. After we finish the Wallace story, we'll fill you in on the other news."

"If the news is that one of Connor's German shepherds went berserk and turned on him, tearing limb from limb, don't make me wait. Tell me now."

"I'm afraid the news isn't that good," Henri replied.

"OK, back to Wallace."

Priscilla continued the story. "The very real possibility that these two exemplary Negro students, Vivian Malone and James Hood, might be denied admittance to the university caught the attention even of the President of the United States and his attorney-general."

"Yesterday morning, when they arrived in Tuscaloosa to enroll," Henry added, "JFK federalized the Alabama National Guard whom Wallace had ordered to the campus to prevent 'Negro rioting.' But we're getting ahead of ourselves."

"Wallace sure likes to be the star in his own theatrical performance," Priscilla said.

"The whole event became a three-ring circus," Henri seconded Priscilla's remark.

"When Malone and Hood arrived at the auditorium where they

were to enroll, the doorway was blocked by Wallace. Members of the Alabama National Guard flanked the governor. Malone and Hood, meanwhile, were directed to their dorms. RFK had dispatched his Assistant Attorney-General Nicholas Katzenbach to the campus to represent him. Katzenbach ordered Wallace to make room and allow the two students into the auditorium to register. Just as he had vowed to the citizens of Alabama during the weeks leading up to that day, Wallace made a show of refusing the wishes of the Attorney-General of the United States and launched into a rehearsed speech about states' rights."

Henri carried the story toward its conclusion. "The time came for Malone and Hood to be fetched from the dorms and try again to enter the auditorium. In the brief interval, JFK exerted his authority and deputized that whole company of the National Guard into federal troops representing federal authority. The commander ordered Wallace to withdraw or be forcibly removed from in front of the entrance. Wallace actually complied, but not before making a few resentful remarks about the violation of constitutional powers by the federal government."

"Act II of the Civil War?"

"For sure," Henri agreed. "That war isn't in the past for some of these Confederates."

"Some of that was pure theater," Priscilla said. "It didn't take long for it to become general knowledge that the whole exchange at the schoolhouse door had been planned, designed, and agreed upon by RFK and the Justice Department, university administration, and Wallace himself in advance. Wallace had assigned the parts in the drama, and everyone left the campus satisfied with the results. Wallace remained Alabama's hero."

"Isn't that all that politics is, a game, a costume drama?" Lucius asked.

"Sure, but a game that by some miracle occasionally promotes justice," Henri said in politics' defense.

"And the other bit of news you mentioned?" Lucius reminded them.

"Well, Lucius, this gets a little more personal," Henri said by way of preface. "Are you ready for that?"

"Give it to me straight, man."

"I don't know if you had a chance to talk person-to-person with Medgar Evers in Jackson after our little vacation in Parchman. I found him to be a delightful man."

"I know some of the other Freedom Riders felt the same way," Lucius agreed. "And his wife...what was her name? I've forgotten."

"Myrlie," Priscilla reminded him.

"Yes, Myrlie. Myrlie had prepared quite a delicious feast that evening for a bunch of young people who had just spent two months subsisting on prison food," Lucius said with a smile.

"Sad to say, Lucius," Henri began, "but Medgar was shot in cold blood last evening."

"God, no! What a loss."

"Such a sweet man," Priscilla said sadly.

"A crackerjack organizer of people and excellent field secretary for the N.A.A.C.P. in Mississippi." Henri added. "This will be a huge funeral."

"Now struck down just that? Where else but in damned Mississippi?"

"Medgar had just pulled into his driveway after a long road trip for the N.A.A.C.P.," Priscilla said on the verge of tears. "When he stepped out of the car, somebody hiding in the honeysuckle across the street from the Evers' house put a bullet in his back."

"Damn cowards!" Lucius evaluated.

"Myrlie and the kids had come out to greet him. The kids had so missed their daddy. They saw the blood-soaked body slumped on the driveway."

"Even if miraculously he gets apprehended, whoever shot him will get off Scot-free, I guarantee it, with an all-white jury," Lucius philosophized. "Isn't that how these things always go?"

"In the past several hundred years, yes," Henri said reflectively. "But, you know, I trust that some fine day things will be different. 'Faith is the assurance of things hoped for, the conviction of things to come not yet seen.' The author of the Book of Hebrews wrote that. But it is Dr. King who is teaching me what such faith and hope really look like."

Chapter Twenty-Four

To those who have said, 'Be patient and wait,' we have long said that we cannot be patient. We do not want our freedom gradually, but we want to be free now! We are tired. We are tired of being beaten by policemen. We are tired of seeing our people locked up in jail over and over again."

John Lewis
March on Washington speech, August 28, 1963

August 28, 1963

Indeed, Lucius was able to travel to Washington, D.C., with Henri and Priscilla in late August for the March on Washington for Jobs and Freedom. He was discharged from the hospital midway through the month of July. The old barber Henri had met on his previous trip to D.C., Gardner Bishop, gave him a copy of the key to his flat so that Lucius was free to come and go as he pleased. But, at least early in his recovery from his surgery, all Lucius could muster the strength and energy to do was walk the few steps to the bathroom to take care of a few basic essential tasks for the sake of his hygiene and health. As Lucius regained some of the strength in his legs, Gardner led him on walks through his neighborhood, ever vigilant that Lucius had his arms securely wrapped around Gardner's waist for support.

"We're fortunate that your rabies test came back negative." Henri tried to initiate conversation that he knew would animate Lucius.

"The damn dog?! What about my life? I've heard a few horror stories in the hospital about humans who were bitten a rabid dog. It doesn't happen in every instance, but the doctors said that often enough, a victim of the bite of a rabid animal would struggle for weeks and eventually go 'the way of all flesh.'

"You'd have enjoyed observing the brouhaha that arose in here when the medical staff scheduled the rabies test for the German Shepherd. It's a police dog, of course. That meant that our friend Bull Connor was going to be in the middle of all the commotion,"

"Of course, where else would he choose to be?" Henri asked sarcastically.

"As evidence for the hearing of the dog before the panel, I wish I had somebody's photos of my pectoral muscles ripped apart and bleeding like there was no tomorrow."

"You were literally a bloody mess, Lucius," Priscilla agreed.

"It looked to some of us as if the dog was intent on separating your arm from you shoulder," Henri added.

"When the medical staff here ordered the test for one of his prized dogs, predictably Bull Connor was provoked beyond anger—more like apoplexy—and said, 'Shit on your damned test. These are the healthiest dogs in the state of Alabama.'"

The public health officer had merely continued as though he was about to administer the test regardless.

"Do you know who you're talking to, son?" Connor asked to establish the pecking order. Connor knew full well that the officer, even as young and green as he was, recognized who Connor was and the extent of the power he wielded. "If that frickin' nigger is sick, it's because of his own filthy living conditions, not because of any of my dogs who are properly cared for in clean cages."

By the time Henri and Priscilla were sure that Lucius could come along to Atlanta to make a threesome, all the available hotel rooms in the District and the hinterland were reserved, Henri managed to locate the telephone number for Gardner Bishop to whom he had introduced himself at the very beginning of their southern odyssey.

"Sure, I remember you, Reverend," Bishop assured Henri when he reached him on the telephone. "You stood out. Most of the preachers who come by for a haircut are more interested in tooting their own horn and bragging about their church. But I remember how you were full of questions about my unofficial work with the kids from the local high school. You made me feel that what I had been doing was important. Of course. My place is not fancy or roomy, but I can make room for you and your two friends. Your friend who is a lady is welcome here, too, if she doesn't mind sleeping on a floor. Man, that civil rights march is going to be something."

The sleeping accommodations in the compact flat of a bachelor barber were anything but spacious. But Mr. Bishop made up for it with his graciousness. He had laid out his best bedsheets on top of sleeping bags borrowed for the occasion from a customer. Both Lucius and Henri were vigilant about making space on the living room floor so that they would not touch her or make any contact with any part of her body inadvertently. Before she retired for the night, she gave Henri a quick kiss on his cheek and wished him a good night. Henri lay down between his sheets but couldn't fall asleep for the longest time. That peck on the cheek and the circumstances of having Priscilla sleeping within just a short distance away for the first time excited him as though he were a teenager again with fantasies of how things might be different if Lucius wasn't within earshot of them.

Better turn off the brain before you lose control, Henri, he remembers chiding himself before he finally fell asleep.

ONE BY ONE, THE TRAVELERS awoke. A humble breakfast was laid out on a table crowded with old newspapers and several unwashed dishes. There was a carafe of coffee and a plate of bread rolls that might have been fresh sometime in the past. They said farewell for the day to their host. They took several buses to the National Mall. This was to be the first day of the March on Washington for Jobs and Freedom.

When they stepped off the bus not far from the Capitol, they were confused by the apparent dearth of people on the mall. They had read in the press that the organizers, particularly the chief logistician Bayard Rustin, had boasted to the media that more than a hundred thousand participants would squeeze onto the mall between the Capitol and the Lincoln Memorial by the time the speakers were scheduled to begin later in the afternoon.

"Well, the hundred thousand won't feel like sardines in a can," Lucius remarked and chuckled.

"It's early yet," Henri said. "You know how long it takes Negro crowds to gather and get set at organized events. At my church in Harlem when we begin the opening hymn, I look around to the nearly empty nave and sometimes think I may be there on the wrong day. But when I turn around and face the congregation at the Amen after the hymn is sung, the church is almost half-filled."

They continued walking toward the majestic Lincoln Memorial at the western end of the mall. In the early morning light, the memorial looked like a mystical citadel rising out of the magical first light. As they got closer to the impressive monument, they began to make out the shape of Honest Abe.

"He's so huge," Priscilla marveled. "I've seen a hundred photographs of Lincoln, but he's never looked this massive and magnificent."

"That's the Great Emancipator himself, looking decidedly godlike and immortal, doesn't he?" Henri asked.

"I wonder how close we can get to him?" she asked.

"Better find out now," Lucius encouraged. "If they expect a hundred thousand it'll be hard to weave through the crowd to get a better view."

"Maybe Lucius and I can lift you up onto his lap," Henri said, then chuckled.

"No thanks. The last man whose lap I sat on was my father. His will be the last before I'm married if I have any choice in the matter."

"Oh, Priscilla, I'm sure someday soon you'll sit on Henri's lap or that of some other dude who knocks you off your feet," Lucius countered.

He and Henri exchanged private mischievous and knowing winks.

They turned around and walked back eastward toward the Capitol. They were faced with a steady flow of people walking in the opposite direction.

"Looks as though the crowds are starting to arrive," Priscilla commented.

"Union Station is in this direction," Henri informed her. "So is the Greyhound terminal. I suspect that these are bus and train passengers just arriving."

"Hey Priscilla." Lucius called out perhaps a little too loudly. "Looks like you're not the only white person here. It's impressive that there are so many of them. They can't all be journalists or cops."

They soon circled and passed the imposing Washington Monument. They looked past the Ellipse on their right to the back of the White House standing impressively and regally. To the left of the foot trail was a makeshift area created for chartered tour buses to park and discharge their passengers. Lucius was impressed by the names of the various tour companies written on the side of the buses, particularly the locations in the part of the country where the tours had originated.

"Look, there's one from Lafayette, Louisiana," he marveled, almost childlike. "That's one long bus ride."

"How about this one?" Priscilla asked. "It says it's all the way from Corpus Christi. That's in Texas, isn't it? This bus brought people here all the way to D.C."

The march itself hadn't started yet. However, small groups of pilgrims walked arm in arm along the mall singing freedom songs, familiar ones to Henri, Lucius and Priscilla, like "We Shall Overcome" and a few that were totally new to them:

Freedom's name is mighty sweet
And soon we're gonna meet
Keep your eyes on the prize, hold on

IT WAS A JOVIAL CROWD, primed to celebrate the success of the Movement, a jubilant school reunion of sorts.

"Oh, my God," Priscilla uttered joyously as she raised her right hand to cover her mouth. "You guys will not believe me, but I am sure I just saw Sydney Poitier and presumably his wife over there."

"Here on the mall? The movie star?" Henri asked her. "It's quite possible, actually. He has been an outspoken ally of the Movement. Why wouldn't he want to be here today, too, to show his support?"

Both Henri and Lucius began to pay better attention to the faces of the people walking past them in the direction of the Lincoln monument. They were a little incredulous initially when Priscilla reported her sighting of the superstar. But the more they thought about it, the more possible they thought it was that in this growing mass of people there might be a celebrity or two.

Suddenly, they saw a familiar face walking with a group of others. It was Diane Nash of the Freedom Rides. She recognized them immediately before they had a chance to greet her.

"Henri and Company. How good to see you here. It's going to be a grand event."

"The crowd sure is electric, and the program hasn't even started," Priscilla said.

"I'm just a little anxious in the presence of so many law enforcement types," Lucius pointed out.

"But you've got to admit that the recent history of these demonstrations has been marred by violence and lawlessness," Diane countered.

"Granted," Lucius acknowledged. "But incited and initiated by whom?"

"I'm actually on my way to a meeting," Diane interjected.

"Another one?" Henri exclaimed good-naturedly. "Is that all you do, Diane, sit at meetings?"

"It seems lately that it is. I was appointed to the Adjunct Directing Committee for the March. Behind the scenes, things get a little tense sometimes. Right now there's an issue about John Lewis's proposed speech. Some of the more traditional older guard of the 'Big Six" as they're called, like Roy Wilkins and Jim Farmer, are very anxious about John's unapologetic and unalloyed radical language. We're meeting at 2:00 p.m. as the Steering Committee to sort it out."

"It's getting pretty close to 'raise the curtain time,'" isn't it?" Henri asked, concerned. "Is there time to make changes in the program now?"

"It all depends on how flexible John is willing to be," Diane replied. "It's essentially four of the organizers against poor John. Even Bayard is counseling caution. Doctor King should be there this afternoon so we'll hear what he thinks."

"That ought to make a difference," Lucius said.

"It's ironic that it was grand old A. Philip Randolph, whose baby this march is, who suggested to the others that, as chair of SNCC, John be given time at the podium to articulate the youth perspective on things. Now even the venerable sleeping car porters' union founder acts like he thinks he made a mistake by inviting him."

Diane reached into her substantial handbag and pulled out some papers. "Here's a sample of what the veteran leaders object to in John's speech: 'The time will come when we don't confine our marching to Washington. We will march all through the South, through the Heart of Dixie, the way Sherman did. We shall pursue our own scorched earth policy and burn Jim Crow to the ground.'"

Henri and Lucius cringed visibly when they heard Diane read the name of Sherman and make reference to "burning" something "to the ground."

"That is more than a little provocative, don't you think?" Henri asked. "Is that really necessary with this crowd?"

"To say you're going to emulate Sherman is offensive in the South, to whites and blacks. I'd tell John that it's a nonstarter," Lucius added.

"I'm from Ohio, not the South, so I wouldn't know as well as you," Diane said. "But I get your point. You would agree with those who want him to lower his intensity and amend his rhetoric so that it's not so bellicose and adversarial?"

"I abstain. I don't have any authority in the matter," Henri answered. "John is young and brave and passionate. I saw that on the Freedom Rides. I wouldn't want to pour cold water on that passion. That's what fuels his whole commitment."

"I beg to differ," Lucius announced. "I've seen a lot of white people walking here on the mall today. They know that this march is for Negro jobs and justice. They must be here to support the idea, not to criticize or oppose it. I think if I were white, I wouldn't want to hear any suggestion today that whites are the enemy and not deserving partners for us. Leave that rhetoric for Stokely Carmichael and Malcolm X. I may be one of those supportive whites of goodwill here today who would agree with the need to be rid of Jim Crow, but I wouldn't want to hear a threat that it will be destroyed by fire set by angry Negroes."

Chapter Twenty-Five

Freedom is never granted.
It is won.

A. Philip Randolph

August 28, 1963

A moving sea of humanity continued to flow relentlessly in the direction of the Lincoln Memorial as the hour for the beginning of the program approached.

Priscilla guessed that Diane Nash Bevel might be finished with the emergency meeting of the march steering committee and led Henri and Lucius to the precise location where she figured that Diane would come after the meeting. The threesome stood by and waited a few yards away from Diane as she finished a hurried parley with several volunteers. When their business was completed, Diane greeted them.

"The march is proceeding swimmingly, don't you think?"

"You're done with your meetings, I hope," Henri asked.

"I had hoped so, but it's not likely. Bayard is a real stickler for details. He never lets one pass without his attention.... We're not done yet with the John Lewis issue."

"What? Not done?" a startled Lucius asked. "The program is just about ready to begin at any moment."

"Apparently, John thought he'd done everything to soften his speech as the others had asked him to do. He went back to his hotel room to rest, but underneath his door someone had slipped a note. It was from Bayard: 'John, come downstairs. Must see you at once.'

"Ever the team player, John told me he went downstairs to Bayard's suite, wondering, 'Who's got a problem with my speech? Who else has seen my speech?'

"Yes, who had seen it in advance and how?" Priscilla asked.

"Apparently, it was Julian Bond disseminating the speech before John or anyone else was ready. He had gone by a display table in the lobby of the hotel and seen a copy of Whitney Young's prepared remarks. Not wanting John to be outdone, Julian made copies of Lewis's speech—as a courtesy—and put them out on that table. By this morning, all the copies were gone."

"A courtesy? I suspect John wasn't happy about it," Henri remarked.

"Sure enough, someone picked up a copy and immediately showed it to Patrick O'Boyle, the Catholic Archbishop of Washington who was scheduled to deliver the Invocation this afternoon. O'Boyle was incensed at what he considered was the inflammatory tone in John's speech so he called Bayard and said that he would have nothing to do with the event if John was allowed to proceed without further major changes to the speech. O'Boyle also called the White House. The Kennedys, especially JFK, were not altogether comfortable with the march, so the President placed a call with Bayard as well."

"Well, congratulations to the damned Catholic Church for fucking things up with their pre-medieval ideas!" Lucius stormed.

"So I've got to rush over to the Lincoln Memorial for yet another last-second emergency meeting. Supposedly, the meeting is in a cramped security officer's space behind Lincoln's statue. See you sometime," Diane said as she rushed away.

THEY COULD HEAR RANDOLPH'S voice over the loudspeakers.

"People," he said, "let the nation and the world know the meaning of our numbers."

The crowd erupted in cheers.

"I've been dreaming of this day for more than twenty years. Thank you for coming to Washington to form the largest demonstration for jobs and freedom in the history of our nation."

Henri, Lucius, and Priscilla were transported by the infectious enthusiasm of the crowd.

"I'm so glad you got out of the hospital in time to be able to come," Priscilla said to Lucius very sincerely.

"I'm so glad I could be here, too," Lucius responded with tears in his eyes as he embraced Priscilla. "I've never been part of anything like this. I'm glad to be a Negro today."

Priscilla was taken aback by Lucius's remark. "You don't feel that at other times?"

"I try not to believe them, but so many white folks just blame us for all the violence and turmoil," Lucius responded, "that we're the source of the 'Negro problem.' On the contrary, however, I think this nation has a 'white problem' but most whites tend not to agree, present company excepted.

They turned to listen to a couple of other speakers address the crowd.

"The crowd looks like it's growing restless to get past these lesser lights to the 'main event' at the end of the program," Henri observed. "Their applause for the Reverend Eugene Carson Blake of the National Council of Churches is tepid at best."

Randoph introduced Myrlie Evans to speak in her first public address since the murder of her husband, Medgar.

"The air is beginning to be charged with electricity now, isn't it?" Priscilla asked.

Myrlie paid tribute by name to some of the Negro women for freedom, including Rosa Parks and Delores Banks, whom Henri and Lucius had met over what seemed like an eon ago in Little Rock.

Priscilla asked Henri and Lucius, "You notice that Mrs. Evers is the only female speaker on the program? I also noticed that Coretta Scott King in the cavalcade of marchers accompanied by her children and other women at the rear of the parade, but not near the men. Imagine making the First Lady of the Movement march without her husband," she commented with a hint of bitterness. "And then to put her in the caboose at the end of the procession almost as an after-thought. The Movement has a few things to learn about life in the second half of the twentieth century."

They heard Randolph's deep bass voice come over the speakers again. "And now, I'd like us to welcome one of the bright rising stars of the Civil Rights Movement, the chairman of the Student Nonviolent Coordinating Committee, Brother John Lewis."

Henri noticed that to the right of the podium stood a sizable group of young members and followers of SNCC, who burst into enthusiastic applause and wild hoots of verbal support for their chairperson. When he saw Julian Bond joining in the applause as well, Henri wondered if Bond had any idea yet of the turmoil, which almost threatened this whole event that his spontaneous mass copying and distributing Lewis's speech the previous evening had incited. If he does, he's not showing any remorse. Perhaps no one, not Bayard, not even John himself, has had a conversation with Bond about it.

Not far from the SNCC supporters was a visibly less enthusiastic group of marchers. Their welcome for Lewis was cordial enough, Lucius thought. "...sympathetic, I suppose, but not exactly what I'd describe as unreservedly supportive. These must be some of Wilkins' people."

Priscilla was quiet and reflective. She looked around at the diverse crowd and contemplated before she spoke, "You know, I see John's proud supporters standing as a group over there on the left. And responding to the Lewis folks' loud cheers with their own lukewarm applause is the group of what are obviously older marchers over here. But can we really afford to be divided into competing groups? I didn't come on this march to be a John Lewis loyalist, or a member of anybody else's party, even Dr. Martin Luther King's faction, for that matter. I came, as I know you have, too, looking at the two of them, to be a member of the Movement, a small part of a huge forward-moving force to bring positive change to the lives of many ordinary people."

Lucius and Henri were stunned into a culpable silence.

Then Lucius spoke. "You're right on, Priscilla, we shouldn't be assigning people to winning or losing sides...or else we'll all end up losing."

"Yes, you're right, Priscilla," Henri agreed. "We can't even be sure anymore that those who advocate for the nonviolent option for racial action are still the majority. Malcolm has been very persuasive in his argument for the need for violent response from our people to the white violence and repression. Day by day, it seems that support for such tactics is growing among our people. I sense a growing gap in the civil rights movement between those who choose nonviolent protest, as Martin popularizes it, and the more aggressive tactics promoted by Malcolm and the Black Muslims. Under those circumstances, do we really have the luxury of further dividing the advocates of nonviolent protests whose numbers may be shrinking?"

Henri put his arms around Priscilla in a grateful embrace when he had finished.

"HE LOOKS UNCHARACTERISTICALLY nervous," Priscilla observed as John Lewis walked up to the podium and laid his papers and a paperweight on top of them on the lectern. For what seemed like the longest time, Lewis looked over the crowd of a quarter million marchers spread out on the mall, beside the Reflecting Pool and in the cramped space in front of the memorial.

"Who wouldn't be at least a little nervous?" Henri asked. "Two hundred and fifty thousand people? I doubt he's ever spoken to a crowd even a fraction of the size of this one."

"He may not be sure of what he can say," Lucius suggested. "His speech has probably been cut to pieces. I wonder if that resistant archbishop even bothered to stay to hear John's speech."

"I doubt it, somehow," Priscilla echoed Lucius's cynicism. "That self-important man believes that he has too many other urgent matters to take care of than to stick around here to be part of the largest racial demonstration in the history of the United States."

Lewis tried to launch into his speech. He opened his mouth, but all anyone could hear was the hoarse wheeze of air from his lungs. The unfamiliar gasp surprised him. He tried to begin the speech again. This time the puff of air expelling from his lungs was more audible, more approximately imitating the sound of human words. John looked more relaxed.

"We march today for jobs and freedom, but we have nothing to be proud of."

All three glanced quickly at one another. They realized that the opening sentence immediately sobered the animated crowd that was expecting some congratulatory statement of triumph.

"For hundreds of thousands of our brothers are receiving mere starvation wages. While we stand here, there are sharecroppers in the Delta of Mississippi who are out in the fields working for less than three dollars a day, twelve hours a day."

"Man, the kid doesn't mince words," Lucius chuckled appreciatively. "He wastes no time beating around the bush."

"The crowd is so intoxicated with high spirits right now," Priscilla said, "that I wonder if it's ready to hear such unvarnished truth right off the bat."

Lewis continued apace. "We are here today with a great sense of misgiving. It is true that we support the administration's Civil Rights Bill, but with great reservation, however."

"Do you think the President is listening in the White House?" Priscilla asked, looking a little dismayed. "I don't think he'd be very thrilled by John's words."

"These words may be some of the ones that folks like Wilkins and Whitney Young would have objected to," Henri said. "I've heard John be very critical of the JFK administration before."

"It takes balls to dare to criticize the federal government and a President who responded to the Birmingham riots with an actual piece of proposed legislation," Lucius said. "Excuse my French,

Priscilla."

"A sentiment like John's surely makes Bayard Rustin squirm," Priscilla remarked. "I wonder what Dr. King is feeling and thinking on the podium with him."

"Likely, he's not too perturbed, actually," Henri responded. "I get the impression that Dr. King has some really mixed and ambivalent feelings about JFK's contributions to the Movement. I think he's smart enough to detect half-hearted support. It seems that John Lewis certainly is."

"Unless there are changes in the bill, there's nothing to protect the young children and old women who must face police dogs and fire hoses in the South while they engage in peaceful demonstration," Lewis said with mounting passion.

Noting the crowd's rousing cheers of agreement as it responded to Lewis's words, Lucius said, "Some of them are cheering for middle-aged clergy, too, I hope, who have had to face police dogs and fire hoses."

"If they knew what happened to you, Lucius, I'm sure they would cheer for you, too," Priscilla added good-naturedly.

Lucius tipped his fedora to her in appreciation.

"As it stands now, this bill will not help the citizens of Mississippi, Alabama, and Georgia who are not eligible to vote for lack of sixth grade education. One man, one vote, is the African cry. It must be ours, too."

"John's really getting into a rhythm now, isn't he?" Priscilla observed.

"He's starting to sound like an old-time black Southern preacher," Lucius added.

"Did you know that John thought of being one once?" Henri asked them. "He told me on the Freedom Ride that his father on the little farm assigned feeding the chickens to the sons and cleaning up after them every day after school. John said he hated getting his boots all mixed up in the shit. When it was his turn, he said he preached to the chickens as though they formed an actual congregation."

"A flock of Baptist poultry," Lucius said, followed by a belly laugh.

People in the crowd looked over to see what Lucius found so funny in Lewis's mentioning the difficulty for the citizens of the deep South to exercise the franchise.

"We must have a bill that will ensure the equality of a black maid who earns five dollars a week in the home of a white family whose total income is more than a hundred thousand dollars a year. We must have a bill that includes FEPC protections."

"JFK won't like being criticized in this way, but I sure hope he's listening," Lucius mused.

"My friends, let us not forget that we are involved in a serious social revolution."

"How did a word like 'revolution' make it past the steering committee?" Priscilla asked. "That's going to become fodder for Nixon and the House Unamerican Activities Committee."

"Thank the Lord that Joe McCarthy isn't around to hear this." Lucius appended.

"Dr. King already suspects that J. Edgar Hoover is on his tail about being a Communist." Henri said.

Lewis must have sensed he was on a roll, for he continued in the same vein as before. "There are politicians who build their career on immoral compromise.... But there are exceptions, of course. Let us salute these. But what leader of a political party can stand up and say, 'My party is the party of principles?' For the party of Kennedy is also the party of Eastland. The party of Javits is also the party of Goldwater. Where is our party? Where is the party that will make it unnecessary to march on Washington or in the streets of Birmingham?"

The crowd's applause and cheering were almost deafening.

Clearly buoyed by the crowd's response, Lewis went on to list some shortcomings of the Kennedy administration in responding to racial tensions in Albany, Georgia. Then he returned to the needs of those in the crowd.

"I think he's setting up the audience for the customary 'ask,'" Henri predicted as everyone present sensed that Lewis was approaching his climax.

"To those who have said, 'Be patient and wait', we must say that we cannot be patient. We do not want our freedom gradually. We want our freedom, and we want it now. We are tired. Tired of being beaten by policemen. We are tired of seeing our people locked up in jail over and over again.... How long can we be patient? We want our freedom, and we want it now.

"We do not want to go to jail, but we will go to jail if this is the price we must pay for love, brotherhood and true peace.

"I appeal to all of you to get into this great revolution that's sweeping the nation. Get in and stay in the streets of every city, every village, and every hamlet until true freedom comes, until a revolution is complete. They're telling us to slow down and stop. We will not stop. All the forces of Eastland, Barnett, Wallace, and Thurmond will not stop this revolution. If we do not get meaningful legislation out of this Congress, the time will come when we will not confine our march to Washington. We will march through the South.... But we will march with the spirit of love and the spirit of dignity that we have shown here today."

Lewis provided enough time and space for applause by pausing and looking around over the crowd.

"By the force of our demands, our determination, and our numbers, we shall send a desegregated South into a thousand pieces, put them together in the image of God and Democracy. We must wake up America, wake up! For we cannot stop, and we will not and cannot be patient."

Applause erupted like an exploding volcano. Marchers embraced each other even if they had never met before. Henri, Lucius, and Priscilla formed a close circle of three and joined in the embracing. The two men squeezed her and in unison lifted her up off about half a foot, causing her to emit a joyful scream followed by laughter. When they had put her feet down on the ground again, Henri kept his right arm snugly around Priscilla's slender waist and squeezed her tightly once more. He contemplated kissing her on the mouth, but for the time being refrained.

Chapter Twenty-Six

God still has a way of wringing good out of evil. And history has proven over and over again that unmerited suffering is redemptive. The innocent blood of these little girls may well serve as a redemptive force that will bring new light to this dark city. The death of these little children may lead our whole Southland from the low road of man's inhumanity to man to the high road of peace and brotherhood. These tragic deaths may lead our nation to substitute an aristocracy of character for an aristocracy of color. The spilled blood of these innocent girls may cause the whole citizenry of Birmingham to transform the negative extremes of a dark past into the positive extremes of a bright future.

Rev. Martin Luther King, Jr.
Funeral Sermon for four girls

September 15, 1963

"Jim and I are pleased as punch that you are sticking to your stated intention of staying with us here in Birmingham to help us with the children's programs. You were a big help with the Children's March. back in May. But I have the sneaking suspicion that Henri may not be as pleased. Am I right?"

"Yes," Priscilla acknowledged Diane's assessment reluctantly. "Not when I first told him about it, at least. But when I told him that I'm still not ready to leave the South and that I wanted to come back with you to Birmingham, he was a lot better about it. I think he sees that I am making a decision about how best to use the gifts God has given me for the sake of the Movement."

"He'll miss you. I can see the sparks flying between the two of you whenever you are together. You guys are good friends and colleagues, but you're more than that, too."

"I suppose that's right. But the relationship is moving along slowly, step by step."

"Which, I sense, is how you want things to progress?"

"I think that that is precisely how Henri prefers it to go, anyway. It might be because I'm white and he's black, although frankly I don't think that's the issue. He's just a little rusty in romance, I think, even a little clumsy. Not sure if he's being too slow. Or at other times he's a little nervous about exceeding the speed limits he judges I may have set for myself in the relationship. I was sure at one moment when the March on Washington concluded, he was going to kiss me on the lips for the first time. But at the last second, he got cold feet. I don't think I put up any obvious resistance."

Priscilla and Henri had talked about it. It didn't seem to either of them that going too slowly was an issue for Jim and Diane. They were married in Nashville immediately after the Birmingham Children's March. Jim had fallen head over heels for Diane, particularly as they worked side-by-side and oftentimes hand-in-hand recruiting and organizing the children and youth before and during the dramatic events of the March. Priscilla struck Diane as someone who was more deliberate about such a major decision, but she knew Diane was as happy as Jim was to tie the knot sooner rather than later.

Diane was visibly pregnant by early September, and Priscilla knew from her own older sister's experience that Diane would need help with baby care and household chores. Priscilla admired the way the Bevels worked together as a team. Jim was the more outgoing and charismatic, especially on a stage or in a pulpit, who caught and maintained the attentiveness of the children by the sheer drawing power of his robust self-confident oratory and his almost frenzied tomfoolery that entertained his youthful audience. Jim would be the first to acknowledge that his wife was the brains of the operation, the organizer par excellence who usually anticipated any potential problem or obstacle.

Diane and Jim shared their sense of vindication and satisfaction with Priscilla and other volunteers after the Children's March ended at the urging of the Department of Justice.

The downtown business leaders were exhausted by the perseverance of the children and their adult leaders and, uncharacteristically, were ready to raise the white flag and agree to the demands of the campaign.

"Dr. King, Rev. Abernathy, and Rev. Shuttlesworth laid out the demands clearly and forthrightly right at the beginning. If the city fathers and business bigwigs had been listening instead of defending themselves with all the usual misleading myths, they could have averted a lot of trouble," Diane said while shaking her head.

Jim couldn't allow the moment to pass without a comment. "Critics kept arguing that we'd never overcome Bull Connor and his dogs and armed deputies by nonviolent means. 'You need firepower. Get yourselves some guns.' Well, they were wrong, weren't they? The nation and the whole world turned against the militants and supported our kids who never reached for a weapon."

Jim said as much to the senior high school Sunday school class that he, Diane, and Priscilla were leading up in a small classroom at the top of the stairs on the third floor of Sixteenth Baptist Church. "It goes to show that practicing nonviolence is not for losers as its opponents like Stokely and Malcolm claim. No, nonviolence is a very practical philosophy and strategy for winners—that's what we are, young people, that's what you are."

Suddenly, the relative quiet of the building was broken by an otherworldly boom that shook the foundation of the church. Even up on the third floor the classroom was buffeted by the violent eruption of hellish explosive force. The eyes of every student were riveted on the faces of one of the three adults. With no prior warning, several of the boys in the room burst in the direction of the door.

Jim reached out his right hand and grabbed hold of one, then two, of the scramblers. "No! Stay in your seat and don't leave the room. We aren't sure yet where the source of the explosion is."

Behind the wooden door of the room at the end of the short corridor a telephone rang and continued to ring unanswered. Jim and Diane knew it was a spare space used to store Sunday school supplies that the superintendent of the Sunday school used occasionally as an office.

"That might be Mrs. Caldwell trying to reach us," Diane said nervously to her husband.

"You may be right," Jim agreed. "But don't poke your head out the door! Stay put where you are. I'll crawl on the floor and see if the supply room door is unlocked to answer the phone. We can't know yet if there's someone dangerous lurking around up here."

Jim slithered on his belly out the door on the floor in the direction of the supply room. He hadn't been gone from the classroom very long when they heard the telephone stop ringing and become silent. Out in the corridor, Jim was able to detect a panicked hubbub rising from the first floor below and the eerie screams of some female children. Jim tried to open the supply room door, and then apply some force against it when he concluded that it was locked. He promptly ducked low again and crawled back toward the classroom with the waiting attuned students. Instead of returning straight back to the classroom, he detoured a few yards toward the stairwell where he hoped he could look down to the first and second floors from where he had heard the screams and commotion.

When he got back to the classroom, all looked toward him expectantly for news.

"The door is locked, and I can't get near the phone. I think, Diane, you and I need to venture down the stairs slowly and carefully to the first floor where it sounds like the action is centered and try to discover what happened and whether or not we need to stay hidden from the source of the danger up here."

Diane nodded her assent to the idea. "Priscilla, would you stay here with the students and make sure no one leaves the room until we come back with more instructions?"

"Of course, Jim. Whatever I can do to help. Just come back soon. Don't leave us waiting here too long."

"A little scared?" Jim asked.

"Yes, a little. But we'll be fine for a while. We've got each other."

"You're scared, too, Miss Laughton?" a boy named Rufus asked her quietly.

"Yes, as I told Rev. Bevel, a little. I've never been in this kind of situation before. That loud boom must have been a bomb of some kind. My stomach just about rose into my throat when I heard it."

"You know, Miss Laughton, that's a relief to me that you feel the fear, too," a tall girl named Yvonne sitting beside Rufus said. "You're a bit older, and you're our teacher, but it's reassuring to me that in the end you're just like one of us."

"Why, thank you, Yvonne. That's a very meaningful compliment. You are being very brave to admit your fear. That's true for all of you."

Little Elena added, "I was scared a few times in the Children's March, but only a few short times. The dogs were scary and so were the fire hoses. But because I knew everybody was at least a little scared, I felt a little braver to face them."

"I have found that to be true of any of the civil rights movement episodes that I've been a part of. The Freedom Rides on the buses through towns where the crowds on the side of the road were raving mad at what we were doing. In the horrible state prison in Mississippi. We had to admit that all of us had a little fear, naturally. No one could guarantee our safety, not even our faith in a good and loving God that wants to protect us. But you're right, Elena. We have each other in times of danger with whom to share our fear. That's why we can fearlessly sing 'We Shall Overcome' and really believe it."

They heard Jim and Diane's footsteps coming up the stairs. When they opened the door and entered, Jim's looked hard and furious. Because her complexion was naturally a lighter hue than usual for a black woman, her face was almost white from being overwhelmed by whatever they had seen downstairs.

"My God! I've never witnessed such destruction, especially in a church," Diane said once she had caught her breath.

The students were literally on the edge of their seats for news.

"The damage from the bomb is indescribable. There are bricks and pieces of stone and concrete strewn all about. Shards of glass that crackle when people walk on them. The face of Jesus has been blown out of the huge stained-glass window. The bomb was put so precisely and accurately as though someone had taken a glass cutter and...." Diane couldn't finish the sentence because her voice quavered, and she broke down in tears.

Jim resumed the report. "It appears that whoever planted the bomb did so underneath the stairs just outside the women's restroom in the basement. The whole restroom was demolished and blown to bits...." Jim cleared his throat before he could go on. "Unfortunately, the initial reports are that at least four Sunday school girls were in the restroom changing their clothes to lead the youth service this morning. We saw some blotches of blood on the floor and sprayed on the walls, the girls' blood." Jim had to keep his eyes fixed on the floor and couldn't look directly at the students.

"All the while, Rev. Cross kept walking in and out of the door facing Sixteenth Street and repeating the refrain, 'Father, forgive them.' He looked to me that he might have been in some kind of trance or shock at what had been done to his church...our church," Diane was able to say.

People downstairs kept on reciting names. "Addie Mae. Cynthia, Carole, Carol Denise. The names of the girls blown to bits in the restroom." Diane was overcome.

"Oh, no! Not little Addie Mae Collins! No, God, please!" Priscilla pleaded. "She marched beside me in the Children's March. She was so very alive. She can't be gone! Why would anyone want to hurt a little girl?" Priscilla collapsed into Diane's arms.

If any of the young people had been observing Jim during this interchange, they would have noticed the intense anger showing on his face. He mumbled a few indistinguishable sounds.

"I feel a deep urge within me," he explained, "to find a high-powered rifle and blow away all vestiges of whoever is responsible for this heinous, unprovoked act of hate!"

The youth eyed one another with looks of shock and consternation. "Mr. Bevel?"

Diane regarded Jim, still trembling in his rage, with spousal disapproval. "Jim! You know that to even think of such a horrid thing violates every single one of our nonviolent values."

Jim's face was less contorted with fury. He looked chastised by his wife.

She wasn't finished upbraiding him. "All that would do is perpetuate the violence and evil you abhor."

She didn't want to discourage his passion, which she loved so dearly. She suggested an alternative path for his fervor. "Just imagine if all the Negroes in Jefferson County were registered to vote, how long do you think Bull Connor would last as sheriff? Or, if every eligible Negro in the state of Alabama were registered to vote, do you think that George Wallace could be elected as governor? Connor and Wallace have created a climate and environment in which someone feels free and encouraged to plant a deadly bomb in a church full of children."

The young people were spellbound by the dialogue. The choice between violent revenge and nonviolent suffering had never presented itself more clearly.

Jim's rage had subsided. "You speak the truth, Diane, as usual. Class, I apologize most earnestly for my outburst. I didn't say I would go out and find a high-powered rifle and mow down the racists who felled the four precious girls. But at that moment, I had an urge to do so. No excuse for that. I'm sorry you had to hear my angry, misplaced fantasy. I hope you learned something valuable."

Both Diane and Priscilla reached out from their seats and took hold of Jim's hand.

THE NEXT MORNING there were fewer cars parked on Sixteenth Street in front of the church and fewer people milling about inside.

Diane informed Jim and Priscilla that she had called Rev. King the night before. King was the guest of his colleague Reverend Shuttlesworth and had preached that morning and evening at Bethel Baptist. Fred Shuttlesworth's announcement during the morning worship service about the bombing and the death of the four girls pulled a veil of shock and heartbreak over the congregation, Rev. King had told her.

"This is the most heartless act of violence in the whole Civil Rights era," King had said. "I don't think that people can go any lower."

"Dr. King talked by telephone yesterday with the FBI people, requesting that the investigation of this bombing take the highest priority," said Diane. "He told me that 'we don't want this matter swept under the carpet and conveniently forgotten like so many other church bombings recently in Alabama.' It was Dr. King among some others who pressured J. Edgar Hoover to be aggressive in their pursuit of the bodies of Chaney, Goodman, and Schwerner in Mississippi. Despite his well-known antipathy toward Dr. King, J. Edgar complied."

"Any leads the feds have on the culprits of this bombing?" Jim asked.

"Dr. King said that if they do, they're being very cagey about naming names except for Robert Chamblis, a notorious racist and member of the Klan. If they pressure Chamblis for any length of time, they ought to come up with the names of the three others.

"There was more bad news from Dr. King. however."

"More? How much can we take?" Priscilla said, throwing up her hands.

"Two teenage youths, Johnny Robinson and Virgil Ware, were shot in the back by Birmingham police seven hours after the bombing," Diane said.

"Just for being black, I'm sure," Jim said skeptically.

"Well, apparently, they had thrown bricks at the officers," Diane corrected him.

The four Sunday school girls were murdered on the same day, but the family of Carole Robertson chose to have a separate, private funeral for her. "Her father Alvin was upset that Dr. King was asked to preach at the funeral of the girls. He blamed Dr. King for interfering in matters in Birmingham and causing trouble that was unnecessary.

"Dr. King did choose to be in the congregation during Carole's funeral and hoped that his presence would not upset the Robertsons. Governor Wallace has signed three hundred state troopers into Birmingham to 'keep the peace.' Jim, Priscilla, and I joined Dr. King at his hotel for lunch after the funeral. As I was returning to our table from the ladies' room, one of the state troopers tried to stop me. I tussled with him a little before he hit my stomach with the butt of his rifle. Jim saw it all from our table in the dining room, rose from the table, and grabbed the officer in a bear hug, preparing to punch him. I cried for him to stop and get back to his death. But it was too late. The officer raised his rifle to bash Jim in the head.

"God be praised! A newspaper reporter standing nearby noticed all this and jumped in to interfere by tackling the trooper and protecting Jim. The trooper was shocked by this interference by a civilian and thought better of continuing so stepped back while a couple of other troopers separated the reporter from the first trooper. Jim needed to be calmed down, and then we returned to lunch with Dr. King."

"Right after lunch, Diane. We go to Dr, Fairchild's office and make sure there's no damage to you. I don't want to hear a 'no.'"

"And check on the health of the precious cargo in my innards," Diane added.

DR. KING DELIVERED A TENDER, sensitive homily at the funeral of Addie Mae, Cynthia, and Carol Denise, simultaneously acknowledging the pain and sorrow of their families and the shock and anger if the Negro community of Birmingham while also censuring the white community, especially the racist and terroristic elements, for this nefarious, willful act of racial hatred.

"But he seems more anxious than I've ever seen him before," Diane pointed out. "It's as if he's looking now and then over his shoulder for someone threatening him with a gun.

"Perhaps he did see someone behind him. First thing he told us after the funeral was that he was distracted during the whole service by a vision of a man sitting in a pew off to the side from others. 'He looked totally out of place in this predominantly Negro crowd, with his grey suit and combed salt and pepper hair held in place by Brylcreem or some other white man's hair cream, not joining in on any of the hymns.

"'I had the haunted feeling,' King had said, 'that I knew him from somewhere...or was destined to run into him again someday.'"

Chapter Twenty-Seven

It's been a long time coming.
But I know a change is gonna come, oh yes, it will.

Sam Cooke
RCA Victor, 1964

"COME ON, GUYS." LAWSON RESPONDED. "You two have been active in the Movement almost since Day One. Think of how far our people have come since you were in Little Rock. There are black kids today in desegregated schools sitting at their desks alongside white kids, even here in the South. Who would have imagined it in 1954 before *Brown v. the Board of Education*? But thanks to the bravery and smarts of our brother Thurgood, the unimaginable has become a reality."

Lucius wasn't in the mood to hear it. "But ten years later, it's still unimaginable for kids in Georgia, let me tell you. I wouldn't let my dog go into the decrepit schools that black parents in Crawfordville have to send their kids to."

"Sure, there are always going to be exceptions," Young added. "Did you really think that after these hundreds of years of slavery and the systematic pilfering of our political rights and economic prospects we were going to flip a switch and reverse all our disadvantages and open the gates to the Kingdom? I don't believe that you're so naïve, Henri."

Henri felt unfairly reproached. "God, it's been a long haul since Little Rock," he sighed. "Maybe I'm just overcome by the physical exhaustion—the irregular meals, the nights of interrupted sleep, the uncomfortable seats on the buses."

"Not to mention your thunderous snoring, brother," Lucius added in an effort to lighten the mood.

Both Lawson and Young joined Lucius in chuckling good-naturedly at Henri's expense.

Lawson made a suggestion. "It really has been a while since you got away from hotspots like Jackson and Birmingham to get some rest. Perhaps it's high time for you to go away, temporarily, of course. Reflect a bit on what you've experienced, reassess the progress of the Movement, perhaps get a better perspective on things."

Henri and Lucius looked at each other to try to gauge the other's reaction to Lawson's counsel. Henri, for one, could hear the wheels of Lucius's mind turning.

"Not many of us are built in a way that allows us to remain in the struggle nonstop without some kind of pause or intermission between rounds." Young paused before his next thought. "Maybe with the possible exception of Dr. King, but the Lord doesn't make many of ones like him. Do as Jim suggests. Go home or wherever you might find restful waters and savor them deeply," Young advised sympathetically, "but then do come back well rested and ready to assume your place in the Movement. You'll be needed here, I'm sure."

THEY DID AS LAWSON AND YOUNG advised. Lucius retrieved his car from the lot behind Ralph Abernathy's church. He drove Henri to the Birmingham train station for him to catch a train north to New York. Before he left for the drive to Atlanta, we sat down at the lunch counter to enjoy a cup of coffee. We chuckled as we could legally sit now in 1965 in any open seat and expect to be served. We were conscious of the fact that Lawson had trained many of those like John Lewis and Diane Nash whose noses had been bloodied at lunch counters in places like Nashville when they tried to find a vacant seat and be served barely a half-decade ago.

Henri and Lucius discussed the merits of Lawson and Young's advice to them.

"I'm more than ready for a break," Lucius declared. "At the beginning I had no clue of how joining the Movement would sap me of so much energy."

"That makes two of us, friend. I thought we were just going on a pleasant tour of a part of the country I had never seen before. I didn't realize that north and south are so very different, did you?"

"Well, since I was born and raised here in Dixie, and came to seminary in New York City, of all places, I had some appreciation for the differences. You know, as a southern Negro, I didn't feel that I belonged all the time I was at Union. But after all we've seen and experienced in these brief years south of the Mason-Dixon line, I'm not sure I really feel that I belong here either."

"Well, I'd like to come back. I want to accept Young's invitation someday. You folks in the land of cotton and peanuts have grown on me."

"I'll wait and see how I feel after a short time away…. But speaking of the hot sultry South. What do you hear from your girl Priscilla? How is she doing?"

"She's had her challenges. The Bevels convinced her to go to Mississippi and participate the 'Freedom Summer.'"

Lucius sounded a semi-sarcastic whistle. "How I detest the Magnolia State. A good white girl from Pennsylvania will learn a lot about the South in a place like Mississippi. I hope she survives to tell us about it."

"I didn't want her to go. We know that bad things happen in Mississippi, not just to our people but people like her who work to advance our cause. Just think of Andrew Goodman and Michael Schwerner. Chaney was murdered to be sure as well, but he was a local Negro. That didn't take much balls. But to add white guys like Goodman and Schwerner to the death toll and risk the ire of all of the American white population—that was bold and more than a little foolhardy.

"Bob Moses assigned her to Sunflower County, to a town named Leland. She recruited some help from one or two of the local parents and started a Freedom School in a Church of God in Christ building. She was teaching the children in the mornings, and then coming back in the evening to try to interest their parents and grandparents in voter education."

"Trying to? If that gem of a lady can't succeed, then no one can."

"Those folks are scared, man. Scared that if they show too much interest in learning about their right to vote, the Man who employs them for their slavery era wages will fire them. But she did persuade a few women to go up to the town hall in Leland and try to register to vote."

"That's our girl! They registered?"

"Are you kidding? The county registrar gave them the traditional literacy test, but none of these sharecroppers' wives had gone past the sixth or eighth grade. After that test, he asked them to name all eighty-two counties in the state of Mississippi. I doubt he could name them all himself. So he stamped DENIED on the front page of their applications. But before they left, Priscilla told him politely but firmly that she would bring them back the next week to apply for their voting card again. She says the women let out a determined whoop."

"Do you think they'll ever get the vote? The odds are against it."

"Priscilla says she has her doubts that they will under the current voting laws. But she cannot let on to the women that she has her doubts. The women understand that they may not succeed now, or next year, or whenever. But they've taught Priscilla that gaining the rights that belong rightly to our people will come slowly, but they will come.... I've been thinking about Priscilla's growth in the Movement, her resilient faith, her rock-bottom confidence that the ultimate victory is ours."

Lucius was listening thoughtfully but clearly a little doubtingly. He broached a new subject, one he had evidently been wondering about for some time. "I noted that you came back to bed at the Shuttlesworths' late last night. You were with Priscilla?"

"Well, it's probably none of your business, brother. But since you ask, I'll tell you. Yes, we were together for a part of that night...but I emphasize only a part. For heaven's sake, it was our last evening together before she got on the bus to Sunflower County this morning, leaving me to move on with the Movement, or whatever. We had a lot to talk about."

"Talk? That's all you did? No passionate kisses after all these months of disciplined restraint on the road? No furtive hanky-panky after being celibate all this time? Are you telling me that there wasn't even a small amount of shagging?"

Henri couldn't disguise his secret pleasure at keeping his travel buddy in a state of curious unknowingness. "As I say, it's for me to know and for you to try to find out. I'm not going to betray Priscilla's confidence. I'd rather leave you guessing."

Henri continued to chuckle to himself as the bus departed the terminal. He had managed to protect his and Priscilla's privacy. He felt a delicious flutter of warmth as he remembered his long conversation with her the previous evening. He was desperate with fear for her safety as she poured out her enthusiasm for the impending Freedom School and voter education project she was about to initiate in Mississippi. He knew this represented a big step in Priscilla's evolution as a civil rights activist. She was being entrusted with the fate and outcome of the project and was delighted with the trust invested in her by Bob Moses and the confidence of the Bevels that she could succeed at the task. But she had accepted an assignment that was well-nigh impossible: running a Freedom

School with children hardly taught in their subpar schools to read, banging her head against the odds, and keeping the small voter education classes away from the snooping eyes of the county authorities and the black neighbors who could be persuaded by threats to snitch on fellow townsfolk too eager and determined to claim the franchise. Where in that forsaken swampland would Priscilla find the support, emotional and otherwise, that she would need to face the nearly impossible? What and who would be her source of strength to rise from the ashes of failure and bitter disappointment?

Having heard and seen Priscilla's fervor for the project and commitment to the goal of an informed black electorate, Henri was sorely anxious about her but felt a slightly reduced fear for her safety.

The bus rolled on through the sandy hills and low mountains of Alabama into Tennessee. He was still thinking of Priscilla now two or three states away. He was filled with a terrible longing for her. Simultaneously, however, he was haunted by a pang of shame. She was just arriving in a western county of Mississippi, full of zeal and energy to get her feet wet and her hands dirty in a new project assigned to her. Meanwhile, he was on a bus carrying him back home because he had grumbled to senior members of the Movement that he was spent from struggle against persistent opposition and wearied of fighting on behalf of a cause whose victories seemed to him few and far between.

Chapter Twenty-Eight

What happened in Selma is part of a far larger movement: It is the effort of American Negroes to secure for themselves the full blessings of American life.

President Lyndon Baines Johnson, 1965

AFTER ALL OF JOHN LEWIS'S ELEVATED talk to them about Selma, Alabama, Henri and Lucius's first impression of the place was less than favorable.

"Isn't this just another one of those off-the-beaten-track burgs like so many we have traveled to throughout the South?" Henri asked his travel companion as their car made its way down the main drag.

Lucius felt the same way. "Just another sleepy, dying municipality that doesn't exhibit many outward signs that it will come to life again anytime soon."

There was a small collection of shops and businesses at one end of Broad Street, like the Rexall Drug Store, the El Ranchero café, and Wallace Craig's Sportsmen's Headquarters, but even they seemed to point more to the past than the future. Much of the rest of Broad Street consisted of boarded up shops and storefronts with handwritten "For Lease" notices taped to the plywood covering the windows.

At the beginning of new year 1965, Lewis, still chairman of SNCC, telephoned both Henri and Lucius imploring them to gird themselves once more for battle in support of the Movement. "You've had long enough in the comfort of your homes in Harlem and Atlanta. You should be well-rested and refreshed by now. We need you back in the fray again.

"Many of us sense that the Movement is close to reaching its climax, approaching the turning point, at least of this phase of the struggle—so close we can feel it in our bones. I tell you, we're on the cusp of breaking through and claiming victory. Jim and Diane have been organizing voter registration drives in Alabama since after the Birmingham church bombing in 1963, and they have made great strides. Our people are primed to seize the vote. As Sammy croons on the radio, 'A change is gonna come.'

"And it's in Selma that we'll see the first rays of the rising sun, I promise you. That's why we want you down here with us. We need you."

They did come, somewhat reluctantly at first, and they wondered whether they had come back to Alabama out of a sense of guilt. Henri, however, had pondered carefully the example of Priscilla and her unconditional commitment to social justice even in the sun-drenched cotton fields, mosquito-ridden swamps, and the sweaty villages and towns of Mississippi that to most looked decidedly unpromising. He felt chastened by her steadfast dedication to the goals of the Movement, unlike his sometimes participation, which often consisted only of observing events from a distance. To comply with Lewis's plea for he and Lucius to recommit to the cause now in Selma would be an opportunity to make amends to the whole Movement.

Lewis had instructed them to meet up with the others at Brown's Chapel, the venerable old house of worship on the northern edge of town. When Henri and Lucius pulled up at the chapel, they were surprised by the sight of what they estimated to be some five hundred or so marchers who were gathering in the softball field behind the school and the basketball court squeezed into the side yard.

"They must be expecting some level of official violence since it looks like they're training march volunteers how to shield themselves from the troopers' blows," Henri remarked to Lucius.

They noticed that James Bevel, his wife, Diane, and Andy Young were off to the side of the crowd, huddled together in a corner of the schoolyard that afforded them some privacy. They were talking animatedly. The distorted frown on Bevel's face was a sure giveaway that they had just heard some bad news.

Indeed, there was bad news. Dr. King, president of the chief sponsor of protests in Selma and due to arrive in Selma shortly after 2 p.m. on that Sunday. March 7 had been designated as the date to kick off the Selma demonstrations. But he had called Bevel from Atlanta to declare that the kickoff would have to be postponed until the following day.

Bevel was clearly incensed and made no secret of his displeasure at MLK's decision. He placed a call to King's home from the office at Brown's Chapel. He spoke so loudly into the phone that Henri, Lucius, and everybody else in the room could overhear.

"Dr. King, you're not in Selma, we notice to our chagrin, but if you were here, as you had planned and we expected, what you'd see are hundreds of men, women, and even children ready and eager to hit the pavement for voting rights. If we send them home now, it would be disastrous. It would feel like an abandonment, a cop-out, by the leader of the Movement."

Dr. King had given as his reason for not being able to come to Selma the fact that he had been absent much lately due to speaking engagements all over the country and had been unable to preside at worship at Ebeneezer, the Baptist congregation in Sweet Auburn, that he co-pastored with his father. He was to deliver the sermon at Ebeneezer that Sunday. As preachers themselves, Bevel and Young could appreciate the difficult tension between Dr. King's role as the public voice and face of the Movement and his love for the people of Ebeneezer and loyalty to his father.

But as he was wont to do frequently, Bevel pushed his mentor, regardless. "With all due respect to the good people of Ebeneezer, Sir, you can preach the gospel to your congregation at any time, fifty-two Sundays a year. But on this particular Sunday, to risk projecting the impression to the citizens of Selma that their long struggle to gain voting rights is anything less than your highest priority would be nothing short of catastrophic.

"Your encouragement of our attempts to persuade Malcolm X to show himself at one of our rallies or demonstrations is much appreciated. We'll have you know that he finally acquiesced to our wish. Malcolm is in Selma. Right now. That's right, the prodigal has come to Selma, prepared to take advantage. Malcolm delivered an impassioned message at a rally last night. Many of us were wary and nervous about how far he would go in defending his program of militant black power and belittling our philosophy of nonviolent resistance. For the most part our concern was unnecessary because Malcolm was surprisingly mellow as Malcolm goes. But will his mellowness last? Our concern and nervousness would be rather heightened were he to catch wind of your sudden absence from Selma today. Do you think he could resist the temptation of labeling the man many of these people consider to be Malcolm's chief rival as a coward whenever the people are facing violent pushback by the authorities?"

Bevel continued in a similar vein until Andy Young made a choke gesture at his throat with his right hand. Bevel looked confused but ended the call as Young requested.

"Jim, you've made your point, only you don't know the whole picture. Dr. King received another threat on his life on the telephone last night. The caller said that if Dr. King showed his face in Selma today, he and his white power friends would blow his head off."

"He's had those kinds of threats before, yet he didn't let a bunch of crazed yahoos stop him," Bevel growled angrily. "What makes Selma any different?"

"Yes, Jim, you're right. Dr. King has not let any threats on his life deter him from moving the campaign forward. But the enemy knows that we may be on the verge of success now in Selma. Just like his master, Satan, the green-eyed demon feels more threatened than ever and is more likely to pull the trigger. I think Dr. King knows that. I've noticed that in recent months he's been making more and more comments about his possible death. It makes Coretta very anxious and blue...and some of us, too. He seems more convinced than I have seen him that a violent death at the hands of those who oppose him is inevitable."

Chapter Twenty-Nine

"John, can you swim?"

Rev. Hosea Williams
Edmund Pettus Bridge, 1965

Selma, Alabama, March 7, 1965

Jim Bevel made a colossal effort to persuade King to at least not wait until the next day but to come to Selma this afternoon. "It's absolutely imperative, Sir, that those who have come to Selma to demonstrate, and the local citizens who are here to support them, see the iconic personification if the struggle at the very front of the procession."

That occasioned another emergency telephone call between Bevel at Brown's Chapel and King in Sweet Auburn after church on Sunday.

"Jim, as always you put forward a convincing argument. It's certainly not the case that I don't want to come to Selma today, as many will undoubtedly be thinking, nor that I am making myself scarce in case the march turns violent, tarnishing the reputation of the SCLC, as Brother Malcolm likes to point out. Your persuasive argument notwithstanding, it doesn't change the reality that I simply cannot be in Selma today. Just tell the people the truth of the matter, and let them think what they want of me and my decision....But, Jim, I want to commend you and your wife, Diane, for the exemplary work you have done these past two years with the voter registration drive in central Alabama. You have laid a strong foundation for the larger march and demonstration we'll commence there tomorrow."

"Thank you, Dr. King," said Bevel. "That's precisely why I am so anxious that you be here as soon as possible. The people look to you to lead them and speak on their behalf."

"As I say, Jim, I will be there tomorrow afternoon to seek the blessing of the Almighty for the march and success of our goal of moving the elected officials of Dallas and adjacent counties, and then the governor and legislature of the state of Alabama to ensure that the laws concerning voting are fair and just so that not one Negro citizen be barred or discouraged from exercising their right as guaranteed in the Fourteenth Amendment to the Constitution of the

United States."

"Sir, the marchers and their supporters will find that goal more credible if they heard those words addressed to them by the President of the SCLC."

"It doesn't matter who speaks those words. They are full of the truth in any case."

"The people look to you to lead them and guide them."

"Jim, you need to learn that an important dimension of leadership is to discern when to take an active role and when to step back from the front of the parade. That's what I have discerned is my call today. The Movement is blessed bountifully with gifted leaders. Tell Andy that I request him to meet with several of them today in the next hour and choose among yourselves who will march at the head of the procession out of Selma in the direction of Montgomery. Tell him to invite people like you and Diane, C.T. Vivian, Joe Lowery, or Hosea Williams…. But tell Andy not to invite Jesse. Jesse is a good leader, but a bit too ambitious to promote his own personal agenda, I'm afraid."

THUS IT WAS THAT AN HOUR and a quarter later on March 7, John Lewis and Hosea Williams led a procession of hundreds of people, many still decked out in their Sunday suits and dresses and hats, off the Brown's Chapel grounds in the direction of Highway 80, which leads to Montgomery.

Both Henri and Lucius had been recruited the day before to serve as team captains for the march, each responsible for attending to a dozen or so marchers. John Lewis told Henri that the captains were to keep an eye on the mood of the marchers assigned to them to make sure there was no violence.

As the orderly crowd was marching down Water Street, Henri remarked to one of his group, Lonnie Douglas, a quiet Baptist Deacon, "I've only been on a half-dozen civil rights marches, but this one feel different. The mood is more subdued. You notice that there's none of the usual defiant singing of civil rights songs and the laughter after each song? Doesn't this march feel a bit like a funeral procession, as though we marchers sense that some something life-changing has happened here in Selma or is about to?"

Lonnie didn't respond right away but eventually said, "This is my first march, but a bunch of us have been demonstrating for the vote many nights in front of the county courthouse. Frankly, if it feels like a funeral procession, I don't care. As long as at the end of the march we have received a pledge from the Dallas County registrar of elections that in the next election for President of these here United States they don't impose an exorbitant poll tax on us folks before they let us vote."

As the marchers stepped off Water Street onto the imposing Edmund Pettus Bridge that spanned the Alabama River below, as instructed, the team captains reminded their team members to be careful not to step onto the road but to stay on the sidewalk because the county had closed the bridge to automobile and pedestrian traffic.

One team captain shouted out, "The next time we apply to the county for a permit to conduct a march, we want to be able to say, 'We don't violate any of the county laws and ordinances.'"

Lucius complained that the bridge was very steep for pedestrians. Several members of his team recited "Amen." As leaders of the procession, Lewis and Williams were the first to reach the stylized steel canopy at the pinnacle of the bridge. They looked down through the metal grate to see the brown Alabama River.

Only then did they notice the unexpected obstacle at the end of the bridge across the sleeping river. Lewis stopped in his tracks abruptly. So, too, did Williams. Their hearts must have jumped to their throats. At the end of the bridge facing them stood a sea of blue-helmeted, blue-uniformed Alabama state troopers, line after line of them, dozens of battle-ready officers stretched from one side of the highway to the other.

Both Lewis and Williams craned their necks to look behind them. A solid wall of marchers in rows two-by-two.

"Can you swim?" Williams asked Lewis, perhaps facetiously, but Lewis was known to be an earnest fellow on whom Williams' attempt at gallows humor was wasted.

"I think we should pray," Lewis suggested instead of answering Williams' question.

"That's a good idea, young fellow. I can't swim worth a lick," Williams agreed.

Lewis burst out laughing at that timely confession.

Before Williams had assented, Lewis was on his knees on the hard sidewalk, sparking imitation from many of the marchers behind them. Henri followed suit and said a private prayer for safety that he had uttered several times before in his and Lucius's run-ins with threatening local yahoos in Little Rock or nasty law enforcement officers in Mississippi.

Behind the rows of state troopers, just coming into view, were a dozen or so armed men, County Sheriff Clark's posse, according to one man among the marchers. Henri learned later that Sheriff was notorious among the blacks of Dallas County for his lack of empathy and disregard for fairness.

Lewis and Williams resumed the march, perhaps marginally more slowly than before.

About fifty feet from the bottom of the bridge, the officer in charge of the troopers stepped forward and pronounced through a loudspeaker, "This is an unlawful assembly. Your march is not conducive for public safety. You are ordered to disperse and go home or back to your church."

Lewis said quietly to Williams, "I'm not going to turn around. We have come this far."

Williams agreed. "We're not going to run and go back. We can't go back even if we wanted to. There are too many people behind us."

The officer in charge of the troopers raised the bullhorn to his lips and reiterated his previous order for the marchers to disband. Only this time he set a strict time limit, saying, "You have two minutes to go back to your church or your homes."

Several of the marchers near the front noticed a new potentially threatening development. "Look. There he is, Sheriff Clark, coming out of his vehicle, and approaching the trooper officer giving the orders. I wonder what he has up his sleeve."

Clark spoke only a few words with the officer.

Very shortly after Clark had returned to the shelter of his cruiser, the officer pointed the bullhorn in the direction of the rows of troopers and shouted: "Troopers advance!"

Suddenly, the air above the bridge was filled with the clunk of the troopers' heavy boots on the highway, the whoops of the rebel yells from the white onlookers along the side of the highway, and the clip clop of horses' hooves hitting the hard asphalt.

Above the din, Lucius heard the shrill voice of a woman encouraging the troopers, "Get 'em! Get the niggers!"

Henri was unnerved as he observed a particularly husky trooper rushing toward Lewis lying on the ground, standing over him and swinging his billy club against the left side of the head of the defenseless Lewis. Lewis raised his arm to shield himself from the blow. Lewis's legs buckled, and he fell before the feet of the zealous trooper who struck Lewis in the head one more time for good measure.

Suddenly, Henri, like Lucius, heard something that sounded like gunshots. "Damn," Henri uttered. "They're shooting tear gas cannisters!"

Many of the marchers began choking and coughing violently. They couldn't get any oxygen into their lungs. Many fell instantaneously to the pavement like hay that was being mown, too overcome by the C-4 gas to get up. Too many to count were vomiting up the contents of their Sunday brunch. Small groups of troopers searched among the prone bodies and, upon finding one, hit him or her with one last swing of a billy club. Several of Sheriff Clark's posse were mounted on horses and rode them purposely over some of the injured and fallen marchers, bringing the animals' hooves down on shoulders, stomachs, and legs.

Henri crawled on a grass median to try to find Lewis. When he did find him, Lewis was sprawled on his back. His head was bleeding badly. Even with pooling over his eyes, he recognized Henri.

"I am sure that I am going to die here, Henri, probably of a head wound or a massive loss of blood. I just want to close my eyes right here and now and enter into my promised eternal rest. I've done all that I can."

"Hush, now, John. This no place to die. Don't use up all your precious energy now. You're going to need every ounce of it to rise and make your way off this plot of land. Let's get you back to Brown's Chapel. Lucius or someone else there who has a car can take you to a hospital to be put back together again. Come on, John, try to get up. I'll help you find a ride to the Chapel."

Henri carried Lewis over his right shoulder away from Highway 80. He took a reasonably clean handkerchief out of his suit pocket and tried to place it over the wound on Lewis's head. Henri approached a man and his wife on the street who were just unlocking the doors of his Chrysler and preparing to get in to begin their drive home. Seeing the bloodied condition of Lewis, the man was more than helpful in his willingness to take Lewis back to Brown's Chapel but would see to it that John is admitted into Good Samaritan Hospital, the only one in Selma that admitted blacks as patients. They delivered Henri back to Brown's Chapel.

The inside of Brown's Chapel was awash with the sounds of

groaning and weeping. Mothers were shouting out for their misplaced children and children were crying out for their mothers and fathers and brothers and sisters whom they could not find. Wives were holding injured husbands in their arms. And unattached men were erupting in anger at the troopers and Clark's mounted posse.

Several men talked audibly about going back home to retrieve weapons and guns. "They're killing us like sitting ducks."

At those words, Hosea Williams winced. He decided to get the people's attention and try to calm the fear and anger in the room that was threatening to get out of control. "Folks, good people. My dear friends, I know the situation today looks bad. I don't deny it but let me assure you. It will be well. I and many others have seen this in the Struggle before. There are no easy victories in the Struggle. Brother Lewis, Praise the Lord, is recovering from his wounds in Good Samaritan Hospital. Tomorrow Dr. King will be here to replace Brother Lewis at the head of our procession. See how God is providing for us. Put your trust and hope in the Lord that he will provide victory the next time as He always has. Back on the road to Montgomery again tomorrow and on to God's victory. He shall overcome!"

Chapter Thirty

The events in Selma galvanized public opinion and mobilized Congress to pass the Voting Rights Act, which President Johnson signed into law on August 6, 1965. Today, the bridge that served as the backdrop to "Bloody Sunday" still bears the name of a white supremacist, but now it is a symbolic civil rights landmark.

Christopher Klein
How Selma's 'Bloody Sunday' Became a Turning Point in the
Civil Rights Movement

Selma, Alabama, March 9, 1965

The next morning, March 8, Henri woke up disoriented. He scanned the fellowship hall for any sign of Lucius. Henri went out to the field adjacent to Brown's Chapel, which the crowd of the previous day had converted into a parking lot for their cars and pickup trucks. Henri was confused when he saw that Lucius's car was in the lot, but it seemed he was nowhere to be found inside Brown's Chapel. In all the pandemonium and turmoil that was incited when the order had been given to the state troopers to advance on the six hundred marchers on the bridge, Henri could possibly have lost track of Lucius. Had Lucius been injured in the skirmishes and been taken to the Good Samaritan Hospital like John Lewis and several dozen other marchers?

Most of the successful participants on March 7 (that is, those who made it back to Brown's Chapel without debilitating injury) were gone from Selma by the next morning. These were working people, either in the small factories in town, or the tenant farms they rented and worked out in the counties. Most had jobs to go back to on Monday. But still lingering over second or third cups of coffee at Brown's Chapel were some marchers who had come to march but had no way to get home.

Once most of those needed at their place of employment had departed and the crowd of those remaining had thinned out, Henri was able to spot Lucius looking tired but chuckling among a group of marchers.

"Hey, traveling buddy. I wasn't sure whether I'd still find you here."

"I've had just about enough of Selma, to be truthful," Lucius said. "There's been enough excitement here in one afternoon as in a month of Sundays in any other town in the South. I think I'm getting too old for too many more days of this kind of agitation and restiveness."

"Speaking of which, have you taken a look at this morning's newspaper? The stories on what they're dubbing Bloody Sunday are pretty accurate. Did you by chance catch ABC's footage of the aborted march yesterday? It was just what Dr. King, Abernathy, and Andy Young ordered. Fifteen, almost twenty, minutes of nonstop film footage of heavily armed state troopers assaulting a peaceful march by blacks who made no effort to defend themselves, much less strike back. The American people may be getting accustomed to seeing this sort of thing and may be ready to come to their own conclusions about what they see with their eyes.

"*The News* even included a short article by one of their correspondents to the effect that it was none other than Governor George Wallace who ordered the Alabama state troopers to be present, to quote Wallace, to 'protect the calm and preserve the peace in Selma.' It was Wallace, the reporter found, who gave the premature order for them to advance en masse on us sacrificial lambs being led to the slaughter on the bridge."

Henri could sense that Lucius had been working up to some sort of sarcastic retort that would epitomize his growing despair about the white resistance in this country. "I hear that Wallace is actually fixin' to try to gain a monopoly of the black vote in Alabama once they grab the right the vote, which, as I understand it, he thinks is inevitable, given what he judges is a namby-pamby, wishy-washy, east coast liberal appeasers."

"Watch it, friend. I happen to believe that JFK and RFK have done a lot to further King's agenda. So has LBJ, for that matter."

"Not every black person is as enthusiastic about the northeastern establishment. But, be that as it may, tell me about Priscilla. Hadn't she said when she left for Mississippi that she might resume her involvement in Dr. King's campaigns once her work with the Bevels is done? After all, the Bevels are here now."

"Funny that you should ask on this particular morning of all mornings. Priscilla telephoned from the bus station in Jackson early this morning to say that she's about to board the bus. She says she should be here in Selma late this afternoon or early this evening—as she often suffixes onto the end of her plans: "If the creek don't rise."

"Well, then. We'll have to encourage prayers for clear blue skies, plenty of sunshine, and no more than a ten percent chance of rain."

PRISCILLA HADN'T EVEN DESCENDED the last step from the Greyhound onto the floor of the deboarding platform before she had reported to the waiting Henri. "As soon as we heard the news about Sunday's catastrophe on the bridge here in Selma, a group of us summer freedom fighters headed immediately for Bob Moses' tiny office in Jackson to inquire about participating in the campaign in Selma."

Henri embraced her and helped her get situated on the platform. "Priss, you're a sight for sore eyes. I have missed you terribly."

"Not as much as I missed you in Mississippi. Oh, Henri, it's good to see you, too, after a summer apart."

"Congratulations, Priss, you made it through a whole summer in Mississippi."

Priscilla wasn't entirely sure whether or not Henri's remark was symptomatic of his original skepticism about the wisdom of a white college grad from Ardmore, PA, immersing herself in the politically and racially taut conditions in the deepest part of the South.

"Are your congratulations because you weren't really convinced that I could survive down here all on my own?"

"No, I'm genuinely impressed and mean the congratulations sincerely.... But you have to acknowledge that there were times when you were made to feel terribly out of place among the rednecks down here, a few occasions when you felt threatened. Like that time when a local yokel tried to grab you as you were leaving the secluded phone booth on the edges of Indianola. He called you a white whore and yelled that you were screwing black troublemakers. Didn't you write to tell me that you managed to escape his clutches just barely by the skin of your teeth?"

"OK, Henri." She said this testily and held up her palms to him to warn him to back off.

He was taken aback by her sudden change of mood.

"Henri, if I knew you would use incidents like that against me, I probably wouldn't have told you about it.... That close call was a part of my learning. All summer I never ventured out alone again on a dark street in an unfamiliar town. See, I'm capable of learning from my mistakes."

Henri could have kicked himself, not for what he had said but for the magnitude of his expectations. It was unfair to both of them to expect that things would go as smoothly between them as the last time they met. "I'm sorry, Priss. I haven't been with you for weeks. This is no time to pick for starting a fight. Can we just declare a truce and enjoy being with each other again?"

AS HENRI INTUITED, THE public reaction to Bloody Sunday was immediate. By Sunday midnight, people from as far away as Massachusetts, Minnesota, and New Mexico were flying to Alabama and renting vehicles to drive to Selma and hold impromptu vigils of their own outside Brown's Chapel or were preparing to. A beleaguered President Johnson had appeared before a national television audience to decry the violence committed in Selma. Andy Young telephoned Dr. King in Atlanta one more time to report on the day's happenings and seek direction for the next few days.

'Why, by all means, Andy, we'll have another march tomorrow or the next day. We've made significant progress today. Clark and Wallace played tight into our hands. Thank God no marcher was killed. I don't want to put anyone in the path of danger and injury, but let's go up to the U.S. Justice Department in Montgomery in the morning and request a federal injunction barring any more state interference."

The federal judge appointed by the DOJ to consider the petition for an injunction imposed a restraining order against march organizers before he could preside at a hearing. He would not rule on the petition before then, and the earliest a hearing could be scheduled was Thursday. Predictably, Bevels and several other SCLC leaders were frustrated by another delay. If Dr. King was bothered by the restraining order, it did not show in his serene demeanor. In a development that reportedly surprised even some of his closest lieutenants, Dr. King led a column of two thousand marchers from Brown's Chapel in violation of the judge's restraining order, and Lucius recognized that they were headed once again toward the Edmund Pettus Bridge at the end of Water Street.

"I can't believe this," a disbelieving Lucius uttered aloud. "Why in the name of heaven would King be leading us over the same bridge where many were beaten to a pulp just two short days ago?"

However, Henri noticed the look of confidence and almost serenity in the faces of Young and Hosea Williams that indicated either they and other march leaders were paying no attention to the route, or else were cognizant of it but felt that Dr. King was a competent captain steering the ship. Henri put his anxiety aside.

But not for long. At the crest of Highway 80, the marchers near the front of the procession like Henri could peer down the length of the bridge and see the blue-clad Alabama state troopers in formation and ready for the order from their superior to crush the marchers. King slowed his pace but did not stop. Henri caught sight of Dallas County Sheriff Clark through the window of a Sheriff Department cruiser, waiting presumably for the chaos and vitriol to be unleashed by the troopers as soon as the order was given.

Like Moses in the Red Sea, King raised his right arm for the signal to the marchers to come to a halt. He announced that they would pause to pray just as Lewis and Williams had done. Following some minutes of silent prayer on the sidewalk, one could barely hear a group of women join their voices together to sing several stanzas of "We Shall Overcome." The singing became more audible as men added their tenor and bass voices until the anthem swelled in the late afternoon.

Henri had his fists clenched, not necessarily to land a knockout punch against a trooper but to be prepared to strike a defensive pose once the blows of a trooper attacked as Henri was certain one would at the officer's command.

But the command to the troopers was to *retreat*. The lines of troopers obeyed. They moved to allow the marchers to finish crossing the bridge and proceed east toward Montgomery. Just as the troopers made way for the marchers to proceed, Dr. King suddenly reversed course and led the procession across the bridge and back onto Water Street toward Brown's Chapel where they had started.

Each evening after March 9, public rallies, each one larger than the prior one, were held at Brown's Chapel. MLK was usually the primary speaker. One evening King announced that earlier that day federal judge Frank Johnson had lifted the restraining order against a march from Selma to Montgomery and ruled that he would grant an injunction against state interference to such a march. Henri and Lucius were among the ecstatic crowd in Brown's Chapel to cheer the legal victory.

Dr. King praised the marchers for their courage to put their lives on the line and thanked the supporters. "But now is not the time to rest in our victories," MLK told the crowd. "We are too close to ultimate victory now to allow ourselves to grow complacent. We will march again starting on March 21, to Montgomery, but this time beyond Montgomery but also the legislature of all fifty states and the halls of Congress in Washington until the right to vote by our people is guaranteed and protected as already assured by the United States Constitution. Tonight I call on every justice-loving American, black and white, from Alabama to New York State and places in between to come here to Selma to cement the victory."

Chapter Thirty-One

Selma is such a place. In one afternoon fifty years ago, so much of our turbulent history—the stain of slavery and anguish of civil war; the yoke of segregation and tyranny of Jim Crow; the death of four little girls in Birmingham; and the dream of a Baptist preacher—all that history met on this bridge.

President Barack Obama

ONE OF THOSE WHO CAME TO SELMA from some distance was one Viola Liuzzo of Detroit, Michigan, a homemaker and mother of several young children, wife of an official of a trade union, a sometime college student—one of the few in that time beyond the traditional age. Upon Viola's arrival in Selma after an eight-hundred-and-twenty-mile drive, seeing that she had an automobile, a group of march organizers assigned her to a team of volunteers responsible for transporting marchers from beyond Dallas County. Some well-known celebrities drove their own vehicles to Selma, but many arrived at Selma Municipal Airport: LBJ's attorney-general Ramsey Clark, entertainers such as Harry Belafonte, Lena Horne, Peter, Paul, and Mary, the Chad Mitchell Trio, Sammy Davis, Jr., Sydney Poitier, Tony Bennett, Leonard Berstein. Odetta, Shelley Winters, and Anthony Perkins, to name a few. They would need rides to and from the airport, as would members of Congress, and likewise, the estimated several hundred Roman Catholic clergy, Protestant ministers, and Jewish rabbis.

Priscilla hadn't been assigned to any particular team or group yet. Although she was hoping to be assigned to Henri's team, and thus enjoy marching to Montgomery hand-in-hand with him, she didn't protest when she was told that she would make a good partner for Viola to accompany her on runs to and from the airport. The volunteer director's characterization of the Michigan homemaker was colorful enough to fascinate her so looked forward to getting to know this woman better.

"Hello, you must be Viola. I'm very pleased to be together with you. I very much look forward to hearing the stories of some of the people we will be transporting to and from the airport," Priscilla said by way of introduction.

Viola held the front passenger door of her Oldsmobile open for

Priscilla who made herself comfortable.

"Where'd you come from to Selma?" Viola seemed very curious. "I can tell you ain't one of the locals but you've had some exposure to these Crackers."

"How can you tell?"

"Why, it's a simple process of elimination. So many of the marchers are from somewhere other than the South that the chances are you are also. But I can tell you've had plenty of exposure to the subtleties of Cracker life."

"You're right again. I traveled here today by bus from Jackson, Mississippi. I'm not from there, but I did spend several summers there. Trying to motivate blacks in Sunflower County to register to vote in the next election."

"Wow! You're a genuine folk hero to me, putting your life on the line here in the South and fighting for the right to vote for people who have been prevented from doing so by the white powers-that-be who like to run things they please. I mean it when say I have a deep respect for your courage and gumption."

"It's Doctor King who keeps reminding us in the Movement not to paint all white people with a broad brush as hopelessly racist. So I try to do as he says. After all, they have been open to the likes of you and me to make a difference even though our skin is white."

"When a field worker from CORE came to Wayne State to recruit college students to come participate in the Freedom Summer in Mississippi, I was this close to signing the dotted line on impulse. But I remembered that I have a husband who works long hours for the union and five little ones at home. I couldn't just get up and leave them for Ole' Miss and say goodbye for a few months. Are you married, Priscilla?"

"Well, I thought I had successfully found the man to build a life and have babies with, but I don't want to rush him. Maybe you'll get to meet him here in Selma. He's here even though we haven't had a chance to find each other so far."

"Where did you meet him?"

"On the Freedom Rides of '62. He's a great black guy from Harlem who was touring sites of the Struggle throughout the South with his classmate from theological seminary."

"Oh, a preacher, is he? Kind of dependable, I bet. The way you describe him and the tone of romance in your voice tells me you had better nab him before some other babe does. Such a good man is hard to find...and harder to keep."

"Henri is quite a deliberate, cautious guy when it comes to women, at least this woman. He loves me alright, I know, but he may not be ready to settle down and commit to one person."

Back in February, Viola and her black neighbor were watching television news footage of a demonstration for black voting rights at the southern courthouse in Marion, Alabama, near Selma. The demonstration had started peacefully when it suddenly turned very violent. Alabama state troopers started clubbing and whipping demonstrators and, in the case of a young local black civil rights activist, Jimmy Lee Jackson, shooting him dead on the pavement.

"Me and Eula were horrified by the unprovoked violence in the clear light of day in Marion. Yet the white leaders have the gall to call the black demonstrators 'enemies of the public peace' by exercising their right to express their protest by legal means. It was as clear as day to us that it was the governor and sheriff's assembled forces that were both the instigators and perpetrators of the hellish violence."

"I know the demonstration you mean," Priscilla said. "The one in which Jimmy Lee was killed. It was shameful, pure and simple."

"You know, I've had just about enough of racial demonstrations in the past few years to be shocked and scandalized by such repressive measures to be infuriated, but rarely overcome by disappointment or despair. Somehow, by my faith, I guess, I am able to still keep faith and hope. But that bloodbath in Marion was the straw that broke this camel's back, and I knew I had to do something."

"I recognize the feeling," said Priscilla.

"That's not all. Several weeks later me and Eula were watching the news on TV about the violence against the marchers at the bridge over the river in Selma. That convinced me that I had to add whatever little contribution I can make to further the cause of the Movement in Selma. I took part in a demonstration by Wayne State students to raise support for a third Selma march the following Sunday. After that demonstration, I heard a closed-circuit broadcast of Dr. King appealing to all justice-loving people, black and white, Protestant or Catholic or Jewish, to gather in Selma to demonstrate to freedom-loving people everywhere that the American people are united in their determination to break the old tradition and grip of white supremacy by peaceful means.

"I took Dr. King's appeal as a personal one targeted for me," Viola said. "'The struggle is everybody's fight,' MLK had said. Before the sun had set in Detroit that very evening, I telephoned my husband to inform him that I had made arrangements with Eula to look after the kids, and that I'll be heading south on I-75 toward Selma, Alabama.

"How did your husband react to that news?"

"I think he understands how deeply I feel about all this…heaven knows I've beat his ear about it for a long time. My husband is a good man and, thank God, not like my ex," Viola confessed, then used a handkerchief from her purse to wipe tears from her eyes.

March 21, 1965

The sheriff and other Dallas County officials might have wished that King and the other leaders of the march might have been satisfied with successfully crossing the Edmund Pettus Bridge, having a clear way to Montgomery to claim victory, and then dispensing with the whole notion of completing the march to Montgomery. Not so. On the morning of March 21, the marchers gathered in greater number than before at Brown's Chapel to launch another attempt to cross the bridge and head for Montgomery.

Campsites had been prepared for the marchers on the properties of supportive farmers, some of them white and willing to risk violent retribution from the local klavern of the Ku Klux Klan.

On the first night, there were few marchers who needed or wanted to turn home; the SCLC paid for overnight accommodations in a motel for Viola and Priscilla.

On the second night, there was a knocking on the door outside Viola and Priscilla's motel room.

Startled, Priscilla looked at Viola, wondering if there in the middle of Alabama they should risk answering.

"Hello, who is it?" Viola inquired through the closed door.

Priscilla was holding her breath for fear of making a sound.

"I regret to disturb your privacy so late in the evening, ladies. My name is James Orange, the Reverend James Orange of the SCLC, and I come out of a serious concern for your safety."

While Rev. Orange was speaking, Viola recalled his name and whispered to Priscilla that he was legitimate and to open the door to let him in.

Orange wasted no time with small talk. "As I say, I beg your pardon for disturbing your quiet time. Thank you for trusting me into your motel room. As you drive marchers to the Selma to the Airport, I have no doubts about your driving skills. Likewise, I have confidence in your competence in navigating through the Alabama farmland. But you need to know, and this is why I came here, that down here the Klansmen rule the roads at night. Their favorite target for intimidation is two unattached women in a car, especially two attractive women in a car with out of state license tags. Particularly Yankee tags. Do you understand what I mean?"

Viola and Priscilla glanced at each other apprehensively. "We are so proud to have a role to play in this campaign that I admit we haven't given much thought to the possibility of physical violence by the Ku Klux Klan," Viola humbly confessed. "We've read about the Klan in our schoolbooks up north, of course," Priscilla added.

"The Klan finds their entertainment in intimidating us black Americans, but what they revel in even more is frightening the shit out of white people, if you'll pardon my French, especially white women from the north."

The women were genuinely grateful to Orange for his errand of mercy. "Before I leave, let me ask: Do you have a black male friend here in Alabama upon whom you could prevail to ride in your car with you as you transport marchers to the airport? There is no guarantee of safety in any case for us black people on Southern highways. But our thinking is that a black male in your car with you might discourage some rednecks from messing with you."

The women were rendered silent after Orange left. They were embarrassed that as two grown, competent women, they needed to be reminded by a man to think through the possible consequences of their haste to accept the assignment offered by the SCLC. They felt a little like naïve freshmen at college.

"Priscilla, do you know any other black man whom we can ask to help us as Orange suggests? Do we really have a choice?"

Priscilla looked away from her roommate and remained absolutely silent.

"I think you do, girl. Will you ask Henri tomorrow?"

After a long silence, Priscilla mumbled an answer. "Well, I can try…assuming I can find him in the march."

HENRI WAS JUST ONE OF MORE THAN THREE THOUSAND people participating in the march. Methodically, Priscilla looked for her love unsuccessfully among the marchers closest to her. *Finding Henri in this huge crowd is like finding a needle in a haystack.*

Priscilla went from one small group of marchers to another, asking if anyone had seen or encountered a "handsome, urbane thirty-fiveish gentleman from Harlem, most likely wearing a white clerical collar with a black clergy shirt."

People responded courteously, but no one recalled seeing or meeting such a person. "Frankly, sister, there are a lot of priests on this march, even one or two who are handsome and urbane. I'm sorry I'm not able to help you very much. I hope you find him," responded one well-dressed woman with an obvious Yankee accent.

On Wednesday night, Priscilla came back to the motel still without Henri's agreement to serve as the women's chaperone, or perhaps his suggestion of someone else. On Thursday night, the caravan of marchers arrived at a point just four miles from the state capitol. The number of marchers had almost doubled since the first day. But it was easier for Priscilla to look for Henri because the marchers had thinned out along the highway for the "Night of the Stars" celebration in which they were entertained by many of the artists and celebrities including Harry Belafonte and Joan Baez who had joined the parade of marchers.

Priscilla stepped back, squinted, and scanned the crowd from across the highway. She was so accustomed night after night to not catching even so much as an ephemeral hint of Henri that she quickly quit the watch. Then she remembered that the next day, March 25, the procession would come to its destination in front of the Alabama state capitol, and there would likely be a high demand for transport to the airport afterwards, meaning this was the last chance to connect with Henri. She resumed scanning the crowd extra thoroughly. This time, Priscilla's patience and persistence paid dividends; she caught sight of Henri in the midst of a group near a campfire.

Henri saw Priscilla approaching. *Something is bothering Priss. She is not running toward me as she did the first time, we saw each other at the Selma bus terminal. A smile is on her face, but it's so forced, so tinged with anxiety somehow. Something must be wrong. I know it.*

In spite of his concern about what was bothering Priscilla, Henri would not allow his own uneasiness to detract from his joy of seeing her.

Affectionately placing an arm on her shoulders, Henri said, "Man, Priss, you're a sight for sore, lonely eyes."

"Henri, I've missed you more than you can imagine. I was about to give up finding you on this march."

"Oh, is that what explains the worried or melancholy look on your pretty face that I saw as you were crossing the highway, that you were frustrated by not being able to find me?"

"Yes, exactly. But I'm over it now. I found you."

Henri didn't find her answer altogether convincing. Yes, the aspect of melancholy had disappeared from her face. But she still seemed uncharacteristically stiff and uneasy.

"Why don't I believe you are completely over whatever was bothering you? Are you not glad we're together again?"

She was irritated. "Henri, how could you ask such a stupid question? I thought you understood me better than that? I've looked frantically all over for you."

"Priss, I'm sorry if I am making such a big deal of a confusing look on your face. I should drop the matter. But when I saw that look, I was frankly disappointed. No, concerned. I've been trying to understand what it means."

"But since you won't drop it, and you insist on cross-examining me about it," she said testily, "I'll tell you some more about my anxiety. I know how meaningful it is for you to have been asked to be a group captain on this march."

Henri took his arm from around Priscilla's shoulders abruptly. "Well, now I'm really perplexed. You're right it is meaningful for me. Why does my finding the captaincy meaningful to have been a cause of your anxiety? I'd think that would make you happy and proud."

"It does, Sweetie."

"Then what the hell is the problem?"

In all their time together on buses, at Parchman prison, she had never heard him utter an expletive in anger, and it gave Priscilla pause before she responded.

"The whole time I've been looking for you these past few days, I've been a bundle of nerves because I have something to ask you that might make it necessary for you to choose between me and your position with the march."

"Surely, you're not afraid that I would not choose you after all the experiences we've gone through together this summer?"

"Admittedly, part of me is afraid of precisely that…not because I don't believe you don't love me, but because I know how much you love the Movement."

Puzzled by her inference, Henri was taken aback.

"Come on, Henri, don't look as if you don't know what I'm talking about. I've seen how much you have sacrificed for the Movement. How loyal and faithful you've been to the principles and ideals and how respectful of Dr. King and the other leaders. How you felt that to be included among the captains of the march was to be given a seat at the table with the decision-makers. How proud you were to have come south as a relative outsider and now to be this close to the inner circle."

"I still don't understand why you are afraid that my commitment to the Movement might interfere with my love and commitment to you."

"Henri, I've been assigned by the march leadership to accompany another white female volunteer in driving marchers to the airport and train station for their return journey home after the march. Dr. King's assistant, Rev. James Orange, came to Viola's and my motel room to suggest to us in no uncertain terms that we need to recruit a male companion to sit with us in Viola's car to dissuade any Klan highwaymen from doing harm to us—preferably a black male companion."

"I don't see what good a black male companion would do to fend off the Klan. Given the Klan's mindset, wouldn't they interpret such a scenario as a case of an uppity nigger getting two pieces of white ass?"

"That's not how Rev. Orange put it. The black male in the car is meant to be a show of strength against the Klan. Viola and I are pretty persuaded that it's necessary for our safety on these Alabama roads."

"And you suggested me to be your ride-along protector?"

"Well, yes, your name was the first to come up. The only name, to be more accurate."

"Priss, I'm flattered, but I can't do it. First of all, do I have any experience as a bodyguard? Do I look like some intimidating dude from the 'hood who would strike fear in the heart of a Klansman armed to the teeth?"

"But we think you would be a deterrent."

"Look, Priss. The march is due to end in a couple of days in

Montgomery. I'm a hundred percent committed to arriving there on March 25 with the marchers in my unit. The march leadership expects that of me. Perhaps when the march is completed, I can help you and your friend. How's that?"

Priscilla was downhearted. "So you're saying you won't ride with us tomorrow night after the march?"

She looked at Henri as he slowly shook his head. "I'm sorry to disappoint you, Priss, but I can't do it."

"It's just as I feared and expected. I'm sorry to make you have to choose. How could I expect you to choose a relationship with me over the doors you hope will open to you in the Movement?"

Chapter Thirty-Two

Somewhere I have read of the freedom of assembly. Somewhere I read about the freedom of speech. Somewhere I read about the freedom of the press. Somewhere I read that the greatness of America is the right to protest for right. We aren't going to let dogs or water hoses turn us around. We aren't going to let any injunction turn us around. We are going on.

Dr. Martin Luther King, Jr.
Memphis, TN, April 3, 1968

February 1, 1968

"Hello, is this the Reverend Henri Esper?"

"Just as surely as every Pope is Italian."

At that, the Reverend James Bevel burst out in his characteristic jolly laughter. "Still the same old Henri Esper of Harlem, I can hear. I'm glad to reach you. I want to talk with you."

"Uh-oh. That might be bad news."

"Just hear me out before you jump to a conclusion. What have you been up to since I saw you last in Selma?"

"Just preachin' the Word. Tryin' to remind folks that the Lord has expectations of his children."

"Amen to that, Brother Esper. Been tryin' to do the same."

"How's that gorgeous woman of yours, Jim?"

Bevel was silent for a moment. "Takin' good care of herself and little angelic Sherri."

"You guys have two little Bevels now?"

"Yes, somewhere between voters' drives and lunch counter sit-ins and meetings of all her committees, Diane has managed to squeeze a little time to drop two babies into the world. But…"

"But what, Jim?"

"But…we may have reached the end of our bliss. We are getting divorced after I get back from the sanitation workers' strike in Memphis."

This time Henri grew silent on his end. "You and Diane seemed so well suited for each other. I'm totally speechless at the news."

"The Struggle can bring a couple together…or it can rend them apart as well, I guess."

"You and Diane were an excellent Civil Rights team. I have trouble imagining one without the other."

"Well, what about you and...the white beauty queen from Pennsylvania whose name I can't recall?"

"Priscilla. Selma was the end of the line for us. We're still good friends, but I'm still as single as before."

"I'm sorry things didn't conclude happily for you. However, it may make you more available for the task I want to suggest for you now."

"I've kind of retired from the Movement since after Selma."

"Old civil rights activists never retire. They just put on their walking boots and march in another campaign."

"That may be true for you, but I'm tending toward a quiet life in Harlem, Jim."

"It's my turn to call you back to the action. There'll be time for a quiet life when the sanitation workers' strike in Memphis is settled. Dr. King has been here in Memphis off and one since the turn of the year. Now there's a man who needs some rest and renewal. The strike here is moving finally to a favorable resolution for our people, and it may happen soon. But he needs good, experienced men like Henri Esper in his brigade to help the settlement to come sooner."

"But I read that there are plenty of you tested and trusted veterans there already."

"Yes. Thank God that Ralph, Andy, and Jesse are nearby to advise MLK. But the strike and the situation in Memphis is complex and convoluted. Guys like Abernathy, Young, and Jackson are useful and experienced, to be sure. But I've been thinking that Dr. King needs a fresh voice in his ear to perhaps suggest a novel approach."

"And you think that's me?" Henri asked, genuinely surprised at Bevel's estimation of him.

On the Civil Rights Road again? The years had passed, but it felts like February 1958 again when Lucius and Henri hit the road from Little Rock to begin their Civil Rights sojourn of the South. *Where have we been? Where am I headed now? What awaits me now in Memphis?*

They were gathered as in days past around a table in the basement of Clayborn Temple African Methodist Episcopal

Church—the directors and officers of the SCLC including Bevel and Ralph Abernathy supplemented by an informal collection of African American clergy from the greater Memphis area. Sitting at the same table facing the African American clergy were the public spokespersons for the sanitation workers, T.O. Jones and Jerry Wurf.

Jones and Wurf had been feeling at a disadvantage sitting with this collection of people because, although the sanitation workers had been granted a union charter by the parent AFSCME in 1964, it had been ineffectual since. The fledgling union had attempted a strike against the city in 1966 but failed in large part because Jones and Wurf were unable to arouse the support of the Memphis religious community, especially many of the very same African American clergy sitting at the same table across from them that afternoon. The union spokespersons were suspected of being Communist just as the city leaders insisted.

Henri felt the tension in the room, which was palpable enough to be cut with a knife. The hostility of the union spokesmen toward the local clergy was unmistakable. As usual in such an environment, Henri felt his spirit confined and cramped, almost claustrophobic, and he immediately started to rummage through his mind and memory for some way out of the tense situation or encounter. Bevel, on the other hand, seemed at home in the midst of such tension and stress, which seemed so close to the surface that it was liable to explode into a thousand shards.

The ringing of the telephone on the kitchen wall broke the awkward silence and caused a few of the more tightly wound people out in the room beyond the kitchen to shudder.

Malcolm Blackburn, the host pastor of Clayborn Temple, sprang up from his chair around the table and hurried to answer the telephone.

"Yes, this is Reverend Blackburn…. Oh dear, that is sad news, sad news indeed…

"Yes, one of them, Mr. Cole, is a member of our church. A very fine and upstanding young man. I'm sure we can find Mr. Walker's church as well…Where can I find Mr. Cole? I would like to extend my condolences and say a short prayer with his parents…. Thank you for informing us, Chief Holloman."

Henri and others in the meeting room adjacent to the kitchen could hear Blackburn's half of the exchange. Henri could hear but could not know the context because he did know who Chief

Holloman was. But it was clear by Blackburn's tone of voice that there was a tragic problem somewhere.

He and the others turned silent as they waited for Rev. Blackburn to return to the meeting. Everyone looked to Blackburn expectantly.

"That was Chief Holloman of the Memphis Police Department. He says that two sanitation workers are dead after being crushed alive in a malfunctioning trash truck. The younger of the two, Echol Cole, and his young family are part of our temple fellowship. Good God. What a horrible way to die."

The men around the meeting table wanted to be respectful of the grief that they imagined that Blackburn was feeling. As he looked at the group, however, Henri could tell that several of the men were anxious to say something but weren't sure if it was socially acceptable to break the silence just yet.

The first to do so was a big, football lineman-sized man, one of the two union organizers, T.O. Jones. "Yes, this young man suffered an ugly, unpleasant death. But we can say with confidence that his death and that of the second victim on the trash truck was unavoidable if management had performed the regular safety inspection they were responsible to perform. Most of you know that I served among sanitation workers in Memphis for many years until January of this year when Henry Loeb was elected as mayor of our city. You recall, I'm sure that these two were not the first sanitation workers of the city of Memphis to die or be seriously injured. There were three men who sustained serious leg and back injuries a few years ago after Mr. Loeb refused to take some of our oldest, most dilapidated trucks out of service. Our labor leaders heard our concerns about the outdated, dangerous ramshackle equipment the sanitation workers were forced to use. They also managed to convince a skeptical and fiscally conservative city council to propose to Mayor Loeb the first wage increase that our sanitation workers would enjoy in over a decade and better city attention to the state of their equipment and working conditions.

"Y'all recall, don't you, Mr. Loeb's response to this timely and most appropriate proposal by the city council? Why, they rejected the council's vote, insisting that only he as Mayor had the authority to recognize the union and, of course, he refused to do so. So, gentlemen and Reverend Blackburn, that is precisely what I mean when I say the violent accidental deaths of these two men were avoidable."

The heads of some around the table were nodding in agreement as Jones was articulating the case for a compassionate and just response to the plight of the sanitation workers. Not all heads, however. Henri felt that although these clergymen whose heads were not nodding in wholehearted agreement to the veteran union leader were total strangers, nevertheless, he knew them well. For although the names and faces among the leaders of black churches in Harlem were different, the underlying conservative, traditional values were not much different from those of these cautious and even timid African American church and community leaders in Memphis. Their essential social and political instinct was not to rock the boat too zealously lest the status quo become too unfamiliar or uncomfortable for their people.

He was reminded of what an uphill battle it must be for Dr. King to persuade such hesitant leaders in the black church to risk revolutionary change even if in their heart of hearts they recognized the urgent need in the church and black neighborhoods for such liberating change. Is this why a whole generation of young African Americans has given up on the black church on the corner? Because of the church's aversion and resistance to change?

Dr. King's associates were visible and evident in the struggle of the sanitation workers for recognition and legitimacy, but Dr. King himself was usually hidden and occupied elsewhere.

On February 12, Jones and Wurf convened a union meeting, which to their vindication some seven hundred men attended and unanimously decided to strike against the city. Within a week the local branch of the N.A.A.C.P. passed a resolution affirming and supporting the strike. On February 24, one hundred and fifty local clergy met in the basement of Clayborn Temple and committed to form Community on the move for Equality (COME), led by Dr. King's longtime associate James Lawson. COME committed to the use of nonviolent disobedience to fill Memphis jails and draw attention to the plight of the sanitation workers. By the beginning of March, local high school and college students were participating alongside garbage workers in daily marches. More than one hundred of them, many of them white, were arrested.

King's associates or allies such as Roy Wilkins and March on

Washington organizer Bayard Rustin rallied sanitation workers at public meetings each night. Finally, Dr. King himself arrived on March 18 and addressed an enthusiastic crowd of twenty-five thousand people, the largest indoor gathering the Civil Rights Movement had ever experienced. King urged the crowd to support the sanitation workers by uniting in a citywide work stoppage. To the delight of the crowd, King pledged to return to the city on March 22 to lead a march through the city.

King was not alone in anxiety about such a march. He understood that the stakes were high. With such high tension between the police and marchers, violence was very possible, if not likely. Back on February 12, police had followed participants in a nonviolent march back to the basement of Clayborn Temple and sprayed the marchers with mace and tear gas. On March 22, although King kept his pledge to return to Memphis on March 22 to lead a climactic march through the city of Memphis, the planned march was cut short at King's request because some scuffling along the route between marchers and white observers threatened to grow into widespread violence.

Concern about violence grew when Mayor Loeb called for martial law and brought in four thousand National Guard troops. A freak late March snowstorm paralyzed Memphis. King almost considered not returning to Memphis but concluded that if the nonviolent struggle for economic justice was going to succeed, it would be necessary to follow through with the movement in Memphis.

King and the SCLC board pinpointed April 3 as the earliest occasion when King could be present in Memphis.

The sanitation union leaders and the black populace were disappointed that a settlement for the strike would have to wait for a new calendar year.

Chapter Thirty-Three

"On some days, John, I feel the ugliness and killing rising up all around me."

Dr. Martin Luther King, Jr.
A private conversation with John Lewis on March 30, 1968

HENRI SAT UNCOMFORTABLY ON A BED in Room 306 on the second floor of the Lorraine Motel, where it was customary for the SCLC leadership to stay in Memphis whenever Dr. King was able to join them. His arrival from Atlanta had been delayed from midmorning to late afternoon. When he did arrive, Henri was struck immediately by how exhausted Dr. King looked from the flight delay, but Henri suspected more than that. The discernible rings around his eyes were often the first signs of a battle weariness from the Struggle. Today King's need to wipe and blow his runny nose, which had caused a reddish inflammation at the base of each nostril. Henri granted it could be a symptom of the poor ventilation in an enclosed airplane; he knew from his own experience what were sure signs of a cold.

'You've probably heard by now. Or, if not, you would not be surprised to learn that my flight from Atlanta was delayed by a death threat. It was aimed specifically at me, not unexpectedly. I know that because everyone had to evacuate the plane on to the tarmac. That's not particularly noteworthy. But this time the police brought dogs with them onto the plane. All I could think of was Bull Connor's German shepherds in Birmingham. I didn't want to let on my fears to upset the other passengers any further, but I have to confess, brothers, that I was unnerved."

Henri looked around the motel bedroom for the reactions of the others. Ralph Abernathy looked the most concerned by King's confession of fear. In fact, Henri doubted that Abernathy had to be told. He and King had been together in the Movement so long that they could almost finish each other's sentences. Surely, Abernathy shared King's alarm.

King tried to alleviate the concern in the room, perhaps particularly Abernathy's, by interjecting, "That lousy airline didn't even offer a cocktail to help me relax. I must write a complaint to the president of Eastern Airlines." He chuckled to try to assure the others that he was unaffected by the experience.

Threats on King's life were not unusual, the SCLC colleagues knew. Lately, neither was hearing Dr. King make mention, or even expound in more detail, on his private thoughts about his potential death.

A few of his colleagues made uncomfortable about death talk would respond to him at such times with a reassuring bromide of some sort: "The Lord doesn't seem ready to call you home yet." Or "You're like the clichéd cat that has nine or more lives."

King seemed to appreciate their attempts at reassurance, but Henri wondered if he would have appreciated more an honest and authentic empathizing from his closest associates. Would it have made him feel alone and isolated?

But he was in Memphis now with an opportunity to "redo" the previous attempt at a nonviolent march in support of the sanitation workers. King was so determined to salve his injured ego and restore the reputation of the march as a peaceful and effective means of change. But his late arrival and the eruption of a powerful storm made a replay of the march from happening that very day.

"Oh, I'm so tired, friends. I am scheduled, as you know, to speak at the rally at Mason Temple this evening. But all I want is to go to bed…. Ralph, you're the trusted Ed McMahon to my Johnny Carson. Will you go to Mason Temple in my stead?"

"I don't have anything prepared. The torrential rain will make for a smaller turnout than we expected, I suppose. Besides, the most celebrated civil rights leader in this country deserves the right to duck a small crowd."

"I'll take that as a 'yes.' I've got to take a couple of decongestants and have a good sleep." With that, King walked into the second bedroom.

King's sleep was interrupted by the ringing of the telephone on the nightstand beside the bed.

"Hello, this is Dr King," he said with much halting effort.

"Martin, it may be storming outside, but here inside, there's a big crowd. I'll speak if you really want me to, you know that. But I don't think this crowd wants to hear the second banana. They won't stand for it, Martin. This is an occasion when they need to hear from the big tomato."

King considered the proposal silently. "They won't hear much different from me than they would from you. You know that, Ralph."

"Maybe not, Martin. But what they came to hear were the words of

Martin Luther King, Jr., not me…. How is the decongestant working? Are you finding it easier to breathe? Come on down here, Martin. I know you've had to preach on some occasions when you're not at your best."

King dressed and was driven downtown to a waiting audience animated by a restless energy.

Abernathy was still at the podium when King arrived. Abernathy was speaking unusually long for a "warm-up act" in order to give King adequate time to arrive at the huge church. He delivered a listing of King's achievements. Then, Abernathy turned more thoughtful and almost contemplative. Henri became aware that King's death threat on the plane was still affecting Abernathy himself.

"Ladies and gentlemen, our leader faces these threats almost every day and everywhere he goes." Abernathy noticed King approaching the front of the cathedral, preparing to rise into pulpit.

"As he takes his rightful place at the podium tonight, I ask sincerely to pray for the health and long life of Dr. Matin Luther King, Jr."

As the crowd realized that King was indeed present and ready to speak, it broke into spontaneous and thunderous applause to match the peels of thunder outside in the Memphis night.

Without a note in front of him, King opened by thanking Abernathy, "the best friend I have in all the world." King's voice, Henri noticed, was very ragged and sounded nearly slurred at first. Henri privately wondered whether King had imbibed a cocktail as he hoped to be served on the plane from Atlanta. But Henri doubted that in their enthusiastic welcome the crowd would suspect.

King thanked the audience for coming despite a foul weather warning. The battering of the storm continued on and sliced through the sentences of King's speech as natural sound effects to punctuate his points. He took his listeners on an imaginative tour of human history. God asked him what period of history he would choose to live in. King imagines a "mental flight" over Egypt's Red Sea and then on to Mount Olympus and the Pantheon in Athens. He'd pass over the Roman Empire and the European Renaissance and only visit the Reformation long enough to see his namesake nail ninety-five theses on the Wittenberg Castle Church door. He would make his way to 1863 and watch Abraham Lincoln finally arrive at the conclusion that he will have to sign the Emancipation Proclamation. King says that he would go past all of these places but say to the Almighty, "If you allow me to live just a few years in the twentieth century, I will be happy."

Henri thought that King had managed to put the present time in the

United States in proper context without insulting the audience's intelligence. Henri applauded King.

"God is working in his period of the twentieth century in a way that men, in some way, are responding to the dream of freedom implanted in them by the Almighty," said King.

"I am so happy that God has permitted to be alive at this time when it is no longer a choice between violence and nonviolence; it's nonviolence or nonexistence.... I challenge you today to make the most of the privilege God has granted you. The plight of the sanitation workers in Memphis is a test of our nation's commitment to justice. Unite while you can under the banner of justice."

Suddenly, in his extemporaneous speech King changes his didactic tone to a more personal one that has obviously been on his mind and heart for a time. "When I got to Memphis today, some began to talk about the threats against me and my life. What would happen to me because of some of our sick white brothers? Well, what will happen now? I don't know. We've got some difficult days ahead. But it doesn't matter to me now. Because I've been to the mountaintop. And I don't mind. Like anybody else, I would like to live a long life. Longevity has its place. But I'm not concerned about that now I just want to do God's will. And He's allowed me to go up the mountain. I've looked over, and I've seen the Promised Land."

The preachers and audience could smell the climax and splice their elation into his oration. "Yes, sir!" "Yes, Doctor!" "Preach it!"

Henri was breathless.

King paused ever so slightly to let them encourage him home. Then he began again, saying "I may not get there with you"—a reminder again of the fragility of life, especially of a progressive, prophetic civil right leader. "But I want you to know tonight that we, as a people, will get to the Promised Land."

"I'm happy tonight. I'm not worried about anything. I'm not fearing any man. Mine eyes have seen the glory of the coming of the Lord."

King began the hymn that he had quoted so many times through the years. Just as he completed a single line of the hymn, King turned suddenly on his heels out of emotional and spiritual fullness. He nearly collapsed into the waiting arms of his faithful lieutenant, Ralph Abernathy. Henri was overcome by uncontrollable tears of joy mixed with unrelenting anticipatory sorrow.

Epilogue

"If a man hasn't found something that he will die for, he's not fit to live."

Dr. Martin Luther King, Jr.

August 1998

King's eyes are riveted to what in the other dimension he would have called "the horizon." The host still has the eyes of a thirty-nine-year-old, 20/20, just as it was day he was cut down and severed violently from the life he had known. A chasm was dug between the world, which so many he loved continue to inhabit and the one into which he had been borne on April 4, 1968. There is no means he can conjure up to cross that deep chasm. He longs for his wife, Coretta, and children Martin III, Dexter, Yolanda, and Bernice so badly that he had tried but failed.

From a distance of fifty yards of less, he discerns that the figure approaching him is indeed a human one—a male dressed in plain brown polyester slacks and a checkered sport jacket that looks like it has been worn regularly and often. The approaching man looks he has already surpassed the completion of his seventh decade of life. Even from twenty yards, he can see that the man's face is pocked slightly. His hair is mostly grey, although the hair on top is almost black, suggesting that at one time in the past his whole crown had been dark.

Who is this guy? The fact that he seems to be headed straight for me indicates that he knows who I am. Would he bother to make this walk from wherever he lives if he didn't know me?

Finally, the figure was within a few feet of where he stood, dressed in a dark, tailor-made silk suit, his right hand adjusting the bejeweled cuff link at his left wrist. The stranger tried surreptitiously to inspect the blemish on the man's cheek that might have been a wound at one time, but all that is left is a slightly discolored mark that had healed over the decades and lost its original blood-red coloration.

The stranger nods self-consciously instead of braving a verbal greeting. Out of a familiar habit, perhaps, he extends his right hand to this visitor. The stranger stares at his host's extended black hand for a long time as though he were unfamiliar with the gesture and does not know how to respond.

"Sir, can I get you a cool drink to refresh you after your walk? I'm afraid that I have only some rum and a little warm Coca Cola to offer."

The stranger discretely pumps a barely discernable shake of his head "No, thank you, Sir. I used to indulge, but ever since my time at Leavenworth I don't touch the stuff. My recovery began there in A.A."

"Excuse me, Sir," the confounded host replies. "You look vaguely familiar to me. But I must admit that I don't know who you are."

"You don't know who I am? That surprises me."

"Sir, I give my apologies, but I have met many persons in my lifetime. I used to have the memory of an elephant, but lately I have forgotten many of the people with whom I marched and demonstrated."

"I'm sure you didn't see me that day. But what I did to you altered the whole trajectory of the movement of which you were the leader. In fact, I hear that some say—even some of your most loyal allies—that what I did to you brought the whole momentum of your movement to a halt, if not an actual end. Does any of this sound the least bit familiar?"

"If by 'what I did to you' you are referring to what many have called my 'untimely death' on April 4, 1968, as I suspect you are, I did notice some changes in the nature of the movement already beginning before that date. Some were positive ones. For example, in the beginning the movement was dependent on the goodwill and favorable support of white sympathizers. If, for instance, the nine justices of the United States Supreme Court, who at that time were all white, had not ruled in favor of the Brown v. the Board of Education of Topeka, black children in America might still be doomed to attend very poorly resourced, inferior schools even today. Or if the white citizens of Birmingham had remained morally comfortable with the strong-arm tactics of Bull Connor and the civic leaders who supported him, Connor might still be Alabama's Commissioner of Public Safety and free to inflict fire hoses and snarling dogs on anyone who dares to question or oppose such police tactics. Do you see what I mean?"

"About Bull Connor, you need to understand that it was not so much your objections to his fierce tactics that made me mildly upset, but rather the weak-kneed, milquetoast reactions of the white powers-that-be, their chicken-livered refusal to wholeheartedly support efforts by men like Connor to preserve the public peace. Jesus, instead, they allowed the forces of chaos and disorder to disrupt the way we've always done things in the South. There had been too many changes in the South. That vexed and exasperated me to no end. I decided something needed to be done about that.

"You can imagine that we have some differences in how we interpret those and other historical events like them. I suspect you and I were working from vastly different assumptions even before you aimed your rifle at me on the balcony of my motel."

Ray relaxed the muscles around his mouth, which heretofore had been tightly locked. A shy smile appeared on his face. "You were a sitting duck on that balcony. I had a clear shot from the bathroom window of the rooming house behind the parking lot. There were all kinds of men—presumably some of your closest associates—up there in the vicinity of the balcony, but not one put himself between you and me several hundred feet away in the rooming house. I couldn't believe how easy it was."

"It all happened the way it was supposed to. If Ralph or Andy or Jesse or someone else had stepped in front of me, he would have been the one who was hit. I'd rather that it was me. I'm obliged to you, I suppose, that you spared them. Obliged, too, for that matter, because I was tired after almost fifteen years of scuffling in the Movement. Too tired to deal with some of the young bucks like Stokely who had started to raise strident voices in favor of Black Power. Increasingly, my voice was that of a lonely figure crying in the wilderness. I was feeling more and more that I was politically and socially dead before you shot me."

"I think I do, Dr. King. How you have just responded identifies you positively as Dr. Martin Luther King. I walked here because I heard a voice telling me to come. But the voice didn't say who I was supposed to look for."

"It's all coming back to me now. You're the infamous James Earl Ray! Finally, we meet. Now you know me so now you have found me... again."

Ray relaxed the muscles around his mouth which heretofore had been tightly locked. A shy smile appeared on his fac. "You were a sitting duck on that balcony. I had a clear shot from the bathroom window of the rooming house behind the parking lot. There were all kinds of men–presumably some of your closest associates–up there in the vicinity of the balcony, but not one put himself between you and me several hundred feet away in the rooming house. I couldn't believe how easy it was."

The visitor gave him a disbelieving look. "I beg to differ, Doctor. Rather I fear that by shooting you as I did, I inadvertently gave you a new lease on life. The bullet in your neck and jaw raised you to the level of a martyr instead of just a victim. It elevated you from the status of a wise philosopher and preacher of a past that was quickly receding to that of a legend, an infallible god who is adored and worshipped."

"That may be, Sir, but you have seen the sad fate of gods and legends in recent decades. They are easily ignored and disregarded as irrelevant to people's lives and real concerns. I sense that I have been idealized into uselessness for the poor I loved, my words immortalized into a 'niceness' that is often quoted but that dilutes the radical political agenda I endorsed. My justice agenda has been smothered by all the adulation."

"My goodness, I caused all that?"

"'Inadvertently,' as you say. "The ignoring and disregarding, the idealizing and immortalizing, and the smothering of my passion was already beginning before either of us arrived in Memphis. Because you didn't know what you were doing or what unforeseen consequences would result, I forgive you, James.... But I must ask, why? When it was plainly obvious to many observers and commentators, that nonviolent protests had run their course and outlived their effectiveness, why did you feel the need to shoot me?

"I have to acknowledge that even now—what is it? three decades later—I still can't answer that question any better than I could then. Isn't that pathetic? Of all my brothers and cousins, I was the one who was considered by folks in Alton, Illinois, to be the one who would make a name for himself, or be the first from the block to go to college. I detest the name I made for myself. 'The man who killed Dr. Martin Luther King.' And the only college I could get into was Brushy Mountain State Penitentiary in Tennessee. But here I am in some strange place, facing my victim, unable to explain my own

actions. I so envy men like you who know who they are, and can give account of what they have done and why they have done it.

"It's ironic, don't you think that the sum total of my life is that I'm the epitome of a 'drifter?' This is the way we drifters are. We drift aimlessly from one ideology to another. We wander without purpose from one religion to another. We meander from one town to the next just because they're located in close proximity to one another on a map. I was drifting aimlessly to Rhodesia when the feds caught up and arrested me in Heathrow Airport. But I couldn't really say to them or anyone else why I was going to Rhodesia. I didn't really know why."

"Sir, thank you for coming to greet me. You've helped me understand some things. You and I will always be joined together at the hip in people's minds. Maybe people wouldn't give you credit for the courage it took for you to come here today. I give you credit, but I don't envy you. Just bouncing from one whim to another with no code to guide you or principles to abide by. That's not really living by any meaningful definition. I will pray for you, James, as I have from the very beginning in April 1968.

"Perhaps you've heard me say at various times, "If a man hasn't found something that he will die for, he's not fit to live."

The End

A Word from the Author

Thank you, dear reader, for accompanying me (and Henri and Lucius) through some of the key events of the Civil Rights Movement. The years from 1954 to 1968 were terribly exciting. They altered the trajectory of a whole nation. Those years, and the dramatic events of that decisive period of American history, produced an impressive list of brave men and women who became the heroes and heroines of a new generation of African-American young people. But not just of African-American young people, but *myself* as well, a white primary and high school student who was excited and proud much later to write a novel that features heroes such as John Lewis, Rosa Parks, Bayard Rustin, Thurgood Marshall, James Bevel, Diane Nash, Daisy Bates, Viola Liuzzo, Elizabeth Eckford, Ralph Abernathy and, of course, Dr. Martin Luther King, Jr.—to name just a few who share the spotlight in *A Long and Stony Road.*

I was just a grammar school pupil in the 1950s, a precocious reader of the newspaper. I don't claim that I understood every article I read, but I had a very approachable third-grade teacher, Miss Pratt, who encouraged her class to look through the newspaper every day and cut out anything that interested or fascinated us and we would talk about the article in class the next day.

For several consecutive days in 1953, there were retrospective articles in *The Star* about the decision handed down several years earlier by the Supreme Court (whatever that was) of the huge neighboring republic, the United States of America. The case of Brown v. the Board of Education effectively made it illegal for any state to provide schools for black pupils that were inferior to those provided for white children. *All* children in schools in the United States were to enjoy schools in buildings that were clean and safe, learn from teachers who were adequately trained and educated, and get information from textbooks that were sufficiently up-to-date and accurate. Miss Pratt explained to us that in the decades before 1953, black children would get access to their textbooks only when the white students were done with them. By that time, the books were often missing pages or had rude racist comments handwritten in the margins.

To a schoolboy in Canada, the kind of unfairness in schools described in the newspaper felt totally alien, scandalous even. I couldn't understand how, if the principals of American schools were anywhere near as nice and considerate as Mr. Fritz at our elementary school, black children would possibly not be treated so unjustly. It was the germ in me of a sense of justice and injustice that has stuck with me to guide my life for the years afterward.

A lot of our news in Canada then focused on events in the United States and were broadcast to us from American news outlets. Less than a decade after the landmark decision about inequality in children's schooling, I was a delivery boy for another Toronto newspaper, *The Toronto Telegram*. The front page of the "telly" as we called it was dominated by photos of black college students in cities like Greensboro, North Carolina and Nashville, Tennessee being beaten by white hooligans solely because the black students had dared to be seated at Woolworth's lunch counters which custom, tradition and even the law reserved for white patrons only.

On the day I was entering high school, the evening news was quite vivid in its depiction and film of a qualified black law student named James Meredith being barred physically by the governor of the state from stepping inside the law school of the University of Mississippi because the university didn't admit black students. Yet another shameful incidence of gross injustice. I proceeded through high school with a heightened sensitivity to the gross bigotry and ignorance endured by black children and young people, particularly in the United States.

I should add that it was only several years later that I became aware of similar injustices inflicted in my *own* country on First Nations children and youth on or off reservations. but which appeared at least to be less blatantly violent and cruel than those in the United States. It was through the lens of the Civil Rights Movement in our southern neighbor, however, that I learned to see and understand our Canadian flavor of injustice.

Ironically, Henri Esper, one of the two primary protagonists of *A Long and Stony Road* is a Canadian transplant to the United States. As a descendant of some of the African-American loyalists who sided with Britain in the Revolutionary War and fled the nascent republic upon its winning independence, I assume he experienced the similar bigotry and systemic racism in Canada which he observed Negroes experiencing in the southern United States on his tour of them with his travel buddy Lucius.

Jack A. Saarela
Wyncote, PA

Bibliography

BOOKS

Baldwin, James, Collected Essays, 1985, Penguin Random House.

Bates, Daisy, The Long Shadow of Little Rock, 1986, University of Arkansas Press.

Branch, Taylor, Parting the Waters: America in The King Years. 1954-1963, Simon and Schuster.

Clark, E. Culpepper, The Schoolhouse Door: Segregation's Last Stand at the University of Alabama, 1993, Oxford.

Dyson, Michael Eric, April 4, 1968: Martin Luther King, Jr.'s Death and How It Changed America, 2008, Basic Civitas Books.

Fairclough, Adam, Martin Luther King, Jr. 1990, University of Georgia Press.

Goodwin, Richard N., Remembering America: A Voice From the Sixties, 1988, Open Road Media.

Garrow, David J., Protest at Selma: Martin Luther King, Jr. and the Voting Rights Act of 1965, 1978, Open Road.

MEDIA

Garrow, David J., Bearing the Cross: Martin Luther King, Jr. and the Southern Christian Leadership Conference, 1989, University of California Press.

Graetz, Robert S., Montgomery: A White Preacher's Memoir, 1991, Fortress.

Lanier, Carlotta Williams, A Mighty Long Way: My Journey to Justice at Little Rock Central High School, Random House.

Leeming, David, James Baldwin: A Biography, 1995, Henry Holt.

Lewis, John, Walking With the Wind: A Memoir of The Movement, 1998, Simon and Schuster.

May, Gary. The Informant: The FBI, the Ku Klux Klan and the Murder of Viola Liuzzo, 2005, Yale University Press.

Meacham, Jon (Ed.), Voices in Our Blood: America's Best on the Civil Rights Movement, 2001, Random House.

Nicholas, Denise, Freshwater Road, 2005, Bolden.

Ogletree, Charles J. Jr., All Deliberate Speed, 2004, W.W. Norton.

Roberts, Gene, and Kilbanoff, Hank, The Race Beat, 2006,

Alfred A Knopf.

Sorin, Gretchen. Driving While Black, 2020, Liveright Publishing.

Sides, Hampton, Hellhound on His Trail, 2010, First Anchor Books.

Watson, Bruce, Freedom Summer, 2010, Penguin.

Wilkerson, Isabel, Caste: The Origin of Our Discontents, 2020, Random House.

FILMS

Daniels, Lee, The Butler, 2013, Laura Ziskin Productions.

DuVernay, Ava, Selma, 2014, Paramount.

Peck, Raoul, I Am Not Your Negro, 2016, Velvet Films.

Acknowledgments

When an author completes the manuscript of a work such as a novel, she or he is filled with the triumph of accomplishment and for having come to the end of a project that has taken him or her over a year and a half or more to complete.

More than that, however, having brought *A Long and Stony Road* to a successful conclusion, I am overcome with gratitude when I think of all the persons who have helped me conceive of and produce the final product. Granted, I was the one who sat in front of a computer screen and fashioned the sentences. Yet, there were many others for whose contributions to the project I give thanks.

This story has been germinating in my mind since I was just out of college. It was in conversation with editor-publisher Karen Hodges Miller of Open Door Publications that we landed on the idea of telling the vast story of the Civil Rights Movement through the experiences of two African America pastor. Karen was with me all the way from conception of the novel to its completion and printing.

Beta readers Kathy Weidner and Marty Weiss were invaluable in pointing out inconsistencies in the plot, grammatical and spelling errors and weaknesses in the text that rendered the manuscript more eminently readable for the reader. As he did for my previous novels, Eric Lebacz designed the absolutely stunning cover.

Fellow author Vivian Fransen (*The Straight Spouse*: *A Memoir*, published by Open Door Publications) gave the manuscript one final read-through as a proofreader.

Some of the invaluable feedback and suggestions for improving the text were provided by fellow members of the Virtual Writers' Group that meets on most Monday afternoons by Zoom to read each other's literary work and give each other constructive criticism as peers and fellow authors. Many thanks to Jan Detrie, Wendy Loos, and Sherrie Lynn, and, of course, our facilitator Karen Hodges Miller. Writing was a less lonely process with your companionship.

I would be amiss if I neglected to thank my dear bride, Diane Saarela, for protecting my valuable, almost sacred, writing time each afternoon from other tasks and distractions.

And thank you, dear reader. You were in the forefront of my mind from the first word to the last.

About the Author

JACK SAARELA of Wyncote, PA, is currently living in his third country. Born in northern Finland in 1955, he emigrated to Toronto, Canada, with his family and was educated through college in Canadian schools. He received his BA in English language and literature from the University of Toronto.

In 1971 he began his theological studies at Yale Divinity School in New Haven, CT, receiving his M.Div. degree in 1974. In 1981 he took up residence in Lake Worth, Florida.

Jack has been married to Diane, a Lancaster, PA native, since 1971. They are the parents of two adult sons: Luke of Wyncote, PA, and Jesse of Gainesville, FL, and the grandparents of two charming granddaughters in Gainesville.

Jack has remained a Canadian citizen.

After forty years as a parish and campus pastor in Canada, Florida, Connecticut, and Pennsylvania, Jack retired to write historical novels. he has written five such novels, including the present one, *A Long and Stony Road,* a fictionalized account of the Civil Rights Movement from 1953 to 1968, four of which were published by Open Door Publications.

Having suffered several strokes, Jack has acknowledged reluctantly that the current novel will be his final one. There are many who are recognized by name in the "Acknowledgments" as particularly instrumental in helping birth Jack's novels. He humbly thanks all those who have encouraged and supported his progress as an author by purchasing his books and commenting on them, regarding their themes and contents earnestly and with curiosity.

May the long-awaited day of justice and amends for the oppressed and underdogs, for whom the novels are dedicated, shine soon like the dawn!

NOVELS BY JACK A SAARELA

I hope you have enjoyed reading *A Long and Stony Road.* I invite you to explore other novels by the same author.

Beginning Again at Zero

Onni Syrjala is still only a teenager when his spirit gets restless and, like many others at the time, decides to follow his dream of emigrating from Finland to Canada in 1938. A whole new world of possibility awaits him there. Onni encounters unexpected challenges and joyful experiences in adjusting to a new land. His thoughts shift back to his native land and loved ones there in November 1939 when the Russians attack Finland from the east as the Winter War begins. Resume his new life in Canada or return to Finland to defend his native land? Onni has a difficult decision to make.

Accidental Saviors

Felix and Algot are two Finnish expatriates who happen to be in Berlin in 1938 to witness the horrors of *Kristallnacht* and begin to learn of further atrocities by the Nazis against the Jews in Germany and across Europe. Felix and Algot have never met each other or even know of the existence of each other. But each in his own way is moved to use his prior expertise to help transport endangered Jews out of the reach of Nazi persecutors into safety. Separately and together, Felix and Algot save thousands of lives. As much as Jack's other novels, *Accidental Saviors* is based on actual historic events.

Love Out of Reach is both a romantic love story and a wartime thriller. The Second World War is raging all around them as thirty-six-year-old pastor/theologian Dietrich Bonhoeffer meets and develops a romantic connection with Maria von Wedemeyer, sixteen years his junior.

What Maria doesn't know in the beginning is that Dietrich has been involved in anti-Nazi activities since 1942. Consequently, he is arrested and imprisoned by the Nazis. However, Dietrich and Maria become engaged when the war is over. They can only continue their love relationship under the supervision of the Dietrich's Nazi keepers. While in prison under the Nazi's noses, Dietrich joins other resistors in a dangerous and ambitious conspiracy to assassinate Hitler. Dietrich remains in one Nazi prison or another until he is executed a mere few weeks before the end of the war in Europe. The couple's dreams of marriage are cut short, and their love remains forever out of reach.

A Perfect Storm of Injustice is a story, repeated all too often in news stories, of wrongful incarceration. Charles is a young black man married to a white woman, Dana—a phenomenon still frowned upon in Florida's Palm Beach County in 1986 when the novel opens.

Charles' very ordinary life changes forever when he is called home in the middle of his workday. The notorious sheriff is on the line informing Charles that his wife has been murdered and that Charles is the primary and sole suspect in the brutal beating and murder, even though he has no prior criminal record.

While Charles protests his innocence, he is arrested and tried for the murder. Charles is sentenced initially to Florida's death row. He spends the next quarter-century in prison before a series of rapid and startling events lead to his eventual exoneration.

A Perfect Storm of Injustice is based on the real-life experiences of several individuals known to the author. Since 1973, at least 172 such persons were wrongfully arrested and in some case's wrongfully executed by the state.

A Long and Stony Road

The author considers *A Long and Stony Road* his most polished and accomplished novel. The setting for the novel is the tumultuous Civil Rights Movement from 1954 to 1968.

Henri Esper (Esperance) is a transplanted Canadian and a newly ordained Congregational clergyman in Harlem who wins a generous cash award that allows him the time and means to tour some of the important sites of civil rights struggles and learn the history-in-the-making first-hand. He is joined by Lucius, a classmate from seminary. Together, they discover that with each apparent step forward in the movement for justice for vulnerable and suppressed African Americans there is often a setback. With more experience in one civil rights campaign after another, Henri and Lucius grow in their commitment to the guiding principles of nonviolent protest. The two protagonists follow the leader of the movement, the Rev. Dr. Martin Luther King, Jr., to the culmination of the struggle in Selma, Alabama, and finally in April 1968 to the movement's apparent dissolution and transformation into something that neither the movement's leaders nor followers were no longer able to recognize.

Made in the USA
Middletown, DE
20 February 2023

24533111R00139